LONDON'S
Wicked
AFFAIR

<u>BOOK YOUR PLACE ON OUR WEBSITE</u>
<u>AND MAKE THE</u>
<u>READING CONNECTION!</u>

We've created a customized website just for our very special readers, where you can get the inside scoop on everything that's going on with Zebra, Pinnacle and Kensington books.

When you come online, you'll have the exciting opportunity to:

- View covers of upcoming books
- Read sample chapters
- Learn about our future publishing schedule
  (listed by publication month and author)
- Find out when your favorite authors will be visiting
  a city near you
- Search for and order backlist books from our
  online catalog
- Check out author bios and background information
- Send e-mail to your favorite authors
- Meet the Kensington staff online
- Join us in weekly chats with authors, readers and
  other guests
- Get writing guidelines
- AND MUCH MORE!

Visit our website at
http://www.kensingtonbooks.com

LONDON'S
Wicked
AFFAIR

ANABELLE
BRYANT

ZEBRA BOOKS
KENSINGTON PUBLISHING CORP.
http://www.kensingtonbooks.com

ZEBRA BOOKS are published by

Kensington Publishing Corp.
119 West 40th Street
New York, NY 10018

All Kensington titles, imprints, and distributed lines are available at special quantity discounts for bulk purchases for sales promotion, premiums, fund-raising, educational, or institutional use.

Special book excerpts or customized printings can also be created to fit specific needs. For details, write or phone the office of the Kensington Sales Manager: Attn.: Sales Department. Kensington Publishing Corp., 119 West 40th Street, New York, NY 10018. Phone: 1-800-221-2647.

Zebra and the Z logo Reg. U.S. Pat. & TM Off.

First Printing: September 2018
ISBN-13: 978-1-4201-4643-1
ISBN-10: 1-4201-4643-2

eISBN-13: 978-1-4201-4644-8
eISBN-10: 1-4201-4644-0

10 9 8 7 6 5 4 3 2 1

Printed in the United States of America

For my parents,
who have always reminded me
I can accomplish anything if I believe in myself

And for David and Nicholas,
who prove—every day—home is where
my heart beats strongest

ACKNOWLEDGMENTS

I have so much gratitude for my brilliant and amazing editor, Esi Sogah, for helping me fulfill my dream of publication. Your clever insight, unfailing guidance, and gracious advice mean the world to me. Thank you for believing in my work.

Thanks to everyone at Kensington Publishing and the hardworking, dedicated staff who are truly committed to excellence in all they do.

Finally, there is no way to adequately thank all my readers. My heartfelt appreciation to anyone who has e-mailed, tweeted, commented, or connected with me on social media. Your generous support has made all the difference.

Chapter One

London, England, 1817

Matthew Strathmore, Earl of Whittingham, examined the array of puzzle pieces strewn across the mahogany table positioned near the paned glass windows of his study. A map of the world awaited his skill and attention. With a satisfied grunt, he completed another portion of the puzzle and reached for what could be Sicily as much as Sardinia, when a knock sounded at the door.

"Enter."

"Milord, you have a caller." The butler stood within the door frame without his customary salver in hand.

"Thank you, Spencer. Has the visitor presented a card?" Whittingham turned and stepped forward, his limp pronounced as he maneuvered with care.

"He did not, nor did he offer his name."

"Then I have no time." The earl retrieved his cane from where it rested against the desk and spared a glance, intent on progressing further with the puzzle before he focused on more purposeful matters.

"Milord?"

Spencer's tone gave him pause and he angled toward the butler in curiosity. "Yes?"

"The gentleman requested I offer this if you refused him admittance." The servant advanced, a suede pouch in his gloved palm.

"What the devil?" Whittingham snatched the bag from the servant's extended hand and spilled the contents. His sharp gasp overrode the foreboding chime of the hallway clock as a wave of recognition gripped him. "Show him up at once."

The butler walked with brisk steps toward the door.

"Hurry, Spencer, before the gentleman takes his leave." Whittingham barely recovered his composure before the Duke of Scarsdale entered. Then a devilish smile broke loose and he embraced his friend in a hale and hearty welcome.

"Scarsdale, I can't believe my eyes." They moved apart, shook hands, and the ten years separating their last visit evaporated as if it never existed.

"Nor can I. You, more than anyone, know how much I despise this city."

His reference to the turn of events that sent Lunden Beckford, third Duke of Scarsdale, as far from England as possible, charged the air with unresolved tension, but Whittingham refused to allow it to taint their visit. He was much relieved to see his old friend and harbored no ill feelings despite how society viewed Scarsdale's unexplained voluntary exile.

For a moment, no one spoke and then Matthew reached for the pocket watch where it rested on his desktop and slipped it into the suede pouch. He offered it with a solemn exhale.

"Thank you." The two words expressed volumes as Lunden returned the pouch to his trousers pocket.

Matthew leaned against the front of his desk and with a wag of his chin, indicated his friend take a chair. "Brandy? Or have you sworn off the poison?" He looked toward the liquor cabinet. "Last time we were together, you were drunk out of your wits."

"Don't look at me that way. You were equally impaired." Lunden declined with a nod. "Besides, you didn't expect me to sink to the bottom of a bottle and stay there for ten years, did you?" He shifted in his chair and his gaze traveled down Matthew's left leg, then upward along the curve of the cane.

"I do all right, you know." Matthew offered no further reassurance, and none was warranted. "So, why have you returned?"

"My solicitor transferred the ducal title and all entailments after my brother's death, but Douglas had some sort of damnable clause added to the paperwork in regard to his town house. I've allowed the property to be leased since I abandoned London, but the tenant has created a problem and I can no longer wait for solicitors and their legalities to unravel the mess. I want to sell it and detach from this city forever."

"No doubt you'll be able to resolve it with your solicitor's assistance now that you're here." Matthew walked to the cabinet intent on a drink. "Perhaps your brother had a specific reason for the clause. I think of him often. Douglas was a good man."

"Yes, he was." Lunden touched his fingers to the suede pouch secured in his pocket.

Matthew didn't wish to resurrect dead memories and silence descended like a heavy rock thrown into a deep puddle. "So how can I help? Do you need a place to stay?" He carried his brandy in one hand, his cane in the other, and took a seat behind the desk. "You're welcome to live here as long as needed. I would enjoy the company."

Lunden viewed his friend, as convivial as always, and a sliver of long-lost reminiscence pricked his conscience. He might loathe the city, but he missed companionship of friends, no matter his chosen isolation. For years he'd declined every invitation sent to his country estate until the few friends he'd possessed stopped requesting his attendance. And no fault could be found. He made it clear he wanted no part of fine society and did not still. Once the business at the bank concluded, he planned to return to Beckford Hall and exercise permanent rustication.

"I do need a place to stay. Thank you. It will be hellish trying to keep a low profile, but that's my hope." The Whittingham town house was situated on Cleveland Row, adjacent to Pall Mall, and not nearly as discreet as he'd prefer, but his choices were limited to one in number. "Do me a favor though and keep my presence here under wraps."

"Done. I will place the staff on notice. The servants have no need to know your name or purpose."

Matthew leaned back in his chair and for a fleeting moment Lunden thought he detected the beginning of a grin.

"Perhaps you would grant me a favor in return."

His friend was an astute thinker, even as a lad. There was no way Lunden could deny him; Matthew had taken a bullet to the leg defending his honor. "Of course. Name it."

Matthew briefly flashed a smile. "Excellent. Allow me to explain. My parents have retired to Lakeview. Father struggles with his breathing at times and the city air proves damp and dense. They've seen decades of Seasons and no longer desire the social obligations, most especially with

Father's health in question. To that end, they've asked me to find Amelia a husband."

"Amelia." Lunden hadn't thought of Matthew's sister in a number of years. He remembered her as a willful chit, more vinegar than sugar, with remarkable green eyes. The kind of eyes that distracted a man so thoroughly, the unsuspected soul never realized she'd kneed him in the groin until scorching pain shot through his lower body. He cleared his throat and said, "How very fine," although his inner voice screamed, *Good luck with that.*

"To no surprise, my sister proves unwilling to cooperate. We are like oil and water, always have been, and I suspect she resists my matchmaking attempts for no other reason than to vex me. Meanwhile, Mother desires results and she worries Father will find scant peace until he sees Amelia settled."

A shadow of unease enveloped the room and Lunden ran a hand along his jaw in an attempt to relieve the sudden tension. "What are you asking me to do?"

A second panicked question rose to mind, but he did not lend it voice. *Was Matthew asking him to wed his sister?* It couldn't be true. All London thought the worst of him. No man would want a scourge for a brother-in-law.

An insufferable silence ensued until at last Matthew replied. "Help me. I'm at wit's end. Find her a husband or facilitate the process. I need her married and out of my hair. The sooner, the better. Life is complicated enough without Amelia's difficulties."

"And how am I to accomplish this and likewise remain undetected? I've been gone for a decade and everyone in this city thinks poorly of me. Once society gets wind I've returned . . ." With a twinge in his chest, he recalled how polite condolences after his brother's unexpected death became veiled inquiries into the circumstances of the accident, and then later transformed into invidious questions and blunt accusations of the vilest nature.

"I'm not asking you to escort her to a ball." Matthew appeared to warm to the idea. "Just help her realize she's fighting an unwinnable battle. She needs to be married, and although I'm not convinced she's opposed to the idea, she objects to any gentleman who pays her favor. Influence her. She hung on your every word when we were children."

"Well, we're all grown up now. I haven't seen her in years." Lunden doubted he could serve any real purpose in the plan. "You're asking me, a notorious blight suspected of murder and collusion, to somehow remain in the background *and* achieve a small miracle?"

Matthew grinned. "I've always believed you invincible."

"Foolish notion." Lunden shifted in his chair. "I hadn't planned on staying in the city overlong."

"Those are my terms. Take it or leave it." Matthew stood and took a few steps, his limp a constant reminder of the heroic deed for which he'd paid a heavy price. "Besides, if you put your mind to it, you can accomplish the task with ease and we'll all be the better for it."

A remembrance of those very same words echoed in his empty chest and Lunden swallowed past the lump in his throat. Matthew was one of the few friends who didn't ostracize him after the sketchy details surrounding Douglas's death became public. How difficult could it be to see his sister matched? He'd make quick work of marrying her off to the first bloke who proposed and then pursue his personal plans.

"Agreed." Lunden took a deep breath and extended his hand for a firm shake.

With more agility than he'd shown earlier, Matthew rounded the desk and rifled through papers spread across the felt blotter. "My mother composed a list for me. I'm sure it will assist."

"Brilliant. Candidates will make the matter much easier." Lunden's apprehension waned. Perhaps he was getting worked up for nothing.

"Not candidates." Matthew laughed a deep rumble. "If it were that easy, I'd have undertaken the task myself. Now here it is." He pulled a sheet of foolscap from a long drawer. "It lists the qualities Mother insists her son-in-law possess. By my guess she assumed I would marry Amelia to the first bloke who proposed and then move on." He aired a wry smile. "What little confidence she has in me. Anyway, here it is."

Lunden accepted the paper with trepidation. He scanned it with a flick of his eyes and then folded it to place inside the left breast pocket of his waistcoat. "Anything else?"

"Just a thought. When you consider candidates, you should avoid Lord Trent. He would not be amendable. Last month, Amelia set his crotch on fire."

"Pardon?" Lunden's bottom half tightened involuntarily and he shifted in his chair. *Again.*

Matthew's expression wavered between humor and exasperation. "We recently attended a dinner party where I planned to pursue my mother's objective. Through no easy manipulation I changed Amelia's seat assignment to a position adjacent Lord Trent. Not only is he a respected peer, but he manages his estate masterfully and is rarely seen out of form. A perfect candidate." Matthew paused for a short breath. "My sister can be charming at times and I hoped she'd become smitten with the young earl, as most other ladies fawn at Trent's every word.

"The dinner was going well, at least I believed so, and the conversation turned to social news. I was thrilled. Surely the Fates were smiling on me. Unfortunately, Trent in a brain lapse I cannot explain to this day, commented that women won all the benefits of marriage, while men were doomed to a future of henpecking.

"Amelia sprung from her chair with such vehemence she dislodged the silver epergne at the center of the table and it tumbled forward, dropping six burning candles into Lord Trent's lap. Had I not reacted so swiftly and doused him with the contents of the water pitcher, the man would have no hope of propagating a future heir."

Lunden cleared his throat. *Twice*.

"Needless to say, I wouldn't bear him in mind." Matthew turned to where his ongoing puzzle lay spread in hundreds of pieces. "It will take a unique man to appreciate Amelia's adventurous spirit."

"Is that how you label it?" Lunden joined him beside the table and assessed the project strewn before them. "Is there anyone else I should avoid?"

"Lords Riley and Lennox." Matthew placed a piece into the Atlantic Ocean near the edge of the new continent. "That should be everyone."

"Clever how you've foisted this task onto me because you detest it yourself." Lunden watched as his friend fitted three more pieces in succession to form a short portion of Egypt's border. Egypt; now there was a place far from the painful memories found in London and the foolish endeavor he'd agreed to accomplish. The puzzle offered myriad escape opportunities.

"You'll do better at it. Amelia resists my suggestions before she considers them, simply because I'm her sibling. She gainsays me at every turn."

"Shall I tell her that you've engineered *this* Machiavellian plot? If she's as sharp-witted as I recall, she'll discover the truth without difficulty."

"I'll leave Amelia in your capable hands. I trust you. You're like a brother to me."

It was a poor choice of words and the look of dismay on Matthew's face confirmed he regretted the statement, but the sentiment was well meant and Lunden wouldn't allow his friend remorse.

"Now show me to my rooms, before I reconsider and flee this house." Lunden waited for no further remarks and aimed for the doorway with purposeful strides.

Chapter Two

Amelia Strathmore twirled the rod of her pink silk parasol, her chin high, as she strolled the sidewalk toward her dearest friend's residence. Her chaperone trailed behind like the ribbons of Amelia's bonnet fluttering on the warm spring breeze. When she reached the home of Lady Charlotte Dearing, she opened the wrought-iron gate and strode up the limestone path to knock on the front door. Thank heavens Charlotte had not moved farther away after her recent marriage.

Amelia would be lost without their morning ritual of a walk to St. James Square, where they sat on a marble bench and confessed secrets before they returned the same way they'd come. At times they would feed pigeons, read poetry, or watch pedestrians, but always they conversed about matters of the heart. Amelia focused on her brother's haphazard attempts to see her married, while Charlotte lamented her current unhappiness, trapped in a practical match when she desired true love.

Amelia dropped the knocker and waited, the butler accustomed to her frequent visits. True to form, the two ladies departed arm in arm only moments later, their chaperones in step behind.

"I'm surprised your brother persists when you've made it clear you will choose a man to marry when *you* are ready."

Her friend's loyal support served as a balm to her soul. With Father's health failing, Amelia suspected time was running out on her independent status. "I don't think Matthew believes me. Meanwhile, I have no idea what he'll attempt next." A sudden giggle escaped. "Although I daresay I'll never forget the look on Lord Trent's face when his pants lit on fire."

"If only I had been there. I would have applauded your valiant defense."

No one knew, save Charlotte, the true reason Lord Trent's comment incited Amelia's temper and spurred her vehement response. "You're my dearest friend. I could never allow anyone to spout blithe nonsense when you're living proof men have all the advantages in marriage and women have none."

Charlotte's expression turned solemn and for a few breaths only the clicking heels of their boots marked their progression along the cobbles. A carriage rolled by and a small dog chased its rear wheels. Amelia watched it pass as her heart ached for her disconsolate friend.

"It hasn't been so bad of late."

Amelia squeezed Charlotte's arm tighter. "That's what I fear the most. At least when Lord Dearing behaves with his usual surly demeanor, we know what to expect. When he's kind, I'm terribly suspicious." An unbidden shiver passed through her and she hugged Charlotte closer. "Did you mention how much you'd like an animal companion? A dog or a cat would keep you company when he's locked in his study or otherwise occupied. Pandora is always there for me no matter my mood, and even though cats cannot speak, she never fails to console me."

"Yes, but consider the trouble Pandora has caused. Lord

Dearing wouldn't be pleased if a pet scratched the furniture or stained the carpet."

Amelia's scoff overrode Charlotte's objection. "Does he plan for a family someday? Children do the very same things and worse. Besides, just because Pandora finds mischief does not mean all cats have the same temperament." She smiled. Her cat was her second dearest friend to Charlotte and she would not trade either companion for all the chocolate in the world.

"When I suggested we purchase a pet, he didn't reply with keen approval."

"Did you mention it would bring you happiness?" Amelia prodded, determined to improve Charlotte's situation.

"Happiness was not a condition to my marriage. My parents needed the security of Dearing's finances. If only I'd had the time to get to know him better. You're lucky to have your brother in control of your future instead of parents sorely indebted and in need of immediate rescue."

They arrived at the square and settled on their favorite bench. Amelia regretted the questions if they forced Charlotte to dwell on her current unhappiness. Though she feared her own situation was not so unlike that fate.

"Luck has nothing to do with it. Father is ill. Last time I visited, his breathing had not improved." Amelia schooled her features, although emotion crept into her voice. "I suppose my brother will be more determined than ever to see me wed." She released a long, melancholic sigh. "Are we both fools to believe in true love? To hope that there is more to life than insipid tea parties and polite conversation?"

"Sometimes I wonder why we ever thought it possible to achieve a love match. Surely it's as rare as a meteor shower on Christmas morning."

Amelia tapped the toe of her boot against the pavement in deep consternation, her heart at war with better sense.

She did believe in love. *True love*. Her parents were devoted to each other and she couldn't recall a time when they weren't affectionate and respectful. It was the very crux of the problem. Her parents wanted her married and infinitely happy before Father's illness progressed or something worse occurred, but how could one find true love on a timetable? Amelia knew exactly what she wanted in a husband and as of yet, the field proved lacking. If she was forced to surrender her freedom, she wanted love and fidelity in return. The fear of not accomplishing this goal left her firmly planted in ambivalence.

Charlotte continued with a note of despair. "I suppose we will have to be satisfied with our lot in life. When I was a child I envisioned a different future, but Lord Dearing has proved very generous with my family. It would be selfish of me to complain he doesn't show me affection or make me feel special when he's saved my parents and three sisters from poverty."

Amelia's right brow climbed high at her friend's resignation. "All is not lost, Charlotte. Marriage is a huge adjustment. Perhaps Lord Dearing has experienced similar reservations, and life will become more enjoyable as time passes." The suggestion sounded as flaccid as the hawthorn branches providing shade above them, but Amelia's devotion to her friend forced her to be optimistic.

"He hardly speaks to me. At times I wonder if he likes me at all."

"Now that's utter rubbish. You're the kindest, loveliest, most agreeable creature on this earth. If Dearing doesn't talk to you, he must be tongue-tied by your beauty." Amelia stood and brushed off her skirts. "Give it time. Perhaps we expect too much too soon." She was carried away now, babbling like a magpie because she couldn't bear her friend's self-deprecating conclusions.

They spoke of mundane topics for the remainder of their

visit and after they said good-bye at Charlotte's gate, Amelia hurried home with the intent to go upstairs to Matthew's study and insist he investigate Lord Dearing's poor behavior. Charlotte's situation proved no one need rush into this husband business. It was a matter to be considered with care, although Amelia knew they should make haste for Father's sake.

Pressing her parasol and bonnet into Spencer's waiting hands, she bounded up the staircase without pausing to inquire of Matthew's schedule. She suspected he'd be playing at his tiled puzzle anyway.

Fearing he might go stir-crazy during his convalescence, and in a bid to ward off the toll on his spirit, Mother bought him the first puzzle while he recuperated from that dreadful gunshot wound ten years ago, her intent to keep his mind busy while his body remained idle. Little did Mother know what she'd incited. Now Matthew devoured them, at times poring over the pieces for hours as if his life depended on the puzzle's completion.

Amelia burst through the double doors of the study and took two long strides before she froze in place, realizing her brother was not alone.

Lunden stared at the majestic beauty who stormed into the room as if she was the queen who owned the castle and someone had stolen her crown. A command stalled on her lips as their eyes locked. Then a ripple of shock vibrated through him, echoing to the depths of his soul with a strange familiarity. Yet, he'd never met the mysterious lady. With certainty, he'd have remembered her unmatched face and statuesque body, never mind her mane of disorderly black curls, dark and glossy as a raven's wing.

He found his tongue, relieved it didn't hang from his

mouth. "Pardon me, Whittingham. You've a guest. We'll continue our discussion later this afternoon."

Lucky devil, to have this beauty so accustomed to keeping his company, she needn't be announced.

Lunden turned to leave but his friend's sharp interjection halted his progress.

"Amelia's hardly a guest." Matthew laughed, this time louder. "Isn't that right, Troublemaker?"

"Don't call me that." She spoke, her voice a rebellious whisper meant for her brother, although her eyes never left Lunden's face. He noted the furrow of her delicate brows as if she struggled to understand the circumstances, her curious gaze as green and brilliant as he remembered.

"My pleasure, Lady Amelia." He sketched a polite bow. "Too much time has passed. The fault is mine, although if I recall correctly your parents kept you sequestered in the country."

"It was a matter of survival," Matthew quipped from the corner. "At least in the wilds of nature, the population had a fighting chance of continued existence."

"Instead I was the one left to perish from boredom." She swung her eyes to her brother with a look of exaggerated tolerance.

Lunden noted how quickly her witty retort nipped at the heels of Matthew's jest. And too, he couldn't stop staring at her mouth. Her lips, full and pouty, were more courtesan than genteel lady and better suited for heated kisses and whispered temptations than conversation in the drawing room. The lower half of his body concurred.

Matthew came forward, a broad smile on his face. "Someday your clever tongue will get you into trouble."

Lunden stifled a cough. *Indeed.*

He stepped away so brother and sister could share a private word, although neither participant made an effort to lower their voice.

"You can't barge into my study whenever you wish. A knock shows due respect. How I will find you a husband I have no idea."

"You've voiced that complaint ad infinitum. With such mundane repetition, one would think that bullet found your head and not your leg."

"Lunden, this is no time to remain quiet. Speak up and fortify my effort." Matthew waved in his direction. "You do remember Scarsdale, don't you, Amelia? You insulted his honor a scant minute ago."

Mortification tinged the lady's cheeks crimson, but there was no need. Her reference to Matthew's wound fell far within the boundaries of normal sibling banter. The emotions that plagued him, the ever-present guilt and regret, visited him during the late-night hours when he was desperate for sleep. Lunden didn't give her glib retort a second thought.

But she did.

He flicked his eyes to Amelia and her unease confirmed she knew she'd proven her brother's point and spoken too callously of his injury.

Lunden sought to soothe her embarrassment. "I'm not so foolish to take sides in a sibling squabble." *So this was the challenge set before him. A termagant wrapped in ribbons and bows. He should have taken rooms at a coaching inn.*

A black cat sauntered into the study with royal poise. It skimmed Amelia's skirts in a habit born of affection and leapt atop the table near the windows.

"Remove Pandora at once." Matthew's stern command sliced the air. "I'll not have that animal destroy the progress I've made on South America."

The cat flicked its tail in deference and settled atop the puzzle, its lean body stretched across the completed portion, its hind feet shuffling loose pieces. Lunden watched the scene with interest, the feline's eyes as remarkable as its owner. Had he not seen them in the room together, he'd be convinced Amelia and the cat were one in the same. A changeling of sorts. She'd certainly transformed in every way imaginable since the young girl he remembered from a decade ago.

Amelia glanced in his direction, all previous bluster gone, and scooped the cat into her arms in a protective gesture.

"Perhaps I should have knocked. I didn't mean to interrupt your meeting."

Her tone indicated she begrudged every word.

"Thank you." Matthew regained his amiable demeanor. "Scarsdale will be staying with us while he attends business. Private business, not to be shared beyond these walls. It's fortuitous you arrived so I could inform you. I only wish you would observe a stricter sense of propriety. Had I been interviewing a husband candidate, your behavior would have obliterated his first impression."

Exasperation narrowed her eyes as she backed toward the door. When her expression mellowed, she turned a brilliant smile in his direction. "It was a pleasure to see you, Your Grace. I would like to stay longer and inquire of your well-being, but my brother forces me from the room with his repetitive blather. I look forward to speaking with you at another time."

She turned on her heel and swept from the room, her cat nestled in her arms as close as an ermine stole.

"Perhaps Amelia wouldn't resist your marital advice if you didn't press so hard." Lunden dragged his eyes from the empty doorway and joined his friend where he lingered near the puzzle table, repairing the damage incurred by Pandora. "It can't bear well that she's being forced into a match in consideration of your father's health concerns."

"She is two and twenty." Matthew placed a piece in the Strait of Gibraltar. "She needs to get on with it and stop dragging her feet. Many of her friends are already settled. It makes little sense to avoid the inevitable, especially when Father will find peace in knowing she's well matched. Amelia finds the most interesting situations, and I wouldn't want her to regret hapless choices." He placed four more pieces before he stepped away and leveled a stare at Lunden that mirrored his sister's earlier exasperation. "In truth, I need her to be someone else's headache." His expression eased. "The poor chap will require the patience of a saint."

Chapter Three

Amelia hurried down the hallway with Pandora pressed against her chest, a shield to conceal her hammering heart. Scarsdale, with his whisky-colored eyes and smooth voice, was an unexpected hiccup in her well-planned day. For some unexplainable reason, he unsettled her. If only she could remember more of his broken history.

She stepped around the coal scuttle and settled into the chimney corner of the drawing room, her favorite place to ponder big thoughts. Tucking her feet under her skirts, a breath of relief escaped. Pandora curled into her lap in a practiced habit and Amelia stroked her velvety fur as the rapid beat of her heart calmed. She rested her head against the smooth stones of the hearth and with effort swept the cobwebs from her memory.

At twelve years of age, she'd been sheltered from societal news, but when Matthew's injury brought him to the country estate to recuperate, she'd gleaned bits of information whenever someone forgot she remained in the room.

Foremost, a vivid memory of her brother's defense of Scarsdale's character sprang to mind. Matthew's protestations had been tinged with sadness, his tone bleak, whether from his personal injury or the circumstances, she could not know. And she remembered her parents' expressions as compassionate and free from anger, despite their only son having taken a bullet to the leg on someone else's behalf. To this day, Matthew still called Scarsdale *friend*.

It was only now, when confronted with the dashing man, that she paused to wonder what he had done to set society on its ear.

Something nefarious enough to send him from the city for over a decade. What prompted his return? Why now?

As a child she hadn't thought beyond Matthew's well-being. What a trial she'd presented, forcing him to play endless games of backgammon while confined to his bed, unable to flee her persistent antics and endless chatter. A smile twisted her lips. He'd proven a good brother, fair-natured and at times overprotective, the precise mixture required of a loving sibling.

The acknowledgment brought about a resonant exhale. There was no escaping the fact she would have to consider a husband in earnest. Father was ill. But how would she find someone she could tolerate for the rest of her life? Someone interesting and spirited, yet also kindhearted and loving?

Perhaps Scarsdale returned to London in search of a wife.

The ridiculous notion stalled her hand and Pandora meowed in protestation. Even now in the familiarity of her cozy corner, she remained undeniably intrigued by his handsome chiseled features and deep baritone. When he spoke, his voice simmered within her and little pinpoints of excitement pricked her skin. It was an unusual and pleasurable sensation. One she wished to experience again.

Discovering his purpose in London would distract from the dismal feat of obtaining a husband, at least until the reality of her circumstances could no longer be ignored. Amelia smiled and pulled Pandora to her cheek in an affectionate nuzzle. She could hardly wait until tomorrow morning to share this news with Charlotte.

* * *

It was later that evening when Lunden had the chance to review the list Matthew foisted on him. He removed the foolscap from the pocket of his waistcoat where it draped across the corner of his bed and settled in the velvet-backed bonnet chair nearest the fire. As he unfolded the paper, the scent of lilacs assailed his nostrils, and he wondered at the frivolities of women and their need to perfume everything.

Lunden brought his eyes to the first item on the list and dismissed his silent musings.

1. Honesty

He scoffed. How serendipitous he needn't fall under candidate review. He would fail miserably at the first requirement. Secrecy and deceit became his two closest allies the cold night of Douglas's death.

He closed his eyes and dropped his head back against the armchair cushion. He should never have argued with his brother. He was foolish and young, an irrepressible bundle of adolescent confusion with an attitude that outsized his britches. His cutting remarks and hurtful accusations were typical rites of manhood, but now he wished he could recant it all.

He opened his eyes, shook his head, and forced his eyes to the second item on Lady Whittingham's list.

2. Fidelity
3. Love
4. Passion

Indeed, Lady Whittingham wished for grandchildren. Lunden attempted some type of smile, but the effort failed. Of course, he knew how it felt to love deeply—first his

parents, then his brother—and was astute enough to realize
these sentiments paled when compared to the intimacy between two lovers.

But love proved a wasted emotion.

His gaze fell to the list clenched in his fist.

5. Courage

Now *that* he possessed in spades. He'd given up an easy
life, adopted the habits of a recluse, and exerted courage
every morning when he forced his eyes open and got on
with the day.

Time was a merciless master. Hadn't his trip to London
proved the speed in which years passed and things changed?
Amelia certainly had. Perhaps repaying this favor to Matthew
would not prove so difficult.

Amelia was lovely. No, that word failed. He was momentarily stunned when she'd entered the room, as fiery and
commanding as he remembered, except instead of a young
pixie who caused her brother and his chums unending
havoc, she'd matured into a breathtakingly beautiful woman.

Something unusual stirred deep in his chest and he
shoved it away. He should get on with fulfilling the agreement so he could pursue his business matter and rid the city.
London held too many memories and too much power to
exhume all the secrets he labored to keep buried.

He rose and returned the folded list to his waistcoat
pocket. He'd keep it there as a reminder to act on Lady
Whittingham's wishes with urgency. Then he walked to the
sideboard and poured two fingers of brandy, relishing the
burn as he swallowed it back.

Fortified, Lunden removed the suede pouch from his
trousers pocket and slid his brother's watch into his palm.
The gold cover once boasting Douglas's engraved initials
was lost in the accident, although the crystal, scratched and

splintered, still protected the inlaid face. He stared at it as he'd done countless times, and the forbidding hands screamed back their callous answer easing none of his pain—the time of his brother's death, eleven twenty.

Amelia was her usual cheerful self when she met Charlotte at the door and advanced to the walkway the following morning. She allowed her friend to chatter until they reached their favorite bench and settled. With a glance to affirm their chaperones remained out of earshot, Amelia grasped Charlotte's hand and informed her of the most current events.

"Scarsdale? I don't know a whit about him aside from what you've just mentioned. We were too young when his difficulties in London arose, and certainly no one has included me in a discussion of dastardly deeds. Lord Dearing hardly talks to me at all."

Charlotte's smile faltered and Amelia watched as her friend struggled to conceal her unhappiness, a condition that grew more evident each morning.

Amelia persisted although her mind wandered down a different path. "I only bring it up because I wonder if there's a connection between Scarsdale and my brother's efforts to see me wed."

"Why so ever would you think that?" Charlotte removed her slipper and shook a pebble free. "Did you hear your brother discuss the matter with him?"

"No, but Matthew speaks of little else with anyone willing to listen. I'd imagine Scarsdale became the next victim of opportunity." Amelia nodded her head in visible disgust. "Never mind about that, I have a brilliant idea. I plan to visit my parents at Lakeview next week. I think you should ask Lord Dearing if you may accompany me. It would be lovely to escape the city for a few days and my parents will be delighted to see you." A secret desire to isolate her friend for an extended period of time prompted Amelia's invitation, but it was truly not subterfuge. She wanted to visit her parents and they would enjoy Charlotte's company. Then she could pursue the quandary of her best friend's melancholy without the boundaries of a thirty-minute morning constitutional.

"I doubt he'll agree."

Charlotte appeared uncomfortable and the change in her demeanor was yet another proverbial nail in Dearing's coffin.

"It can't hurt to try. One never knows until one poses the question. Does Lord Dearing so intimidate you that you can't propose a simple request?" She hadn't meant to sound harsh, but when tears threatened Charlotte's eyes, Amelia regretted the words as they rushed from her mouth. "Forgive me. I didn't intend to upset you, but I have it all worked out in my head. Traveling will be fun. Remember when we were younger before you became a wife? I miss our time spent together."

Charlotte's face softened and with a little sniff, her tears vanished. "I know. I miss you as well. This has all become difficult, but I'll make you a promise. I'll ask Lord Dearing about journeying with you to Lakeview, if you confront your brother about this marriage business. You should uncover his plans so we'll know whether he intends to bind you to the next available bachelor or include you in the decision. We must do everything in our power to ensure you escape as mismatched an arrangement as mine. Do we have a deal?"

Shrewd business indeed, but Charlotte made a fine point. A shudder skittered down her spine at the thought of marriage to the wrong gentleman, the commitment itself inevitable for no other reason than to ease her father's concerns. She was a dutiful daughter and cared for her parents deeply.

That being true, she should at least understand how much control she would wield in the process.

"Deal." She extended her hand and they shook on their agreement in the same manner she'd seen her brother do on many an occasion.

The walk home seemed quicker and the future a tiny bit brighter as she climbed the stairs and strode into Matthew's study, not bothering to knock. But he was not there.

Scarsdale, his midnight hair and broad-shouldered stance a clear indication a different man waited near the windows. A mixture of world-weariness and secrecy hung around him as if he possessed so much of the qualities they overflowed onto the floor like a death shroud.

He turned before she could finish her assessment of his stature . . . *or recover her breathing.*

"Lady Amelia."

He announced her name, each syllable a deep timbre, and she smiled, all at once her stomach at odds. "Your Grace, you must call me Amelia. You did so when we were children. It seems rather foolish to stand on formality now."

"I agree, and you must return the familiarity. We've known each other through decades."

A stilted pause ensued although Amelia could feel the thunderous beat of her heart as if it played a concerto on her rib cage. Little made her nervous, but she knew no other label for the strange sensation.

"Your brother isn't here at the moment."

She noted the quiet intensity in Scarsdale's gaze, a somber concentration that overrode any other emotion that dared enter his eyes. He appeared the same yesterday. Did his expression never change?

Her memory produced his smile, although she couldn't have been more than six years old when she'd first met him at Lakeview. For some odd reason, she could still see his lopsided grin, the left cheek dimpled, as he yanked on her braids and ran from the sitting room, acting on her brother's challenge. Peculiar, how the single memory stayed with her. Matthew had a fondness for issuing tests of risk-taking conscience and daring spirit. Perhaps that was the reason.

"Thank you. May I ask you a question?" When he made no indication, she attempted an explanation of sorts. "To satisfy my curiosity."

Cold fury darkened his eyes. Apparently she'd struck a nerve, but she dared not study him long. It would be all but impossible to concentrate on her objective if she drank too much from his intoxicating whisky-brown eyes.

Lunden stiffened and forced himself to relax a breath later, unwilling to permit this forthright hoyden to pry into his past. The events surrounding Douglas's death were a millstone around his neck, at one time a noose, and he would not allow anyone to dredge up information he fought so vigorously to keep buried.

"Pardon?" His voice had lowered to a malice-filled whisper. He would listen to Amelia's inquiry, if she'd proved so bold, and then remind her gossip preyed on the weak-minded. The sharp memory of the unending censure of his brother's death hardened his jaw. Those rumors, born as mournful whispers, seamlessly evolved into lascivious exaggerations. He could not imagine what version of the mistruth Amelia meant to explore.

"Are you here to acquire a bride?"

"What? No." He had no idea how she'd conjured the ungodly notion he needed a woman in his life and he almost laughed with relief. He'd been too quick to judge her motive.

"Oh, very good. I thought, perhaps my brother . . ." She

did not finish, the awkwardness of her suggestion loud in the room.

"Have no fear. I would be your brother's last choice." He kept his sober expression in place despite his self-deprecating response.

Her posture softened, all at once at ease. "Then Matthew did not speak to you about finding me a match?"

Her eyes communicated skepticism and he noted a touch of rebellion in the question. A variety of answers, all capable of avoiding the truth, leapt to mind and he discarded them. He'd accomplished enough lying for a lifetime, the result stranding him in an untenable situation, labeled a liar, and ostracized from society as a consequence for showing loyalty to his brother.

"Now that's a different question altogether." He stepped closer to where she lingered near the door. Did she think to make a fast exit after her brazen inquiries if the answers proved unacceptable? "I was under the assumption all young women dreamed of balls and similar delectations, a life lived in the social spotlight on the arm of their husband."

"Not me."

She didn't say more, the two words softly spoken, yet something had changed. She stood almost as tall as he and there was nothing about her that professed defeat, although her words signaled a deeper meaning to her admittance.

"Your brother wishes to see you married as soon as possible. You're two and twenty. Most women are settled by that age."

Her chin shot up and her emerald eyes, framed with inky black lashes, flashed in defiance. "Settled, yes, and unhappily so. The very word implies compromise and dissatisfaction. Am I to have no say in the matter? It's my future he plans, not some insignificant puzzle he seeks to complete before moving on to other things." She pushed past him to the table and shuffled a few pieces in her distraction as if to emphasize her anger.

"It's the way of things. The world's rules are not of my making." If they were, then his past wouldn't haunt him still.

"I have no wish to be sentenced to a life of unhappiness, forced to wed by convention, or matched by convenient arrangement." She turned with a shake of dark, silky curls and pinned him with a stare, her words as sharp as her perspicuity. "I would prefer to live independently if left with a dismal choice. I've nothing against marriage unless I'm not to have a say."

The girl possessed spirit enough to drive a man to Bedlam. The sooner he resolved this business, the greater his chance at finding some small scrap of peace.

"I see." Defiance tinged her cheeks pink, the contrast of innocence at odds with her confident stance. *Damn it, she looked fetching.*

"I have no desire for Matthew to find me a husband, never mind involve a virtual stranger in the private affair. He accuses me of wasting time and lacking effort, but I've discovered no suitor who sparks my interest." She sighed. "Why would you assist him?"

He tempered his anger. "Your brother almost died defending my honor. There is little he could ask that I would not endeavor to achieve."

She dismissed his reply with a straightening of her shoulders. "It will be no easy undertaking. I can't imagine why any intelligent man would desire a contrary wife." She strode forward and met his eyes in challenge, nearly upsetting the puzzle with the abrupt twirl of skirts. "Matthew tells me I'm outspoken and difficult. A square peg for a round hole or nonsense like that."

Something ached inside his soul but he forced the

emotion away. "There's nothing wrong with being different. I'd imagine you possess qualities that overshadow any fault you find in your nature." *Pouty lips and endlessly long legs, for example. How glorious those legs would feel wrapped tightly around his hips. And those lips pressed against . . .* He cleared his throat and realigned his thoughts.

"So you've agreed to assist him. I understand." She closed her eyes for longer than a blink. "I don't suppose I can change your mind."

"Is there something about marriage that disturbs you?"

Her previous determination wavered and her eyes dimmed the slightest. "Yes, that's true."

Her response was both sufficient answer and obscure confession. Lunden eyed her with avid interest. For such a cheeky girl, she seemed exceptionally closemouthed in regard to her reluctance to marry. Was it a matter of control? Fear? "Why have you dragged your feet and delayed your fate? You possess beauty to catch a bachelor's eye. I am sure, were you to set your mind to it, you could charm any gentleman." His mind conjured an image of Lord Trent's flaming crotch and Lunden mentally corrected himself.

Amelia paused, her lush lips pursed as if she wanted to reply but decided otherwise.

"And there is the matter of your father's declining health," he pressed. "Marriage seems the best path forward."

"I detest the idea of a binding decision made in haste, although I would never disappoint my father. If you're bent on pursuing this objective, we should come to an accord. A guarantee of sorts to smooth the process."

Lunden gathered his patience close. How entertaining. What would the lovely termagant propose now?

"I will meet the gentlemen necessary and make a genuine effort to find a suitable husband if you'll agree to a short list of requests." She raised her chin a notch, her silken curls in unruly disarray.

"You have demands?" The lady was a shrewd opponent, a devious charlatan disguised in burgundy fustian and blond lace.

"Requests. Once married I will have little freedom. Label it foolish, but I wish to experience a taste of excitement before I become a wife."

Marriage with the right man would fill your life with nothing but exciting experiences. All of them delicious.

He banished the observation with no desire to enlighten. The whole situation was none of his concern beyond resolving one obligation, so he could attend to his personal affairs. "You hold a surprisingly dismal perception of marriage. I believed your parents happily married for decades."

"Oh yes, and it further proves my point. My parents are a love match. Marriage for convenience or any other reason is a trap. I know that to be true."

She didn't expound on her statements and Lunden didn't inquire of her certainty. Marriage was a waste of brain power, but love, that was a topic on which he had very strong views. "Love makes life complicated and is the stuff of childish dreams. A life without love is the purest existence."

She gasped, her slender brows furrowed as if his words shocked and saddened at the same time. The moment did not last and she angled her chin higher.

"Do we have an agreement?" Her spectacular eyes glinted with purpose and determination.

The lady had one goal in mind, although any purpose that helped him speed the process was welcomed. She stepped closer, almost too close, and he was struck by the brilliant spark in her gaze and the subtle scent of jasmine. It suited her, all uncommon beauty and wildflower. A thrum of desire ignited under his skin. She extended her hand to further her proposition.

The corner of his mouth twitched at her businesslike pose and he clasped her bare hand in a firm shake. Her fingertips trailed across his palm as she withdrew them and when she rushed from the room, he stared to where her delicate caress lingered, no matter they no longer touched.

Chapter Four

Had she pledged her soul to the devil? Scarsdale claimed an unscrupulous reputation and she not only bargained, but aligned with him to work toward a common goal. *Marriage.* Something she didn't desire at present, but would be forced to accept. Was it wrong of her to want love? The duke would never understand. His opinion of the emotion left her flabbergasted.

Before he'd reconsider their agreement, Amelia rushed to her bedchamber and flipped through the pages of her journal intent on finding the list in question. Measuring her eagerness, she gently tore the page from the stitched binding and hurried downstairs to Matthew's study. No gentleman would agree to such outlandish behavior, not even one rumored to disregard propriety, but she fanned the flames of hope nonetheless, determined to latch on to an opportunity to accomplish her goal.

Her boots couldn't carry her fast enough and she returned to the study, relieved to find Lunden remained. Had she thought he would flee? This man who left the city amidst outrageous scandal a decade ago and never once looked back.

"You're still here." The words escaped before she could

stop them and he inclined his head as if he misunderstood her doubt.

"I'm a man of my word."

His deep tone emphasized the hard edge of the statement and Amelia resisted the urge to withdraw, yet at the same time his gaze conjured images of heated brandy and goose down, a secret promise of all warm, wonderful things. She could eye him forever and never become bored of the view. She steadied her hand as she extended the paper in his direction. "Here is my list."

He accepted the foolscap and scanned her writing. His dark brows rose by the time he neared the end but he did not laugh, nor did he thrust the list in her direction with a flat refusal.

"Your brother won't be pleased."

"I make no presumption you'd be foolish enough to inform him." Something associated with a grin twitched his lips as he slipped the paper into his right breast pocket.

"And if I accomplish these three demands . . ." His voice held a lovely mischief.

"Requests." She interrupted. They were in fact, exactly what he stated, but she refused to allow him the upper hand.

"Then you will be amenable to marriage?"

"Yes." She blurted her answer, anxious to have it out of her mouth as quickly as possible and thereby tried not to fidget, although the tip of her boot tapped a nervous cadence on the hardwood floor.

"Why?"

She could never tell him the truth, that accomplishing her list would ensure she held power within her marriage, and with power came freedom. *Freedom to escape if her husband proved unbearable and her life as unhappy as Charlotte's appeared.* A beat of fear, unwelcome and terrifying, chased these conclusions. "Those are my terms. Do you agree?"

Her refusal to answer his inquiry and instead pose her own question didn't seem to bother him. He walked to the liquor cabinet and poured a small measure.

"Where is your chaperone?"

His question caught her by surprise and without answer Amelia went to the bell pull and summoned a servant to fetch her maid, Mary. An inescapable shadow of doubt mocked her actions. When Mary entered, wide-eyed and silent, Lunden cast a speculative glare in her direction and Amelia shifted with unease.

"Does she speak any English?"

How he'd discovered the ruse so easily was beyond her comprehension. "I've taught her a few rudimentary phrases, but she mostly succeeds with a smile and nod."

"And your brother approves of a chaperone who has no command of the language?"

"He allowed me to choose my own maid and has barely conversed with her, at least not at length or of a subject that could not be answered—"

"With a smile and nod." He watched her for several long minutes, and Amelia refused to break the hold of his gaze. Against her better judgment she became lost in an assessment of his entrancing eyes, a delightful shade of brown rimmed with an edging of gold, all heat and liquid, decidedly uncommon and unexpectedly beautiful. As deep and secretive as the man himself. For reasons unknown, the farther she sank into their silky depths, the more her body tingled in private parts, intimate parts.

She looked away with a gasp of objection as she spied her maid, stalled near the doorway and thoroughly confused. Amelia flitted her hand in a blithe wave. "You may go, Mary. I will join you shortly."

* * *

Lunden could make neither heads nor tails of Amelia's convoluted perception of marriage, but the why of it didn't matter. He'd accepted her terms and would see them done. Another list in his waistcoat pocket. Like mother, like daughter. He slid his focus to where she remained poised for escape. Bloody hell, she was mischief barely managed, all feminine beauty on the surface and sensual hellfire underneath. A man could go mad from wanting a woman like that. Her words were sharp, her tone tart, but what would she taste like were he to capture those plump, luscious lips in a deep openmouthed kiss? He finished his brandy in one swallow and set the empty glass on the sideboard with deliberate ease.

There was a time when he wanted what Amelia represented: a wife, children, a home. By his own poor decisions, he now lived on the outskirts of convention, chewing on life's gristle. Secrecy cleaved his existence to pieces, regret obliterated his dreams, and the ashes of both were best left scattered. Perhaps this knowledge made him amenable to her harebrained proposition. Something akin to vulnerability flared in her crystalline eyes when she'd handed him the list.

"I suggest we begin tomorrow." He cleared his throat and forced his thoughts to the problem at hand. "I will meet you at noon in Hyde Park. There's a section to the rear of Oxford Street across from the Tyburn Gallows. I passed the area as I arrived and it will serve our purpose well, for it is little more than an abandoned field, unnoticed by pedestrians. Does this arrangement suit you?"

"It does."

Her voice sounded breathy, as if he'd surprised her with his ambitious plan. It only made sense to begin with haste. Then he'd be one step closer to fulfilling his commitment, able to focus on resolving the problem with the town house, and rid of the city once and for all.

"I will take care of all necessities." He spoke slowly, each word marked by his boot heels on the study floor. "You'll need only to arrive." She appeared anxious, her green eyes wide and glittering in the reflected light, but he couldn't imagine why. This was what she wanted, for what she bargained.

"I will be there. I'll bring Mary."

"For all the good that will do." The words rolled languid from his tongue and for some reason her cheeks tinged pink. He meant to intimidate her, to assert he would control the situation, complete her list of requirements, and see her matched as soon as possible, but instead her nearness disconcerted him, and an intangible friction charged the air as each step pulled them closer together.

Perhaps his tactic worked after all. Her spine was as rigid as a fireplace poker. Unfortunately, he suffered the same condition elsewhere.

"Until tomorrow then." Her voice rang strong, although her actions revealed something different. She jumped out of his path like a startled cricket and hurried from the room.

Later in the evening, after Lunden finished a dinner tray in his bedchamber, he stood at the window and stared into the black night contemplating his day. He'd skirted the truth when acquiring a carriage for the morrow and Matthew had obliged with few questions and an invitation to make free use of the stables. His generosity compounded Lunden's regret. If past experiences taught him anything, it was that secrecy led to heartache.

A cloud covered the moon, blanketing its glow in a foggy veil, and without effort the years rolled away, depositing Lunden once again in that alley as he shadowed his brother on horseback, anxious for any scrap of information to share with Matthew who waited diligently at the town house stable. He'd accepted his best friend's challenge, equally curious to see where his brother, the duke, spent each evening. Certain it was somewhere nefarious and dangerous or better yet, as forbidden and intriguing as a brothel or gaming hell.

Things had not turned out as planned. Little had since.

Pushing from the window frame he walked to the bed and climbed under the inviting linen sheets, aware sleep would elude him. With a wry grimace he recalled the spell of nightmares he'd suffered after his parents had died. His brother had hushed him to quiet, advised him not to cry, and turned off the bedside lantern as he left. At the time it was not the comfort he'd needed, but in retrospect, perhaps it prepared him for the harsh bleakness that composed his future.

He blinked away the dank memory and willed himself to calm. By degrees his body relaxed and his thoughts drifted to Amelia and his promise for tomorrow's afternoon.

Why couldn't she be nondescript and mousy, plump in all the wrong places? He would still accomplish the task of seeing her matched, but his body would not be so spell-bound by her presence, so in tune to every detail of her bewitching appearance. Her hair would be the death of him. Those unruly curls begged for his touch, their silken sheen so tempting, even now he itched to tighten his fingers in the lengths as lush as black silk and wind her closer until the fall of her tresses blanketed his bare skin. And her legs, her lips . . . His body tightened and he cursed into the darkness. Had she been anyone else, he would have closed the scant distance between their mouths earlier and captured her full lips so he might learn her taste. *Honey or lemon?*

His heart pounded against the wall of his chest and he

scrubbed a palm over his face as if to erase the images. Damnation, he'd gone too long without a woman. No other explanation for his reaction made sense. He'd rusticated to his detriment if it had come to this.

Any idea of rest was out of the question if he didn't abandon these thoughts. With a string of curses meant for no one's ears but his own, he forced his eyes closed and decidedly shut out the world.

"You're in a peculiar mood this morning." Charlotte offered a handful of bread crumbs to the pigeons gathered at her feet. "Usually you're the chatterbox. Is something wrong?"

Amelia smiled, full knowing any effort spent disguising her emotions would be wasted indeed. "I'm sorry. Have I been quiet? I have a lot on my mind. I've agreed to meet three gentlemen selected by Matthew and Scarsdale. It's my hope I'll gain some control in the matter, but one can never be sure."

"At least you'll have the opportunity to meet the candidates beforehand and share in a courtship. That's a good sign for an agreeable future."

"I suppose, but what if all three prove boring and insufferable? What if they don't understand my perspective on life or disregard my opinion?" Amelia thrust her hand into the paper bag and collected a handful of bread. She sprinkled the crusts to her left, allowing the crumbs to fall slowly through her fingers like the sands of time. Several birds rushed forward for the choicest bits.

"Oh, now you're beyond silly. Don't borrow worry." Charlotte touched her arm with an affectionate pat. "Besides, with your plan in place, you'll have a voice in the decision."

Both ladies went silent, staring at the cooing pigeons as if studying the birds was an extraordinary experience.

At last, Amelia broke their disquiet. "Well, I have kept my end of our agreement. Have you asked Lord Dearing if you may join me next Saturday when I visit my parents?" She brushed any residual crumbs from her skirts and pinned her friend with a determined glare.

"Lord Dearing disapproves." Charlotte's words were barely a whisper.

"Good heavens, he's a tyrant." Amelia shot up, scattering the startled pigeons. She paced a hard line in front of the marble bench, ignoring her friend's surprised gasp. "What harm can come from you accompanying me to the country estate? We would have our maids with us and outriders for extra security. It's barely a day's worth of travel." Worked into a fit of temper, she spun around, her hands akimbo as her left foot tapped an agitated tempo against the gravel. "We need to convince him otherwise."

Charlotte sighed with discontent. "Perhaps I can ask again in a few months' time. He may change his mind by then."

"Or you will need to change it for him." Amelia reached to clasp Charlotte's hands in her own. She pulled her friend from the bench and linked their arms, set to begin their return walk home.

"Whatever do you mean?" Charlotte squeezed Amelia's arm tightly. It always felt better to have a friend by one's side when things were at their bleakest.

"I'm not sure, but I'll think of something. I can't bear to see you this unhappy and I promise you, we'll find a way to make things better."

Chapter Five

Lunden arrived at the rear entrance of Hyde Park, across from Tyburn Gallows, fifteen minutes before the designated time. He'd chosen the calmest horse in Matthew's modest stable for Amelia, a mild white mare with soft brown eyes. Then he'd harnessed the horse to a curricle alongside his stallion, Hades. His horse was black as midnight, high-spirited, and faster than the wind, an unsuitable mount for someone first learning to ride astride, but the perfect match for a man who wished to turn back time whenever he allowed the horse free rein, galloping at breakneck speeds across the grassy fields of Beckford Hall.

He released both horses from the equipage and wondered if he wasn't making a terrible mistake. His boots crunched on the gravel walk, lined with bracken and bilberry, as he tied the animals to a tree with a temporary tether. Next, he removed the mounting block from the carriage boot and carried it toward the white mare. Amelia would look lovely atop the horse. The fanciful thought struck him with unexpected intensity and he shook his head and turned his eyes to the vast meadow of low grass and wildflowers extending before him, the perfect pathway for a novice rider.

He was an excellent horseman and held no doubt he could teach Amelia to ride with little effort. Why the impetuous lady wished to ride astride when all of society dictated she use a sidesaddle, was beyond his reason. He suspected Amelia considered it rebellious, on the cusp of scandal to learn the skill, but he did not spend time on the why of it. It was her first demand and it would be satisfied with ease. And that brought him one step closer to resolving his business and leaving the city.

He checked both saddles and reviewed his approach to the lesson. They would start with the basics—a shy walk, then a lively canter, and at last a gentle gallop. He hoped she harbored no fear of the large animal. Horses were highly intelligent and intuitive. The mare would sense her discomfort and any apprehension would make the lesson more difficult.

By the day's end Amelia would have the security of knowing he meant to keep his promise, thus binding her to reciprocate as per her shrewd negotiations. A smirk played at his mouth. The lady pricked his curiosity, among other things. It was a miracle of sorts any emotion other than anger and regret lived in him still.

No time was left to consider the revelation as a carriage approached and the driver pulled beside the curricle. Undoubtedly, Amelia had charmed the man to a vow of silence, otherwise Lunden knew she'd receive hell from her brother for meeting him here and undertaking this lesson. And he would receive an invitation to leave London. The chaperone was of no consequence.

He mulled these conclusions until the carriage door creaked open. Amelia exited and his heart slammed against the wall of his chest.

"Is something wrong?" Her smile faltered as she moved forward, her brilliant green eyes marked with concern.

He dragged in a deep breath in a valiant attempt to

collect himself. "I didn't anticipate—" His tongue struggled to form the final two words. "The trousers." His eyes skimmed her length a second time. Fire, white hot and hungry, lit his veins and spread to every cell of his body before it settled in his stomach in perfect position for the flames to lick at his heart.

Amelia sauntered a slow circle and smiled.

The saucy minx.

"How else did you expect me to ride astride?"

Her voice held a familiar mocking tone, as if she assumed him daft. His temper bristled and he lied. "I honestly didn't give it a thought." In truth, his mind was filled with little else besides her and the unforgivable notion that he'd like to taste her kiss. Donning a scowl, he rechecked the mare's bridle. His brain would cease proper function if he didn't rid his desire for her full, delicious mouth. Damn it to hell, he was lust-struck.

"Well, are you teaching me to ride or not?"

With his thoughts so muddled, it was a wonder he could fasten his boots. "Of course. I'm a man of my word." He cleared his throat. "Just as you'll keep your half of the bargain and find a husband at the end of all this foolery." He waved his hand in a dismissive gesture.

"You need not remind me as if I'm a petulant child."

He half expected her to stamp her foot.

"We made a deal. One I've every intention of seeing through to the end." She jutted out her chin and poised her mouth in a mocking little frown that accentuated the sweet plumpness of her lower lip. Lunden bit the inside of his cheek and indicated the mounting block with a sharp jerk of his head.

She advanced to the wooden steps and climbed up, the scent of jasmine, soft and subtle, teased the air while the action placed her perfectly formed derriere at eye level.

His whole body tightened, most especially his groin, that development sure to make his ride enjoyable.

She took an impatient sidestep, her toe tapping, and he forced himself into motion.

"I can only label myself a half-wit for allowing this." *And the other half, pure genius.* Buckskin breeches never looked so attractive fitted to the gentle slope of her slender calves. "Where did you acquire these?" His question sounded like a growl and he brushed the tip of his glove against her hip to reference the tight pants, although his bare fingers itched to coast over every inch of her endlessly long legs.

"One of the grooms left them flung over a stable stall. He'll never miss them." She beamed down at him, her green eyes glittering in the noonday sun. "Now let's get on with this. Tell me what to do."

Oh, how he'd like to do just that. "Put your foot in the stirrup and bring your other leg over." Lunden kept a firm hold on the mare's harness, although Amelia and the animal appeared at ease. With hope she'd mount with haste. He could not bear to look at her tight bottom one minute longer.

"Like this?" She landed in the saddle with little effort and his lips quirked with pride. *Damnation, she was a delightful surprise.*

"Yes, you seem to have everything in hand." He threw her a casual glance, then turned to his horse and pulled up into the saddle with one swift movement, before aligning Hades beside her. "I suggest we begin with a slow walk." He wasn't sure she'd heard his suggestion as she prodded her horse ahead of his into the grass-covered meadow. And true, he was distracted with the sight of her lovely bottom as it moved in sensual rhythm against the leather saddle.

"Now, the first thing I'd like you to do—"

"Yah!"

With a strong nudge of her heels, the mare lunged forward and obliterated the end of his sentence. Lunden followed directly behind, but Amelia caught him unprepared and held a significant lead. He cursed into the wind, his mind racing faster than the horse's hooves. Farther ahead the grassy field narrowed in approach of a copse of hornbeam trees. He kicked Hades into a full gallop, determined to catch Amelia before her horse breached the thicket. His heart pounded with an unwelcome and familiar tension, while his chest clenched tight, a tangle of sorrowful lost memories. Sweat broke out across his brow. Did she know what she was doing? Was she frightened? He thought he heard her gasp but he couldn't see her face or judge her reaction, all concentration spent on leading his horse in the chase.

He leaned low over Hades's mane and focused on closing the distance between them. His jaw tensed and the hairs on the back of his neck pricked high. He nearly had her now although the tree line grew ever closer. Her horse would never manage the undergrowth at this pace. Were the mare to react with abrupt rebellion, Amelia would be thrown. His pulse drummed in tune to Hades's hooves. He had to catch her. *In this, he could not fail.*

Lunden pressed his heels into Hades's flanks and the horse charged forward at a breakneck speed. For a timeless span he returned to that long-ago night when he rode like hell through the dark, flooded with fear as he raced against hope to reach his brother's horse.

He pressed Hades with a cruel kick and gained on the white mare, thundering up in her wake. Almost. Another yard. He had to push harder, make ground. With a wild thrash of his arm, he captured the mare's straps in one hand and yanked tight. His muscles burned as he sawed at the reins. The mare let out an earsplitting whinny as Lunden leaned from his saddle at a careless angle and brought both horses to a stop.

His roar, meant to bellow over the slowing pound of

hooves, startled Amelia, her look of elation transformed into one of instant dismay. "What were you thinking? This horse barely knows you. Are you daft?" His anger spiked, his jaw rigid, and he speared her with a glare as comprehension registered. Hades snorted and pawed the ground to underscore the explosive questions.

At last she matched his eyes. The tears that brimmed her lids meant nothing. Good God, how easily she could have been thrown.

Like Douglas. Dead like his brother, through an act of recklessness and impulsive stupidity . . . an act he'd instigated. Again.

A terrible ache replaced the hard beat of his heart and sliced his anger in half. "I'm insane to have allowed this." He muttered an expletive and forced himself to calm, although every word cut through the air like a fierce strike of lightning. He released the leather straps from his fists and begged his fingers to cease their tremulous rebellion. His eyes went to the tree line, only a stone's throw away, and he struggled to mollify his temper.

"I didn't intend to upset you. You worry too much on my behalf." She blinked twice, although her green eyes glittered with tears.

"I'm not upset. I'm angry." He snarled the words. Amelia's apology did little to balm his fury. God help the girl were she to challenge him on this, although the usual note of defiance rang through. "You do as you please."

"It's just . . ." She paused before she continued. "It was wonderful. Thank you. I've never experienced such a moment of pure exhilaration in my life. Trotting along in a side-saddle is nothing compared to this."

Lunden breathed deep and assessed her proud poise atop the mare, as regal as a queen holding court. Her crown of glossy black curls was tousled in disorder from their chase, her cheeks as rosy, her luscious mouth ripened by the wind.

Pride shone in the depths of her brilliant gaze, as well it should be. She'd managed the mare with controlled ease.

Yet he hadn't overreacted. Only an expert horseman could maneuver the underbrush of a dense forest.

He swallowed, unsure of how to explain his irate reaction. "Matthew would take great pleasure in beating me to a pulp were he to know what just transpired. At least we can depend on the discretion of the driver and your chaperone." He looked over his shoulder, unable to see the gravel walkway at their starting point.

"No one will share a word."

She smiled, as if he'd given her the greatest gift, and something shifted inside him. A quiet calm blanketed his restless soul.

He clicked his tongue and nudged Hades to turn so they could make their way back. Amelia mimicked his actions. She looked majestic indeed astride the white mare, a right and royal duchess. Perhaps he ought to consider only worthy dukes for her husband list. With due consideration, no one came to mind.

Amelia didn't know what to say after her apology. Lunden appeared furious and for once a smart retort escaped her. She stole a glance in his direction as their horses wended across the field. His head was bowed and his hair, thick and dark as the secrets he kept, caught the breeze. An errant lock lifted to reflect a glint of sunlight. She studied his profile, all sharp angles and smooth planes, as polished and cold as a marble statue and devoid of any revealing emotion aside from anger. Perhaps if he'd glance in her direction, she'd detect understanding in his eyes, but since his outburst and chastisement, he'd failed to look in her direction. When he'd spoken, his words were enraged, yet there was something else evident. Sadness? Remorse? She couldn't label the troublesome emotion.

He turned unexpectedly and her breath caught. His eyes darkened as he studied her but neither spoke a word. Did he have any happiness in his life? Did he ever smile? She realized he was a man of deep emotion, but did he allow himself joy? She couldn't fathom a life lived without contentment. Her mind flitted to Charlotte's marriage and how much it troubled her. She refused to sacrifice her own future with little regard to her personal happiness, yet her future was dependent on the decision of a man, either her brother or Lunden, both men long disillusioned that happiness was a possibility.

When finally Lunden spoke, the smoky quality of his voice rippled through her with the same exhilaration she'd experienced while she raced breathlessly across the field.

"I will consider the first requirement of your list well met."

Amelia breathed a sigh of relief. The quiet tone of his voice held no gruffness.

"No matter how harmful the undertaking."

Detecting a note of humor, she offered a genuine smile. "Thank you." Emotion crept into her voice although she tried to conceal it. "You've given me something no one else would allow."

He stared at her a moment longer, then averted his eyes to the path ahead. They were nearly returned to their starting point.

"I will begin to assemble a list of suitors." His voice rang out across the field, as if a proclamation of sorts.

Amelia whipped her head up and the mare whinnied, sidestepping with her sudden motion. "Not until all three items on my list are satisfied. That was our agreement."

"Of course. I would not wish to upset the lady. Matthew warned me doing so could prove dangerous." His teasing tone pleased her and Amelia defended herself with a cheeky smile.

"I never intended to knock Lord Riley unconscious." She turned away before he eyed the grin expanding across her face. "A smarter man would have backed away from the door. Besides, I'm sure my brother distorted the retelling."

She returned her eyes to his and a shadow of amusement passed over his face although he did not reply. When the horses approached their waiting carriages, they parted with polite salutations.

Regardless of their congenial conversation, in the silence of the ride home Amelia could not forget Lunden's anger and the wild, terrified gleam in his eyes as he'd leaned over and pulled her horse to heel. It scared her, intrigued her, and most of all, caused her heart to ache with unanswered questions and the unprovoked desire to learn the dark secrets that tortured his soul.

Chapter Six

The house stood silent when Amelia entered through the rear door and tiptoed up the back stairs to her bedchambers. Relieved she hadn't encountered a single servant, she washed and changed into a day gown, then hurried to the front hall to question Spencer concerning the household's whereabouts. Discovering Matthew remained out of house and suspecting Lunden had not yet returned, she strode to the drawing room intent on finding Pandora. The morning's emotional confusion pestered like butterflies caught in a net and she wished only to nestle cozily in her favorite corner.

But Pandora was not curled atop the coal scuttle near the fireplace fender, her much loved location. Nor was the cat in the dining room, sitting room, or lazed across the wide sill of the hallway grand window. Perplexed, Amelia scurried up to Matthew's study, her consternation ablaze, several of his careless threats to rid the house of her pet piquing her concern.

The room stood as it always did, its dark woodwork and aristocratic presence, staid and authoritative, a mirror of the man her brother wished to portray. On a whim, she opened the storage closet on the far wall, its contents bare aside from a stack of boxes near the rear and an old broom. Pandora was not there. She meandered to the unfinished puzzle near the window, viewed it with absent concentration and chose a few random pieces to drop into her skirt pocket for no other reason than to cause her brother annoyance. Pivoting on her heel, she left to continue her search.

At a loss to where Pandora wandered, Amelia dismissed the more logical consideration of the kitchen and ventured down the short hallway. There were only three rooms, one of them now in use by their houseguest. It was unlikely her cat would choose either of the two empty rooms, as they stood cold and vacant, but Lunden's bedchamber presented a feasible possibility. Perhaps Pandora slinked in when a maid changed the linens or delivered fresh water.

She stopped in front of the door and with a flit of her eyes asserted the hallway remained empty. Should she knock? There was no logical way Lunden could have returned without her knowledge. At Hyde Park she'd watched through her carriage window until she could no longer see him, and the whole time he'd made no effort to hitch Hades to the curricle. And too, she'd inquired with Spencer concerning his whereabouts.

With a shadow of hesitation, she turned the brass knob and eased inside. Each nerve in her body screamed in objection, for surely to venture into a guest room, never mind one of a gentleman bachelor, chafed against every rule she'd learned as a lady. She huffed an impatient breath. Pandora would forever lure her into hot water.

Amelia whispered her tongue against her lips in a familiar sound that never failed to summon the cat, but the feline didn't appear. Curiosity rose to the forefront and any earlier trepidation melted away to soothe her nerves as she advanced across the hardwood floor.

The bedchamber appeared meticulous. She knew Lunden had no plans to visit overlong, but his rooms looked unoccupied, all in its rightful place, with very few personal items visible. A pair of ankle jacks stood near the foot of the bed, the black leather boots positioned in wait of their master. A leather traveling valise rested in the corner, closed up tight.

She took another step and inhaled, filling her lungs with the exhilaration of the daring venture. Notes of cedarwood and bergamot teased her nose and the intimate masculine scent intrigued her. Somehow her feet carried her to the wardrobe where a shaving kit and brush lie atop a white linen towel. The smallest sliver of soap rested beside the cup. She picked it up and rubbed it across the back of her hand. A rush of warm pleasure slithered through her at the woodsy scent and she replaced the soap where it once rested, her fingertip lingering for an extra caress.

Pandora long forgotten, she turned and eyed the massive guest bed. The draped linen canopy shadowed the mattress under mahogany posts. *Lunden slept there.* The man of mystery who took her to ride and then fiercely rescued her when he feared she was in danger, whose very presence seemed to swallow a room with overwhelming handsomeness and dark forbidden secrecy. Yet his deepest emotions lay locked up as tight as his valise. Truly, his rooms held no revelations, their contents as confidential as the man.

The bed loomed before her, the sheets hardly crumpled, where only a slight indentation confessed his head ever rested on the pillow. Had the maids already replaced the daily linens? Amelia fought against the panic of discovery fluttering in her chest. Instead she edged closer, her curiosity leading her on a short leash.

Someday, not so far away, she would lie with a man on her wedding night. The activities of such remained a mystery. Oh, she understood the mechanics of the intimacies shared between a husband and wife, and the function of each gender's anatomy. She'd learned that when she smuggled the appropriate volume from Matthew's study years ago.

And while she would be labeled an innocent, she'd been kissed and embraced on rare occasions. But of the carnal delights and forbidden sensations women whispered about when they assumed no one could overhear, she possessed no experience. While gossip assured pleasure could be taken from the act, lovemaking remained a foreign concept.

With a small degree of disappointment, Charlotte had not confessed a single iota concerning her affections with Lord Dearing. Amelia believed in utmost privacy, but if her dear friend had shared a well-placed comment as to whether the experience proved enjoyable, Amelia could put her own mind at ease. The alternative, that she remained defenseless as she went to her wedding bed, exposed not only of her clothing, but of her most hidden insecurities, renewed her vow to rebel.

She completed her journey across the room driven by more than carnal fascination and insatiable curiosity. On the one hand, she yearned to know every aspect of sexual relations and on the other, feared the vulnerability and loss of control when one succumbed to passion. Therein lay the paradox. And passion, though she'd never tasted that forbidden fruit, was alive in her as much as the blood in her veins. She would not be forced to wed a man who did not touch her heart as much as he yearned to touch her body.

Amelia studied the empty sheets of Lunden's bed and swallowed the heavy considerations. She pushed back an errant curl that fell forward on her cheek and the heady fragrance of cedarwood across the back of her hand fortified her bold entreaty. Her fingers trembled as she smoothed her palm over the bed linens, and before she could change her mind, she reclined on the mattress, her head on the pillow, careful to keep her boots from the counterpane.

Good heavens, she'd lost her mind. What would Lunden say were he to walk through the door and find her sprawled in his bed? Would he be as enraged as earlier in the day, or would he laugh, her presence in his bed the unfathomable scene that cracked his solemn resolve?

Or would she become another of his secrets?

The outrageous and sensual question tempted her with a forbidden intimacy that tightened her lower belly. The unnamed pleasure undulated through her, settling with warmth between her legs and she gasped, all at once enthralled. She squeezed her legs together as if to capture and hold the intriguing sensation even though it confused her just the same, then turned her cheek to brush against his pillow. For a fleeting moment, her eyes fell closed.

The mattress felt the same as hers, but knowing Lunden had lain there the night before, made the act decidedly wicked. She smiled, delighted with the revelation, and nestled her head more firmly atop the soft down.

A sound in the drive outside the window pulled Amelia to attention and she scrambled from the bed. She checked twice that everything appeared as pristine as when she'd entered. On unsteady legs she tiptoed to the doorway, opened it a crack, and slipped through. The hallway stood empty and she left, grateful she hadn't been caught experiencing the unthinkable.

Lunden led Hades across Downing Street and on through Belgrave Square. The rumble of distant thunder announced his arrival and the clouds opened with a sorrowful drizzle that suited his mood. After Amelia's riding lesson, he'd sent the curricle back to the stables and headed to a nondescript tavern at the outskirts of the city. The Bleeding Wolf proved a seedy, undesirable establishment where the patrons, sober or otherwise, were unlikely to recognize him. Once settled in a dim corner, he'd purchased a bottle of liquor, and considered his options for the evening.

Now as he approached his old town house under the

cover of night, he wondered if he'd made a wise decision, this glance into the past.

Little in the area looked the same. In many ways, London had changed as much as he. Still, the feelings that flooded him remained consistent: regret, hopelessness, and guilt. Those emotions did not waver.

He never wanted the title, which made it all the more frustrating when people presumed he possessed so strong a desire for the duchy, he'd machinated his brother's death. The word *murder* was never uttered in his presence, but he was aware of the gossip and the whispers that detailed a malicious deed embellished by each conspirer's gullible imagination. Nothing gathered strength faster than a lascivious secret in a room of curious fools.

The day his brother died was the worst day of his life. How dare London suggest he welcomed the pain, when in truth his desolation was the result of a yawning lapse of good judgment. He slipped his hand into his pocket and brushed his fingertips across the pouch holding his brother's pocket watch. *Had he the power to turn back time . . .*

A lamplighter cast a curious glance in his direction as he led Hades down Oxford Street. Lunden bent him an abrupt nod. He suspected his childhood residence would appear familiar, yet tension stole over him as he neared the address. It seemed the right decision to come here on a day already saturated with regret, but he wasn't prepared for the rush of emotion that slammed his chest as he viewed the three-story town house from afar. No light lit the windows, the street as silent and caliginous as his memories, and his heart pounded as if to remind he did not dream. No, that night was carved into his memory like the inscription on his brother's tombstone, deep and everlasting. With a final glance to absorb every detail, he kicked Hades into a sharp gallop and retreated down a nearby alley.

He returned to his rooms at Cleveland Row nearly an

hour later having taken time to tend to his horse and unravel his thoughts before entering the house with silent steps. Fatigued, he shed his clothes to his smalls as if dispensing of the emotional layers of the day. Stretched across the mattress, his head on the pillow, he scrubbed his palms over his face and closed his eyes, his body emotionally wrung.

Amelia's image, her long legs encased in tight buckskin trousers, burned into his brain to taunt his body. He released a loud groan. It would be the devil's pleasure if he ever found sleep again. What the hell was wrong with him? It was the vilest form of disloyalty to lust after his best friend's sister, to envisage her straddling him, her tangle of dark curls strewn across her bare shoulders, her head thrust back as she rode him to fulfillment.

Bloody hell, if he continued this way, the devil would welcome him with open arms.

Without a doubt, Amelia was beautiful, but something about her, something intangible and tenuous, provoked his senses, summoned desire as if she penetrated his skin and insinuated his soul. One look at her and every wall of defense, carefully constructed over years of seclusion, threatened to fracture, tilt, and crumble. He shifted on the pillow. Even now he could smell her, jasmine and delightful loveliness, mixed with vivacious laughter and ripe pink lips. His groin hardened and urged him to pursue the thought. Fantasies would have to suffice. Fantasies and secrets. Always secrets. With another groan, one more of agony than pleasure, Lunden flung to his back, desperate to find relief.

Whittingham climbed the steps leading to the address scribbled on the paper clenched in his right fist. His other hand kept a secure hold on his cane, the stairs unusually steep and difficult to maneuver when confronted with his limp and the dismal state of the evening weather. A steady drizzle fell and the damp conditions caused his leg to ache, his shortened temper an outcome of the combined predicaments. Still, he relished the evening's opportunity to participate in the scheduled meeting, no matter the location had been changed on short notice, and he now feared a late arrival. Pride intertwined with punctuality and he scoffed, not wishing to present a poor impression, most especially as elections grew nearer. He pursued a nomination, his goal finally within reach.

The Society for the Intellectually Advanced was highly respected as one of the most elite associations of academia in London. Matthew participated as a member for almost a decade, rising from newcomer to esteemed contributor. He was determined to become chief officer with the upcoming election, no matter the failure of his past attempts. The opportunity was never more attainable as Collins, the retiring officer, was also a comrade. Matthew hoped to obtain a glowing endorsement from the gentleman.

He managed the last few stairs with effort and then moved into the silent hallway. A butler stood ready to accept his dripping overcoat and hat, and Matthew wished he could offer his boots forward, as the laborious struggle up the front steps left the leather soaked through to his stockings. Instead, he made haste to enter the sitting room.

"Good show, Whittingham. I began to doubt your attendance." Lord Winthrop extended his hand for a hearty shake as Matthew advanced. Gentlemen conversed in small pockets around the room, some more animated in their discussions than others, and Matthew released a huff of breath, relieved he'd arrived before the meeting was called to order.

"I didn't receive word of the meeting's relocation until this evening. Had the message arrived a minute later, I would have missed it. But I'm here now. What do you make of this impromptu gathering? Why has the location changed in such slapdash fashion?"

The men moved to a more private corner near the bookcases, although Matthew yearned to find a seat. His leg throbbed from the pressure exerted as he climbed the slippery marble steps. He grimaced as his eyes darted around the room in assessment of the situation. He needed to locate an open chair.

"It's quite the story and one that might aid your efforts, my friend." Sensing his unease, Winthrop tapped him on the arm and motioned toward two recently vacated wing chairs near the fireplace. "It's my understanding Collins has suffered the most unlikely turn of events. His brother and sister-in-law from Manchester have suffered a tragic accident."

"How terrible for Collins." Matthew settled and extended his leg toward the flames in hope the warmth would coax the steady throb of pain to subside and not impair his enjoyment of the evening. "I'll make it a point to extend my condolences."

"That's not the half of it." Winthrop leaned in, as if imparting a confidential secret, although Matthew suspected the entire room discussed Collins's misfortune in low-toned whispers. "According to his brother's will, Collins has been named guardian of their six children. Collins has no wife and no desire to be a family man, but we're all aware of his fondness of money. His brother's testament stated contingent for Collins to inherit the bulk of the family fortune, the children must remain in Manchester to be raised on their estate, continue their schooling, et cetera." Winthrop waved his hand in the air as if to explain everything he hadn't stated. "Collins plans to relinquish his position at the society as soon as matters are settled and relocate to Manchester. He's not as discomforted by the idea as I would be, and instead has turned his focus to finding a wife as soon as possible. Money can purchase the assistance of servants and tutors, but Collins isn't so brave as to embark on this venture without a woman by his side. The youngest children need mothering, most especially after their tragic loss."

Matthew considered a number of replies. Indeed, he held sympathy for Collins and the sudden detour his life had taken, but there was no denying this turn of events offered a fortuitous advantage. He wanted, with every ounce of his being, to become chief officer of the society. Here was an opportunity to achieve that goal with ease. All he need do is convince Collins to extend a ringing endorsement for his ascension to the position. Considering the man's need to leave London, it shouldn't prove a difficult proposition. If necessary, he would devote himself to aiding Collins with his transition in any way possible. Perhaps he could find the fellow a wife. An unexpected smile curled his lips. Assisting in the marriage mart seemed a popular topic of late.

"This is very good news, Winthrop. Aside from the deaths, of course." He spoke with measured deliberation as he slued his eyes across the room. "Nevertheless, I should pursue my cause before the meeting begins."

But he had no time to debate the proposal as the sound of a gavel striking wood resounded in the sitting room and the meeting was called to order. Reassembling to the chairs set before the long meeting table, Matthew noticed his leg no longer throbbed and that in a remarkable shift of mood, he didn't bemoan his wet boots.

Chapter Seven

"Hurry along, Mary." Amelia set a stirring pace down the sidewalk, not minding her maid's stride equaled half her own, while Mary struggled to shorten the distance between them. Sleep came with ease the night before and Amelia fell into bed exhausted from exhilaration, only to awake this morning with remnants of pleasant dreams, the scent of cedar and bergamot against her cheek where her hand lay folded.

She met Charlotte at the door and the two ladies scurried down the sidewalk as was customary, although Amelia could not contain her conversation and lunged into current news with a lack of ladylike finesse.

"Oh my goodness, I have so much to tell you." She twisted to speak to her friend, their arms looped as they followed their familiar route to the park.

Charlotte glanced in her direction, her eyes wide with curiosity. "Please don't wait a moment longer."

"I scarcely know where to begin." Hardly a pause followed Amelia's announcement before her words burst forth in an exuberant flurry. "Lunden took me riding yesterday afternoon. Astride. I've never felt more alive."

"You call him by his Christian name?"

The disturbed tone of Charlotte's question cut her enthusiasm by half, although Amelia dismissed the opportunity to address the stringent rule Lord Dearing established dictating Charlotte and he employ formal titles. She didn't wish to bring pallor to their conversation and instead continued in a jubilant tone.

"It's not improper. I knew him as a child. Matthew invited him to Lakeview on occasion. It feels quite natural. Besides, this is no time for dithering over details." They settled on a bench under the trees although nothing could shade Amelia's enthusiasm. "It was magical to race across the field with the power of the horse beneath me. Nothing at all like a sidesaddle. I can easily understand why men prefer to keep women confined to the cumbersome contraption. If every woman were allowed to experience the freedom found in riding, we would never hear horror stories about ladies trapped in marriage with no escape." She finished on a high note and tilted her head at a jaunty angle, pleased with her illuminating speech.

"I wish I possessed but a thimble's worth of your courage. You told me you were determined to accomplish your list and you're succeeding. I'm proud of you. If only I could experience the same joy." Charlotte continued to smile, although her words didn't echo the expression.

"Oh, but you can. I'll teach you. Lunden did very little aside from choosing the proper horse. True, I did startle him when I kicked the horse into a gallop, but I've watched gentlemen ride for years and studied their motion. There's nothing to it. If you travel with me this weekend, I'll show you and no one will know." Amelia captured her friend's hands in her own. "Have you attempted more discussion with Lord Dearing concerning the trip?"

A shadow of dismay entered Charlotte's eyes and she

cast them to where their hands knit together in her lap. "The matter has not changed, I'm afraid."

Both friends fell silent, but Amelia harbored far too many opinions on the subject to bite her tongue for long.

"I implore you to address this matter again. Today is Tuesday and I plan to leave Saturday before noon. There's still time to convince Lord Dearing a trip to the country will make you happy, as well as express benevolence to my ailing father. I've seen the way he looks at you and must believe he can be reasoned with, otherwise all will be lost. How could anyone deny such an act of kindness?"

"Kindness is never his consideration." Her tone edged on melancholy. "I fear I can't breech the subject again. Dearing asserts you put improper ideas in my head, first with the suggestion of a cat and now with this weekend travel."

"Utter rot. You know that's rubbish." Amelia released her friend's hands and stood up in a swirl of skirts. "Our thoughts are very much aligned. I merely inspire you to give them voice. Lord Dearing is proving an inordinately stubborn man. Do you think I should talk to him directly? Explain how much I would enjoy your company and how welcomed you would be at the country estate?"

"Dear no." Charlotte stood up with such alacrity, Amelia stepped back in alarm. "That's a terrible idea."

"All right." Desperate for a change of subject to mollify her friend, Amelia grasped on to a topic that never seemed far from mind. "Lunden is extremely handsome despite the absence of any semblance of a smile. I studied his face yesterday when he didn't know I was looking." She closed her eyes and conjured an image of his severe scowl. With such rugged, attractive features, he no doubt claimed a charming grin. What would it take to coax it out? When her lids fluttered open, Charlotte's perplexed expression demanded a quick explanation.

"He tempts my curiosity. That's all. Everything concerning his departure from London is cloaked in secrecy and now he's returned, willing to do my brother a favor and satisfy my list of demands. Curious, indeed. He seems very accommodating, yet likely something else drives him. It's fascinating, the intriguing mystery that surrounds his actions."

"Well, I daresay your brother will marry you off to the costermonger on the corner if he learns you were out riding with Scarsdale. Aside from the scandalous nature of your activity, no dignified lady in lack of a proper chaperone should venture anywhere with a bachelor. You're breaking every rule."

Amelia tried to stifle her laughter. "I brought Mary with me."

Charlotte rolled her eyes and Amelia ignored her friend's smirk of disapproval.

"Rules are made to be broken." A smile punctuated her sentence. "I've done nothing wrong unless one analyzes my actions according to society's antiquated expectations. The *ton*'s dictates are ridiculous. Your marriage serves as a prime example. Given the opportunity, you would have chosen a husband and accomplished the security your family needed within a union based on love and not convenience. Instead, because society didn't allow you to be privy to your family's financial woes, you were thrust into a marriage without any preparation or warning."

"Yes, although it might have been worse." Charlotte looked out beyond the fountain in the middle of the square. "I shouldn't complain."

Amelia placed her hand on Charlotte's shoulder in a gesture meant to comfort. "Yes, you should. Please know you can always talk to me." She leaned in closer and cast a sideways glance toward their maids. "Be assured, I dare not abandon your situation. We will help Lord Dearing realize what a treasure you are. I need to give the subject deliberation."

She stepped away and tapped her finger against her lips in a thoughtful pose. "How much pin money have you saved?"

"I'm afraid I haven't any. Lord Dearing is very frugal with the accounts. He reminds me often that he incurred a great financial burden when he settled Father's debt."

Amelia suppressed a breath of frustration. "I'll continue to think on it. There is a solution. We just haven't found it yet. Love might not have been a requirement in your marriage, but affection can grow given the opportunity."

A whippoorwill sang in the distance as both girls remained silent. Amelia knew not what else to say.

Then Charlotte turned to her, a twinkle in her soft brown eyes. "What is he like? Scarsdale, I mean."

A wistful smile wound its way around Amelia's mouth. "He's very handsome, wickedly so, and when he speaks to me, his voice does peculiar things to my insides. I am sure it's nerves on my part." Considering Charlotte's state of shock concerning the use of first names, Amelia thought better than to mention she'd reclined in Lunden's bed the night before, although the suggestion she might confess the words caused a ripple of excitement to shoot straight through her. A secretive smile spread across her face.

"Amelia, you're never nervous." Charlotte didn't remark on the expanse of her grin.

"I suppose it could be attributed to all this marriage talk. I wish Father was not so set on finding me a match. I believe I can find happiness as an independent woman until I meet a man who promises me a content future. I wish to fall in love, not be bartered away in an agreement. Perhaps I will attempt to convince Father of this fact when I visit on Saturday."

Charlotte shook her head in the negative. "But what of children and a family? You've always told me you wanted to be surrounded by babes."

"Yes, that much is true. It is a slippery slope I'm afraid, but mark my words, I will not marry without love."

Lunden dismounted and handed Hades's reins to the waiting footman outside the Dobson residence. John Kendall, Earl of Dobson, was an honest fellow, a past acquaintance, and at current, Lunden's best possibility. Most pointedly, Dobson was a huntsman and knowledgeable in the use of firearms.

He presented his card to the butler, disgruntled the task forced him to make his presence known, but no other option seemed viable. He didn't own a pistol and needed the use of one. He'd best borrow the blasted thing and be done with it. Purchasing a firearm would resurrect distasteful speculation, not to mention his unexpected appearance at a weapons store would recharge every gossipmonger who wished to exhume the arcane secret he worked for a decade to keep buried.

And too, he would ask Dobson for discretion, if such a thing existed. He remembered the man as trustworthy and uninvolved in societal scandal. Still, the days following his brother's death were a blur and he could no better tell which man fortified his explanation or cast suspicion in his direction. As heir presumptive, the transfer of the title was tainted by rumor and doubt, ultimately crucifying Lunden as a manipulative, bitter second son, hungry for revenge and assumption of the title. The erroneous depiction, combined with his grief, the obligations of funeral arrangements and customary visitation, and the tremendous guilt that grew stronger with every breath, smothered him in a haze of perfunctory survival until finally he escaped the city for good.

A whisper of despair winnowed through him.

Were he not bound by his word to Amelia, he wouldn't be at Dobson's in the first place. The curmudgeon inconvenienced him in more ways than he could explain, and yet on another level, a deeper, richer one, she amused him and somehow ignited a small spark of light in his otherwise dark existence. She was all contradiction, long legs and short temper, incredible beauty and guaranteed hellion. A lovely bit of mayhem.

Any man that volunteered to put up with her tart tongue was the biggest fool in England and he would find that fool, fulfill his promise, and then be on his way.

"Lord Dobson will see you now."

The butler, a middle-aged man with a stoic countenance, stared at him with little interest. Perhaps his imagination had gotten the better of him and no one cared he'd returned.

Doubtful.

He followed the servant and entered a somber drawing room decorated with various-sized game, stuffed and mounted for display. It would appear Dobson kept the local taxidermist in expensive leather boots. Intrigued, Lunden wandered the perimeter noting the varying degrees of death on display, from bear cub to large spotted cat. He was examining the latter when the earl made his entrance.

"Beautiful specimen, the lynx. Rare and elusive. Some cultures believe it to be mythical." Dobson extended his hand with a half grin of acknowledgment. "Almost as uncommon as a visit from you, Scarsdale. How are you?"

"Well enough." Lunden shook Dobson's hand in greeting. He had a favor to ask, but no plans to share any shred of his past. "Good of you to see me. I realize my card may have taken you unaware."

"Any hunter worth his salt is prepared for the most unexpected situations." He speared Lunden with a stare and an astute nod of the head. "Although I never thought to see you again. At least not in this city."

"And I assumed the same. Nevertheless, circumstances have drawn me here."

"Brandy? Whisky? What's your pleasure?" Dobson moved toward a liquor cabinet behind a free-standing gazelle. "I have the finest brew imported from Scotland when the law was looking the other way. You won't taste anything smoother."

"No, thank you. As much as I appreciate you seeing me, I have a favor to ask and won't take unnecessary time out of your day."

"Don't mind if I enjoy one then." Dobson reached into his pocket and removed a small key from a ring that held several others. He made quick work of unlocking the cabinet, and poured a glass of amber liquid before he motioned toward two overstuffed chairs facing the clerestory windows. Lunden sat without pause.

"Intriguing to see you after all this time. You seem much as you did ten years ago."

On the outside perhaps; certainly not the inside.

"Must be the country air." Lunden shifted in his chair and the pouch in his pocket wedged against his hip in protest. He straightened and aimed at the goal of his visit. "I need to borrow a gun."

Before Dobson could respond, Lunden continued, not wishing to offer an opportunity to delve into his past. "An unlikely request, I know, but a friend has asked me to teach of the weapon and I foolishly agreed. Now I'm bound by my word, but have no firearm in my possession. I thought to visit you rather than venture into town and spark unwelcome speculation as to why I need purchase a firearm."

"I see." Dobson took a long swallow from his glass. "You've come to the right man. I have a large collection of weapons, but I assume you mean to borrow a gentleman's pistol. We can practice out back. Living here provides me the acreage to hone my skills before I venture abroad." He stood and walked to the French doors that led to the back of the property. "It's a perfect day for target practice, bright with just the right amount of cloud cover. We can begin at once."

Startled by the man's enthusiasm, Lunden rose and followed Dobson to the slate-covered terrace. That Dobson offered immediate acceptance and did not trouble him with an inquisition concerning his reasoning proved a tremendous relief. He only wished the earl hadn't drained his glass so thoroughly before requesting the butler retrieve two weapons.

True to his word, Dobson spent the better part of the morning instructing him on the proper use of the flintlock pistol. Lunden was confident in his ability to teach Amelia the same. Why the willful chit desired to learn such outrageous behavior escaped him and he again attributed her desire to thrill-seeking rebellion. Without a doubt, Amelia was like no other woman he'd ever encountered. Whether that was a favorable attribute or not remained undetermined.

"That should do it. You've managed to hit the target in the center for ten straight shots. I'd say you're a natural, but then . . ."

His words faded, although Lunden understood what the clumsy comment implied. He steeled himself and strove to keep his tone even. "My brother died from a broken neck incurred when he was thrown from his horse." In a swift change of position, he turned toward the board and fired the last shot. It hit dead center. He busied himself with collecting the bag of ammunition, cleaning rag, and solvent, to avoid Dobson's scrutiny.

"I never gave credence to the hearsay." Dobson took care to return his pistol to the box. "Never mind then."

A short pause followed while they reassembled the supplies.

"I leave for Ghana, Africa, on Thursday. You're welcome to use this area to teach your associate. My butler will supply you with fresh targets and powder, as well as fetch the pistols when you're ready. I'll leave the key in his possession, although I grant the other servants holiday when I am out of the country, so there will be no other staff on hand."

Lunden nodded and extended his hand forward. "I appreciate this, Dobson, and your discretion in the matter. I wish you luck in your travels."

"And I'll need it. I'm after the big one this time. Rhinoceros. Are you familiar?"

"Not at all."

"Then you'll have to visit again, if for no other reason than to see the horned beast in the middle of my drawing room."

Chapter Eight

Amelia entered Matthew's study with Pandora nestled in her arms. There were a number of items she wished to discuss with her brother and his absence from the town house of late caused her impatience. She strolled to where he stood hunched over his puzzle and lowered her arms. Pandora executed a graceful leap to the windowsill.

"Keep that infernal animal out of my study. Why can't you do as you're told, Troublemaker?" His mouth flattened to a thin line with the question.

"What a bore life would be if I obeyed all the rules." Amelia eyed Pandora, stretched in a languid pose across her brother's desk chair. She issued a silent prayer the cat didn't choose to shred important papers or worse, the leather cushion. "I've needed to speak to you, but you're hardly in the house these days."

"I'm vying for the position of chief officer with the society. And of course, I have other obligations. I know from your point of view, I solve puzzles all day, but I assure you, I'm buried in work before you're out for a morning walk with Charlotte."

"I plan to visit Lakeview this Saturday and I invited Charlotte to accompany me, but her dreadful husband will not relent. Why is it, dear brother, that men find it their duty and purpose to lord over their wife? I cannot imagine a single reason why Dearing wouldn't allow Charlotte to accompany me."

"I can." Matthew turned in her direction, a mocking smile on his face. "And as far as his decisions, his title dictates he *lord* it over her, although Dearing is one of the last men I would have thought a good match for Charlotte. Of course it must be considered her parents were in great financial debt. I suppose accepting a wife with no dowry and agreeing to alleviate the family's money woes allows him latitude in his choice of behavior." He fitted two pieces into the puzzle and stepped right to examine a particular section in the sunlight.

Amelia changed the subject. "Why is Lunden here?"

Matthew whipped his head up and shot her a fierce glare. "The matter does not concern you. And do not share his presence here with anyone. The whole world is aware of your proclivity for causing trouble and Lunden's had more than his portion. You steer clear of him unless he finds a man for you to marry. In that case, we'll hold a party in his honor."

"That's unkind of you." She looked to him, her arms crossed over her chest and displeasure evident. "Is it so wrong for me to want a love match?"

"No, it's not."

This time her head shot up, confident she'd heard incorrectly, but her brother continued.

"Other factors are at play. Father's health of course, your penchant to ignore every bit of ladylike advice offered in your direction and, of course, your unwillingness to consider a single suitor set in your path. Whatever this fear is—"

"I am not afraid." It was a statement of fact.

"Whatever your hesitation"—Matthew gentled the words

and angled to face her—"you will have to abandon it and realize marriage is part of your future. Mother and Father will not live forever, dear sister."

His final words left her speechless. A rare occurrence indeed.

"But don't despair. I may have a solution sooner than you think."

She had no time to object as Lunden entered and the focus of her attention shifted. He looked terribly dashing. His thick hair appeared wind tousled and a shadow of whiskers darkened his chin. Amelia despised whiskers. Usually. Now she wondered how the scrape of his skin across her cheek would feel. Similar to Pandora's tongue perhaps, but much more sensual, she suspected. An unexpected burst of goose bumps dotted her arms and she slid her palms up and down their lengths to soothe the sensation away.

"Ah, just the man I wanted to see. I've informed my sister I may have a candidate worthy of her attention." No one could miss the brotherly teasing in his words.

"Things move at an unusually fast pace here." Lunden walked farther into the room. "I'm afraid I've spent too much time in the country, or worse yet, will be restless when I make my return." He swung his gaze to where Amelia lingered near the puzzle table. "Have we a name then?"

Something lurched to life inside him as he asked the question. Perhaps it was only desire to see his part of both bargains completed that caused the sudden unease, although his promise would become a moot point were Matthew to match Amelia off so easily. Still, he hadn't gone through the trouble of shooting a pistol all morning if he wasn't going to have the opportunity to teach the green-eyed vixen proper form.

"No. As usual, Matthew has not extended me the courtesy." She skewered her brother with a forthright stare.

"Don't be flippant. It's unbecoming," Matthew's stern tone admonished as he sent a chiding look in her direction.

Most women would lower their chin. Amelia notched hers higher. For some unnamed reason, Lunden took pride in the small movement.

"I have business to attend across town so I must leave you both." Matthew picked up his cane from where it leaned against his desk. "I'll send Mary in." He turned in Amelia's direction. "Classes in deportment were a waste of Father's money. You need to become more aware of propriety, most especially if I'm to find you a good match." Then he nodded a good-bye and departed the room.

Lunden eyed Amelia during the entire exchange and noted the shadow of dismay clouding her crystal green eyes at the mention of marriage. In that, he understood. He had no wish to be married. Love, and any type of affection necessary for a successful relationship, represented the last thing he wanted in life. Considering the industrious effort put forth to make her a match, Amelia's fate was sealed. Yet she admitted she could be happy if she married for love and not convenience. The odds were stacked against her. Pity that. He sided with her abject rejection of being manipulated. On some level, it mirrored his past.

"I've secured a location and the items needed for your second demand."

Her features softened and a twinkle of mischief lit her eyes. Good. His words met the mark and he'd cheered her.

"Request," she persisted, although an impish smile played on her lips. "When can we come together?"

His heartbeat stuttered at the question until he realized she inquired of the gun lesson, nothing more. Despite the clarity, his eyes roved over her from head to toe. She appeared so damned beautiful in clothes, what would she look like without? Something about Amelia conjured images of empresses and goddesses. Perhaps the defiant set of her shoulders or the line of her slim neck. But then, in a contradiction he'd come to expect, her untamed curls, mischievous eyes, and full ripe lips prompted thoughts far from gallantry, and instead plunged headfirst into naughty fantasy.

He made a concerted effort to pull his mind from that dark, forbidden place.

"Does Thursday afternoon suit you?" His voice went husky and a shot of desire quickened his pulse. He stalked to the fireplace to poke at the logs, uncomfortable with how easily Amelia provoked him on a visceral level.

"Yes. That's perfect. Saturday I travel to Lakeview. Our bargain is moving far faster than I expected, but then so are my brother's plans."

Her eyes followed his every action and he stilled, entranced by her glittering green attention. With effort he replaced the poker and crossed the thick Oriental rug to where she stood near her brother's desk. Mary showed up at the doorway and Amelia waved her away. When she turned in his direction, he cocked an eyebrow at her dismissal of the maid and her velvety laughter contradicted his condescending expression.

Delightful minx.

"In this, I'll need your full instruction." She whispered the words.

Lunden swallowed his immediate retort. Somehow they'd moved much closer, and although the double doors stood wide open as it was the middle of the day, an edgy tension thickened the air between them.

"I have confidence you'll take well to the skill, provided you don't point your weapon at my heart." *That organ withstood enough damage for a lifetime.*

"I'm a fast learner."

Her words were breathy, as if she feared the same thing she wanted, and the quality kicked his pulse another notch, despite it already thrummed in his veins. Their eyes locked as he moved closer, their bodies scant paces apart.

Why would a woman shun the idea of marriage and determinedly pursue how to fire a pistol? The intriguing quandary convinced him further, like he, she kept a silent secret locked away tight.

"I have no doubt." He focused on her lips, held in a full pout. No one should possess such an irresistible quality. He took another step, obeying the insistent tug of desire, and her gaze faltered. Her eyes dipped to his mouth and back up again. "You know, learning how to ride or shoot a pistol won't give you the control you seek."

"I disagree." She tipped her head and her eyes flared with willfulness. "Marriage leaves women with very few choices. My list ensures I have a sense of . . ."

"Security? Power?" His low-voiced questions seemed to cause her unease.

"Freedom. Choice." Her voice caught on the last word. Color flared high on her cheeks.

She looked absolutely bewitching.

"A woman can have all the control if she acts wisely. A flirtatious glance, a subtle suggestion . . . women possess more power than they realize and yet they sublimate the control and lose all opportunity."

Her lips parted as if she wished to object or agree. He would never know. For the span of several determined beats of his heart, they faced each other and time stilled. He watched the smile leave her eyes as laudable challenge took a firm hold.

The tip of her tongue poked out to lick over her enticing lips and desire was on him in a white hot rush of heat.

How would she taste? As tart as her words or as sweet as temptation?

"Milady?"

The butler's voice cooled his ardor; still with great reluctance Lunden slid his eyes toward the door in tandem with Amelia.

"Yes . . . Spencer."

She answered in a remote voice and the perceptible pause between her words revealed more than the brief flash of emerald.

"What is it?"

Her normal tone seemed recouped. Lunden's lips climbed to what others considered some semblance of a smile, but he fast schooled his features with a sharp exhale.

"Pardon the interruption. A note has been left at the door. I believe it is intended for the gentleman."

Spencer turned in his direction and Lunden advanced to claim the message. No one knew of his arrival, save very few. Could it be Dobson with a change of plans concerning the firearms lesson? He broke the seal as Amelia dismissed the servant and returned to his side.

His eyes scanned the page and regret sunk its sharp claws into his soul. Sadness crawled over his heart with such heaviness, even the scent of jasmine and Amelia's light touch to his arm could not permeate his despair.

"What is it?"

"If you will excuse me." His voice sounded peculiar. *Emotions*. He could do without them all.

He hastened from the room, intent on his bedchamber, the note gripped in his fist, the foolscap already dampened from the sweat of his palm. He kicked the door closed, dropped into the armchair nearest the window, and focused on the twisted branches of an ash tree planted in the sparse side yard.

Hell and the devil, things were not proceeding as planned. Why would this stranger ask for a private meeting and implore Lunden withdraw his inquiries through bank and solicitor? His brother's past was complicated enough without another roadblock to interfere with settling the matter once and for all. Worse, the letter held a dire tone. It stirred memories he'd chosen to bury under years of mundane living and blankets of regret. *Painful memories.*

He dropped his head to the cushion of the chair and closed his eyes. In sleep he could escape, surrender to the bleak despair that consumed him from the inside out. He'd find peace there, in the darkness, for at least a little while.

Chapter Nine

"So you see, Collins"—Whittingham employed his most decorous tone—"this will serve both our favors. I seek an exemplary husband for my sister, while you require a wife. The matter warrants little deliberation. It's as simple as the monthly riddle at the society." He strove to stifle an impatient note. Collins would never agree if he felt cajoled.

"It's an unexpected and interesting proposition. Tell me more of your sister. Does she enjoy children? Know well how to manage a large household?" Collins drained his glass and leaned against the leather bolster in the dimly lit tavern. "I will have six younglings to raise once I relocate." A bark of laughter escaped the older gentleman. "A duty better managed by a young wife."

"Amelia loves children, I assure you." An image of his sister and her bane of a pet flashed to mind. With a slight grimace, Matthew pressed on. "She has a vivacious spirit and likable disposition younglings find appealing." He took a long swallow of ale and then another. He'd never seen his sister take an interest in children simply because there were none in the family as of yet, but that didn't mean she would not enjoy their company. And he wanted a sterling endorsement. Best keep his mind on the prize.

"With all due respect, Whittingham, hasn't your sister caused a stir with her antics? Did she not light someone on fire recently?"

Matthew buried a cough. "A terrible misunderstanding. It was my fault in truth. I bumped the epergne, but you understand how ugly rumors begin. Considering all being said about your hasty departure from the society, I surmise securing a new chief officer weighs heavily on your mind," he finished in his gravest baritone.

"True, the matter needs to be resolved." Collins drew a long breath. "If only the demands of the society were not so time consuming, I could retain my position."

"But you're relocating, aren't you?" Matthew tempered his inquiry as idle curiosity, afraid to reveal he'd dug into the man's personal business.

"Yes, it's a condition of my inheritance although I'll frequent London on occasion. I have no intent to leave off with my mistress just because my life is being turned inside out." Collins eyed him with too-keen interest. "You're vying for my position?"

Perhaps his efforts appeared transparent. Damn Collins's high intellect. "It would be a great honor. With your endorsement, who could stand in my path were I fortunate enough to secure that document?" No need to slice hairs now. He breathed a long sigh, uncomfortable with the avenue of the conversation and uncertain of the outcome, yet so much was at stake. On the verge of becoming the laughingstock at the society, he'd already endeavored to ascend the ranks twice and failed. This would be his last attempt due to the rules of eligibility. Pride and ambition hung in the balance. So many parts of his life had become a matter of compromise, but he remained guiltless in this one pursuit. It was nothing less than luck the two main issues preoccupying his time overlapped.

"I presumed so." Collins smiled and the action was not

at all what Matthew expected. "Any man willing to trade his sister for a position in the society meets my criteria for candidate." He banged his fist upon the table in the same manner he employed the gavel. "I will need to meet Amelia of course, and find her amenable, but otherwise, I would say this conversation has provided what we both desire. Arrange things, Whittingham, and I'll do the same." He stood and grabbed his hat where it perched on a nearby hook before he bustled out the door.

"Charlotte, you mustn't allow him to speak to you like that. Oh dear, I've failed you. I need a plan." Determination locked Amelia in place until she broke free and strode triumphantly toward the park bench. "I'm taking you with me. What will Dearing do? Hunt us down as if we're criminals? You're his wife, not his chattel. And you're my friend and I need your assistance." Amelia hemmed her bottom lip, her mind busy.

"I could never disobey my husband. I took a vow. And frankly, women are as much chattel as a wing chair or a storage trunk. What if he rescinded on my family's loan payments because I angered him?" Trepidation chased her words.

"He wouldn't dare." Amelia rushed forward in a scuffle of pebbles. "Does he offer you any reason? Does he dislike me so?"

"No. Now that's ridiculous." Charlotte rose from the bench and looped their arms. "Let's not dwell on it. There'll be other opportunities. I'm sure your family will want you to themselves anyway. A Saturday spent in the country is delightful."

"It is. That's why I wished you to join me. Today is Thursday." Amelia's expression mellowed and a small smile tempted her lips. "I've an appointment with Lunden at eleven o'clock."

"An appointment? Of what sort? Has he found you a husband already? I thought you had the situation in hand."

Amelia could not contain the sudden laughter that bubbled to the surface. "Which question should I answer first?" The day seemed brighter. Surely it had nothing to do with the mention of Lunden. Learning to shoot a gun set her body all a-jitter. "I'll answer every question if I have your promise to take a firm stand with Dearing. Surely he cannot be unbearable all the time. Speak to him after he's eaten a large meal. Men are usually more agreeable when fed." She squeezed her friend's arm with her free hand and smiled as Charlotte nodded agreement. "Now let me tell you the details of my day. I know you'll agree its guaranteed excitement."

Lunden eyed Amelia with keen interest. She settled on the carriage seat and made a big show of arranging her skirts. Then he handed Mary up and the maid slid across the banquette and promptly wrinkled Amelia's efforts. A rueful twinge stung his lips, but he stifled the reaction. He did not smile, and rarely allowed any desire meant to invigorate the effort.

He climbed aboard and rapped on the roof.

They'd only traveled a short distance before Amelia's jasmine fragrance set his body afire. He flung the velvet curtain aside and cracked open the glass window in hope of deflecting his arousal. One slim velvet brow arched at his sudden action, but otherwise the lady made no comment. Her expression conveyed everything she meant to say. His cheek twitched. Damn, he enjoyed the eager glitter of mischief in her eyes.

"We'll be there momentarily. Mary will remain in the

parlor. Dobson's estate is vacant aside from his butler, but your maid may read, embroider, or do whatever women do when they wait."

"Have you been so detached from society, Your Grace?"

She cast an imploring glare in his direction and he rankled at the question. He would not discuss his absence from London and the reason that forced him to flee. He'd left the city a boy and returned a man assuring him little knowledge of society's dictates. It made the prospect of securing a bridegroom ridiculous. He ran a palm over the pocket of his waistcoat, the candidate requirement list tucked inside. His punishment was complete, gone too long without purpose other than to keep a secret buried. "I've never been one to visit the maids after hours and with no sister to chaperone, the explanation is clear."

His gruff tone hinted at restraint tethered on a short rope. Amelia's eyes flared.

"Friendship is unlike the false pretense of formal society. I hope you consider me more friend than obligation to be fulfilled." Her voice held a solemn tone but then she grinned, and he liked it too much.

Amelia offered only danger and temptation, evidenced by the swift ache of regret and longing currently lodged in his chest. She represented everything he could not possess no matter how time faded memories or blurred the edges of a decade past. Without a doubt, scandal was always one whisper away and she deserved better than the shallow happiness he could offer.

"I appreciate your kindness." His eyes shifted to her lush succulent mouth as desire pulsed through him. He forced himself to complete his reply. "But I have no other goal than to settle my brother's estate and leave London." Somehow his eyes found their way to her lips again, in anticipation of her reply, no doubt.

You want to kiss her so badly, you ache from it.

He cleared his throat and shoved the thought from his mind.

"I understand," she capitulated with a grudging tone. "I suppose finding my future husband will be accomplished in equaled slapdash fashion."

"By your brother, I presume." He turned his eyes to the landscape, unwilling to read the sentiment in her eyes. "I'm currently too preoccupied with fulfilling your wish list to pay attention to your quest for everlasting happiness." He meant to jest, but the terse words came out ruined by some nameless emotion that unsettled his resolve.

"Is it wrong to hope for contentment?" Her voice rose on the imperative. "Men have such power—"

"But possess equally poor judgment."

An uncomfortable silence enveloped the coach equivalent to the shadow in Amelia's eyes.

Memories wormed their way to the surface. He missed his brother no matter their vociferous disagreements. Thoughts of childhood foolery and sibling worship before their parents died, and even afterward, fought valiantly with bitter regret and confusion. He would always love Douglas and feel the loss of his early passing, no matter his brother's unorthodox choices. Douglas had come into the title too young, barely sixteen. Yet despite their father's untimely death, he was born to it, much the same way Lunden inured the casual careless nature and near responsibilities of a second son. Second sons were expendable. How ironic that the social enigma would ultimately prove undeniable truth.

He dared a glance to the unusually quiet lady seated across the coach and relief infused him. Remembrances proved discomforting. He would not allow further memories of Amelia. If he did, *when he did,* it would be to succor his tremendous loneliness and for no other reason ever.

In the meantime, he'd need find a way to squash his physical awareness of her: the petite slope of her nose, that delectable chin, the graceful curve of her neck. Every jilt and jiggle of the carriage set her riotous curls in motion begging for his touch. Today she was a quiet storm, powerful even when demure, lest no one doubt she wouldn't cause devastation of all temptation given the opportunity. Truly, he needed a lengthy lecture on friendship and loyalty, anything to abolish this wordless compulsion.

The coach slowed to a stop.

With Mary deposited, Lunden dragged Amelia from the intriguing display of taxidermy littered throughout the estate. He noted with unfounded delight she preferred the lynx, just as much as he. Not that it mattered, but on some unexplained level, the observation pleased him.

They followed the gravel path to the same clearing where Dobson and his butler had arranged for pistol practice and Lunden's thoughts filtered to that afternoon and Dobson's curt insinuation he'd been maltreated by society. If only the rest of London would concur, he needn't skulk around vacated homes and dark alleys. A shot of anger flicked him raw.

"So how does this thing work?"

Lunden jerked his head in Amelia's direction, his eyes fixed on the flintlock pistol turned sideways in her palm and pointed in his direction. "Put that down." He charged in a fury. His hand found the barrel and he eased it from her grasp. "No need to hurry my journey to hell."

"I don't know what you're talking about."

"Exactly." He watched as she squared her jaw with a resolute tilt of her chin and wondered if she was aware of the habit. He certainly was. And the tendency she favored, all righteous indignity and straight-shouldered stance, coupled with the sunlight as it played havoc on each blue-black ringlet falling down her back. Her eyes bright with strength and vitality made him imagine the unthinkable.

If only life had played out differently.

He tightened his grip on the reaction and blotted out the thought. "If I'm to teach you how to shoot, you'll follow my directions. Let's not have any improvisation reminiscent of your riding lesson when we're dealing with firearms." He replaced the unloaded pistol on the low-lying brick wall and slanted his face nearer. "I'm the instructor. You're the student. Clear?"

She had to look up to meet his eyes, and when she didn't immediately answer, he blew aside a rebellious ringlet from where it rested against her cheek. That gained her attention.

"Crystal." All haughty defiance was absent this time, her lips set in a firm line.

"Then we will begin." He stepped to where the powder bag waited. "First, measure out the proper charge." He demonstrated once, and then allowed Amelia to mimic his actions under close supervision. She did well and only appeared unsettled with the awkwardness of the powder horn.

"Next, we'll need the ball and patch." He loaded his pistol, making slow deliberate movements before overseeing Amelia's preparation. "Last, you must tamp down the charge."

She followed his directions and completed the load. An irrational sense of pride reared its head and he hammered it down with the same force as the bullet.

"This isn't difficult at all." She straightened her shoulders with the declaration. "Men make such a to-do about every iota of life. Women should be allowed the privilege of riding or shooting without having to bargain away their independence. I imagine I will hit that target with ease." Conviction shone in her eyes.

Then a proud smile curled her lips and Lunden swallowed a groan. He'd dreamed of that mouth, the silky warmth of her kiss, and spent endless minutes wondering if she'd embrace lovemaking with the same vivacious spirit she exuded for all other activities. He muttered a low curse and answered with a derisive snort. Best get on with the lesson or he might do something that warranted he take a bullet to the heart first thing in the morning.

"Where should I stand?" She folded her arms under her breasts while her toe tapped an impatient beat on the gray slated patio. The action accentuated the fullness of her bodice and he clenched his teeth to stifle his appreciation.

"Stand here. In line with the target. I'll shadow you and help you pull the trigger. The first—"

"I can do it myself."

Any trace of lingering pride vaporized. Hadn't the termagant learned from their riding lesson? Her headstrong disposition wrought nothing but trouble. "Amelia . . ."

"Oh yes. You're the teacher. I'm the student. I almost forgot." Her rueful smile and mocking tone eviscerated the sincerity of the declaration.

"Move. Here." He indicated the spot Dobson utilized when instructing him. The technique worked well, and as of yet, Lunden believed the lesson was a success despite Amelia's mutinous attitude. "Face the target and spread your feet apart." He glanced to the ground and nudged her slipper with the toe of his boot. "A bit more." He shadowed her form, careful to avoid getting too close to her skirts, and brought the flintlock forward with care to place in her grasp. Then he braced his arms against hers, ready to pull the trigger while he supported her hands. The report would be unexpected and he didn't wish her to be frightened or hurt.

She resisted his guidance, shrugging free from his hold so only her finger rested on the trigger.

"What do you think you're doing?" His question skimmed the silky skin of her lobe.

She twisted to view him over her right shoulder and her lips nearly brushed his chin. He resisted the urge to step back. Why did she have to be so bloody damn arousing? Hadn't he already paid his price to the devil?

"I want to pull the trigger." Her eyes volleyed from the gun to the target and back. "That's the only way I'll enjoy the full experience."

Her answer resonated on a physical level and his annoyance deepened. He noted the defiant set of her jaw and the clever glint in her eyes. Her irises were the most unusual shade of green, as addictive as absinthe, strong and hypnotic, yet astonishing in their brilliance. A silence opened between them and her gaze met his with quiet force. For a fleeting moment, her brows furrowed and then her lips parted, as if another retort singed the tip of her tongue.

"Think about what you're doing. Otherwise we'll both get hurt." His voice sank to a deep growl, the advice meant for his ears only.

She resettled the pistol and turned shrewd attention to the target while he ordered his heart to find its normal rhythm. The traitorous organ disobeyed. In his peripheral vision, he caught her smile of victory. If she only knew.

Chapter Ten

The recoil plastered Amelia flat against his chest. Distracted by his ardor, Lunden struggled to make sense of the situation as momentum carried them backward. They flailed in a synchronized tangle of limbs, past the low wall and onto the grass, first he, then she, now spun forward and sprawled atop him, her hair a curtain of silk against his face.

"Where's the gun?" It was the only thing he could manage. His pulse thrummed an accelerated beat, each muscle in his body hard as the ground at his back.

"The gun? I dropped it."

Her words, hot pants of breath, struck his cheek and his body tightened. Was it possible for him to grow harder? She shook her head to the left in an attempt to clear their vision and her body pressed against his, soft and inviting, while every ebony curl glossed over his face until only defiant strands lingered, caught in the stubble at his chin.

"Are you in pain?" He forced the words in an aggrieved tone. She seemed in no hurry to stand. Perhaps she'd twisted an ankle.

"No. Are you?"

None he could express to a lady. He tried in a Herculean

effort to ignore the weight of her breasts pressed against his heart, and focused on her face. The usual confidence was absent and her eyes held a question or perhaps an observation she could not dismantle. Some unnamed emotion cloyed at his chest, vibrant and unfamiliar, as Amelia's bewildered expression played havoc with his emotions, and the urge to kiss her, to tighten his arms around her shoulders and press their mouths together, drenched his every pore.

He shouldn't.

Only the devil would take advantage.

He wouldn't.

He was a better man than people believed.

Her tongue peeked out to lick her lower lip and temptation tipped the scale.

Confusion held Amelia hostage. Surely the air knocked out of her when she launched back from the pistol's recoil, otherwise how could she explain her inability to regain an even breathing pattern?

Lunden was under her.

Her brain intruded with the feasible answer.

Lunden was under her. Hot, hard, and pressed as firmly as the stays in her corset. Good heavens, the man was a rock. Her skirts were flung to the side when she'd fallen, and the muscular outline of his thighs perceived through the barest layer of fabric caused a warm, wonderful feeling to flood her lower extremities.

She forced her gaze upward. His eyes seared hers with an intensity that robbed all breath.

When he raised his hand, her gasp escaped. She rolled in a swift effort to her right and stood with the assistance of the half wall. By the time she righted her gown and turned, he'd retrieved the pistol and his glare inferred he stood ready to use it.

"I wanted—"

He launched forward as if a bullet from the gun, and each stride punctuated his powerful words.

"Yes, Amelia. Everyone knows *I* is your favorite word. *I* don't listen to my brother. *I* don't want to get married. *I* wanted to race the horse. *I* wanted to shoot the gun. *I*, *I*, *I*. Have you thought of the consequences of your choices? Have you considered how your quest to please *I* endangers, impinges, and affects the people around you? The people who care for you?"

He'd reached her, yet he kept on coming, their strides matched measure for measure, hers moving backward, his pushing forward.

"Your brother has assigned me a futile mission because never will *I* find a man who will subject and surrender himself to your eternal pleasing."

Her palm found his cheek in a resounding slap. It echoed in the barren clearing.

She gasped on a half-taken breath, shocked at the truth in his statements more than the angry delivery. *And her reaction.* What had she done? How could she repair the damage?

They stood quiet, motionless, until he closed the distance between them and his mouth found hers.

All resistance dissolved like sugar in hot tea.

She should chastise his arrogance, rail at his audacity, but similar to her legs, the proposition was weak and unsupported. There was nothing for her to do but surrender to his assault.

He kissed her hard, as if his argument continued without words. His hands plunged deep into her hair, the few pins that held its weight scattered on the ground, and his tongue . . . His tongue stroked the soft interior of her mouth as if he wished to coax a secret free. She leaned into his strength, no longer trusting her fickle spine to hold her upright, his arm a band around her back.

In the length of a deep sigh, his mouth withdrew the slightest distance and then slanted to the left to possess her in another hot openmouthed embrace. She'd never been kissed like this, never consumed the way he devoured her. He tasted of danger and secrets, his kiss something of daydreams, and night dreams, forbidden temptation, and unspoken fantasies.

Suffused with pleasure, she trembled from the inside out. Perhaps he perceived her reaction. He pulled from her lips in a swift dip of the head, his hot breath lingering between them before the brisk air interceded.

"You deserved that." They spoke the same words, although a slap and a kiss balanced opposite sides of the scale.

Then a few breaths more and an easy camaraderie erased the anticipated awkwardness, as if she didn't discharge a pistol without permission, or he hadn't kissed her to heaven and back. With an inscrutable expression, he dropped his arms, pausing to ensure she stood firm on her feet before he busied himself with reclaiming the equipment. Her eyes followed each of his movements, and while he made no comment as to the depth and wondrous magic of their kiss, she sensed he remained affected. She saw it in every lineament of his body.

They returned to the house in amiable silence. Inside, Mary slept in a wing chair, her head inclined against the rump of a shaggy brown bear. A smile played on Amelia's lips as they continued to the carriage, and she mused all three occupants harbored a secret shared.

Matthew drummed his fingers on the tabletop, the puzzle pieces vibrating to the cadence of his impatience.

"Where the devil is she?" His question evaporated in the empty room as frustration held him captive, any work on his map futile until he spoke to Amelia. The nomination for chief officer dangled like a prize held out of reach. How convenient Collins was on the hunt for a wife. No doubt luck had finally shifted in his favor. He'd convince his sister to marry Collins and move to the countryside to take care of the newly acquired brood if it killed him. Granted, if forced, his sister would scare Collins to purgatory. He blew out a frustrated breath. Finesse. He would need to contrive a plan and employ every ounce of aplomb he possessed.

Pandora slunk into the study like a precursor of doom. Amelia swept in at the tip of her tail. Perhaps luck did smile upon him. He would begin the groundwork. Time was of the essence.

"Where have you been? I questioned Spencer and the rest of the staff. No one had an inkling to your whereabouts. It's not the behavior of your station to disappear without notice."

"I would think you welcomed my absence. You complain about my staying home, and now you complain about my going out. Make up your mind."

Why was he cursed with such a contrary sibling? Collins would never accept such impudence. "It's only because I mean to speak to you. Have you given thought to Father's wish that you marry as soon as possible?"

"How can I not, when you perpetually remind me? I'll speak to him when I visit this weekend." Amelia bent and scooped Pandora into her arms, but did not say more.

"I've secured a solution. Trust me to handle this matter." He strove to keep his tone even.

She turned to him with one brow arched, her mouth curved in some semblance of a grin, and his jaw tightened with frustration. Was she amused or set to slice him to ribbons? His inability to read her mood fueled his temper.

"Don't trouble yourself, brother. I've the matter in hand. I already bear the embarrassment of your petition to Scarsdale. What's next, an ad in *the London Times* to advertise my need to marry?"

"Make no mistake, we don't have the luxury of time." In part the statement was true, and he used the flimsy fact to bludgeon his conscience. "Another year or two and you'll be considered on the shelf, while Father . . ." His words faded in a veil of concern.

"I will honor Father's wishes even if they don't mirror my own."

Her voice wavered and a glimmer of compassion flickered to life within his chest. He knew Amelia had no wish to be forced into an arrangement, yet the stakes were too high for him to be weakened by emotions. If things proceeded as planned, he could accomplish multiple goals. Why shouldn't they all benefit?

"Very good, then. There's a gentleman I'd like you to meet tomorrow evening. Lord Collins will join us for dinner. Be sure to dress in your finest silk." He nodded his head to signal the discussion concluded and then braced for the anticipated rebuttal, yet none came. Still, his eyes narrowed as he watched her exit, her shoulders straight and her chin held high.

Chapter Eleven

Amelia entered the breakfast room and buttered her toast with a solemn lack of enthusiasm. She never walked with Charlotte on Friday as Dearing required his wife attend all household duties and correspondence before the week's end. The reminder of her friend's inflexible schedule and current unhappiness stilled her knife. She had to find a solution to Charlotte's misery. Otherwise, where lay her worth as a friend?

With effort Amelia forced herself to consider Charlotte's discontent, otherwise she'd lose herself in the remembrance of Lunden's heated kiss. She'd already spent most of the night straight into morning reliving the divine perfection of his mouth upon hers. And all was lost when she'd attempted to rationalize her obsession with the memory, placate herself with platitudes, or suggest she was enthralled with discharging the pistol, emotions high, self-control at its most vulnerable. The bald truth remained whether she chose to confront it or not. His kiss was magic. Pure sin and eternal paradise combined.

Good heavens, she'd been kissed before, but nothing, nothing in all her imagination, compared with Lunden's kiss.

However would she face him when they were next together? Impossible, indeed.

The click of silver on china alerted she was no longer alone and she glanced to the sideboard where the subject of her contemplations filled his plate, as if by reflection alone she'd conjured his presence.

"Good morning." He nodded in her direction and accepted a steaming cup of black coffee at the table. "What causes such sullenness so early? The sun is shining and we've made excellent progress in your list of demands."

The intended jibe did not find its mark. Reality replaced fantasy and the threat of tonight's dinner and Lord Collins's appearance, robbed her conviviality. "My brother has proven quite nimble. He's invited a candidate to dine this evening, and I fear Matthew is more serious than ever."

"I'll be sorry to miss it."

The tone of his voice defied his words. She threw a warning glare in his direction meant to curb remarks involving flaming pants and unconscious suitors. "You must attend. How will I defend myself against my brother's ill-meant intentions if I have no ally at my side?" She paused to gauge the flicker of emotion in his whisky-brown stare. "We made an agreement. We sealed it with a handshake." The memory of his branding kiss prodded her heart.

"Of course." His voice dipped lower. "But my meeting is of great importance and shouldn't be delayed."

"Then I'll ask a personal favor." Could he hear the desperation she struggled to conceal?

"I don't recall a good turn as an item on your mercenary list of demands."

One dark brow cocked as he challenged her. She noted an invisible smile at the corner of his mouth, the slightest bend of his lips, and the liquid depths of his warm eyes lit with an amused glow. A breath later he acquiesced.

"I'll rearrange my schedule."

"Thank you." This time she achieved a smile, though she worried still. "I feel better already. You've saved me yet again." It was barely an improvement. If Matthew pursued the issue, any objections meant little. Her fate sealed.

"Don't mistake me for a hero." His voice edged with a harsh quality, forbidding and relentless. All amusement fell away as his curt edict stifled further discussion. "The role doesn't suit me."

Her eyes searched his face for understanding, but a shadow veiled his expression. The only discernible evidence of emotion was the tick of a muscle in the line of his jaw. Amelia bit the inside of her cheek to keep her questions contained.

"And don't forget, I have the same purpose. To see you wed and settled. Your brother sought my assistance and I intend to fulfill the bargain."

Pity he fit but one requirement on the husband list. Lunden eyed Amelia and stifled a rare urge to grin. How the girl provoked his humor eluded his comprehension. He'd given up smiling years ago. All romantic notions better left unexplored. Amelia deserved true love. His heart remained unavailable to the emotion. Masked beneath his calm demeanor he seethed with anger aimed at himself, furious he'd given in to temptation, succumbed to misplaced desire, and kissed her. No good could come of it, and in the light of a new morning, with firm resolve, he vowed to smother the passionate vestige of their embrace, and never repeat the mistake.

She sat across from him, a vision in violet silk, her mane of unruly curls tossed over one shoulder as she studied her tea. The long sweep of dark lashes against soft ivory skin declared delicious femininity no matter what skills she learned or the sharp rebellious edge of her replies. He dragged his eyes away in an act of salvation. If he looked at her too long, he couldn't catch his breath.

This evening, he'd planned to investigate the perplexing letter he'd received, but if she truly needed his help in allaying the conversation at tonight's dinner, his business would keep for one more night. If only he could ignore the remembrance of her body pressed against his or the startled gleam of sensual awareness in the depths of her eyes. Disgusted with himself, he forced the anxious images from his mind.

Right now, he was due to an appointment with his solicitor. That would not wait. Douglas's affairs were in order, and barring any unexpected obstacles, the matter with the town house sale should resolve with ease. He'd conclude his business in this damnable city once and for all.

Thirty minutes later, he arrived at the modest law building of Bolster Hamm, Esquire, and was shown into the office with haste. Questions bumped against each other in his mind. Who sent the mysterious letter and why would anyone wish to prohibit the sale of Douglas's town house? Was this complication connected to the tragic events of that evening? He slid his hand into his pocket, the suede pouch protecting his brother's watch secure in his possession.

Not one to enjoy idle time, he slew his eyes across the room. Bookcases grew from floor to ceiling against three of the four walls. Leather tomes of every size and color filled the shelves, although he doubted Hamm needed to reference their information often. A good solicitor was worth his weight in gold. Lunden held no reservation in spending funds if the matter resolved with expedience.

The last wall was comprised of three parallel windows. He stepped near the glass, his eyes fixed on the view below. London's busy thoroughfare rushed through daily life. A young boy hawked wares on the corner. An energetic pup, bouncing near his feet, mimicked his cries with high-pitched yelps. A fishmonger rolled his cart with concerted

effort, his attention drawn to a group of finely dressed
ladies admiring gowns in a shop window. This was the
world he'd escaped. He would have no trouble abandoning
it once again.

He spun to face the door at the sound of someone's entry.
Bolster Hamm, a well-built man in his midforties, shook his
hand with vigor and settled behind his desk.

"Forgive my tardiness, Your Grace. I'm working with
purpose toward clearing the sale of your brother's town
house, but your message mentioned another concern. How
may I assist?"

Lunden cleared his throat and produced the letter he'd
received. Hamm skimmed the contents and returned the
message a minute later.

"This could be a scam. Gossip brings about the most
preposterous circumstances."

Lunden needed no lesson on the rumor mill. Damn them
all. Society didn't know the palest shade of truth. He grimaced and offered a nod of affirmation.

"Perhaps your brother left behind an unresolved matter.
I can delve deeper, although I've been thorough in my com-
pilation of information."

"I don't doubt your ability, Hamm." Lunden's voice was
low, indicative of his pensive consideration. He'd hired the
most discreet investigators and they'd all yielded nothing.
"Douglas was an efficient peer. It's unlikely he harbored
illicit involvement." The lie rolled from his tongue with
practiced ease.

"Pardon me, Your Grace. That wasn't my intention." The
solicitor touched his forehead as if deliberating the right
choice of words. "I meant to reassure I'll leave no subject
unexplored."

"Of course." His mind spun with painful remembrance.
Douglas was strict, forbiddingly so, and private, yet Lunden
loved him dearly, no matter their quarrels. He was a child,

unable to understand the depth of his brother's need for privacy. Despite their vast age difference, he strove to emulate his brother, comfortable in the role of second son, never coveting the title. Still, fate forced the duchy on him anyway and it proved an unnatural fit. He straightened his shoulders, as if to shake off the uncomfortable conclusion.

"I plan to meet this man at the time and place indicated. I've no patience for games. If it proves a scam, we can move forward with resolving all complications and be done with the sale." Lunden stood to indicate his intent to leave.

Hamm rose in kind and extended his hand. "Yes. Please keep me apprised if I may be of assistance."

Dark thoughts clouded his mind as he settled in the hack and rapped on the ceiling. The coach lurched forward with a jolt as it maneuvered the crowded street. He yanked the curtain closed, anxious to shut London from his view, and leaned against the worn banquette. The appointment had accomplished little. Despite the most pointed questions, Hamm knew of no one interested in the property or poised to interfere with the sale. What could it all mean? He would confront this man under the cloak of night as indicated, but he doubted it would erase the sorrow of his heart. He bit back a ready curse at the tormented twists of fate. Romulus killed Remus, one brother left to a life of regret.

The carriage pulled to a stop at the corner of Lamb Street and Lunden shoved aside the crimson curtain to slant a glance out the window. Across the way, shadowed in the afternoon shade, stood his brother's private residence, tucked neatly into a well-heeled community of quiet money and scholarly gentlemen. Until the night of his brother's death, Lunden had no awareness of this address. And it should have remained as so. But everything was different now. Time changed life's circumstances whether one wished it or not. If only he hadn't followed his brother and interrupted his evening plans.

He opened the drawstring pouch and slid Douglas's broken watch into his palm. The hour was long past for resolution, forgiveness an unattainable absolution. Still the desire to discover something, anything, linked to Douglas and the events of that evening pulled at his soul with unanswered yearning.

Amelia slipped into Matthew's study intent on discovering any shred of information involving Lord Collins, the man due to arrive for dinner in less than an hour. She rifled through the files on his desk then darted a sideways glance to the door. Had she heard a sound or was it the thrumming of her heart that deceived her brain there was footfall on the hall carpet?

She jiggled the top drawer and feeling resistance, removed a pin from her hair to slide into the lock. Pandora sauntered into the room. Startled by the feline's silky shadow, she dropped her makeshift key. With a strong mutter, she rose from the floor with pin in hand and froze. She *did* hear footsteps.

Blast, Matthew would wring her neck.

Palming the hairpin, she gathered her skirts and rushed across the room. A bemused smile twitched her lips as childhood memories flittered to the surface. She'd overheard a good share of conversation meant to be kept from her ears by hiding in the study closet. Tonight would be no different. Perhaps her ruse would supply more information than her clumsy investigation of the desk.

The door barely clicked before the soft weight of heels on carpet entered the room. She strained her ears to decipher a voice, but could hear nothing aside from the familiar rustle of paper and the dull jangle of brass pulls on desk drawers.

What was Matthew looking for? If only she'd managed

to open the locked cabinet. What if he'd had the paperwork arranged? *Good Lord, a marriage contract.* She meant to discuss it with her father this weekend. Could her freedom be taken tonight? Would her brother act with rash abandonment?

A heavy pulse thrummed in her ears. How would she ever hear a word spoken in the room if she didn't calm down? Straining to decipher the sounds, she set her body flush against the wood panel and as the room fell silent, her breathing slowed. Perhaps Matthew had left. At seven o'clock Lord Collins was due. She pressed her ear to the door again, desperate for the assurance needed to emerge from the closet and scurry to her bedchamber. Instead, the distinctive sound of Matthew's voice and another deeper baritone, echoed through the wood panel. *And the rush of heavy footsteps, discordant with the approaching voices.* She gasped when the doorknob jiggled, withdrawing to the farthest corner, swallowed by shadows in a heartbeat.

Lunden released a string of expletives known only by those bound for hell, and closed the closet door with a swift silent pull. He breathed a sigh of relief as two male voices entered the study. Matthew and Lord Collins, no doubt. He'd almost been caught inspecting his friend's personal papers. Not an easy matter to explain having one's hands in another's desk. Almost as dangerous as having his hands on his best friend's sister.

Amelia.

The hellion would cause him nothing but trouble, yet she ignited his curiosity, his humor, and passion for living, long thought dead. He'd finish his business and leave London as soon as possible, or else risk an obsession. An image of her midnight curls, plump, seductive lips, and curvaceous body, formed with vivid clarity no matter he stood in pitch-black darkness.

He muttered another round of expletives and stifled a groan.

It was too late.

She lived in him.

He squeezed his eyes shut and drew a deep breath, assailed by jasmine and unmistakable female. Bloody hell, what was wrong with him? He could smell her, alive and vibrant in this musty closet, as if they shared a lover's rendezvous. He cursed into the dark. Still the fragrance teased him as clearly as the evening he'd smelled her on his pillow. She'd bewitched him, the beautiful minx. This wanting would addle his brain. He clenched his fists to force the yearning free and shifted in the darkness.

Then every muscle stilled.

Bloody hell and jasmine.

"Amelia." His best attempt at a whisper sounded harsh as it sliced the air.

"Yes."

At the sound of her voice, he leaned forward as if tugged on a leash, his body harder than stone. Then his heart prodded his blood flow with a sexual jolt so strong he rocked with vertiginous force in the opposite direction. Any well-respected gentleman would stifle naughty thoughts involving his comrade's sister. What a mercy he didn't fall into that category.

"Why are you in this closet?" He'd dismantle his desire with mundane conversation.

"I'm hiding from my brother. I thought I heard him coming. . . ." Her voice, a strong hushed tone, reached for him in the darkness. "I suppose it was you."

She shifted in the corner and it was though he could see the sway of her curls, the defiant angle of her chin, her long silk-stockinged legs.

"Why are *you* in this closet?" Her voice, part curiosity, part provocation, begged him to grin.

"Never mind that. A little quiet will buy us time until we can leave this cursed confinement and follow to dinner." She made a small sigh and he heard her smile, if that was even possible.

A lively conversation took hold on the other side of the door, but the predominant voice belonged to Matthew and revealed little. Lunden forced his attention to decipher the words. Bits and pieces filtered through. Talk of an intellectual society occurred with frequency, and Collins's deep baritone reiterated the theme. Then finally, when Lunden couldn't bear the confined torture of knowing deliciously tempting Amelia was hidden in the darkness an arm's length away, the word *marriage* stabbed through the closet with pristine clarity, and she rushed to the door, nestling beside him in an attempt to discern the conversation.

Had any muscle, *that muscle,* relaxed during the interim, it awakened now. Unfortunately, it had never disregarded Amelia's presence and grew harder still. Desire skittered to every corner of his being, invigorating a rush of blood through his veins, saturating him in carnal lust. What the hell was wrong with him?

The rustle of her skirts brushed his thighs as she shifted position and his brain begged he step away. His body refused. The knowledge they stood sequestered in privacy hung heavy in the air, while only the impatient tap of her slipper marked time through the silence. He located her shoe with the tip of his boot and effectively pressed down.

She swore with a startling knowledge of vocabulary, and her words, a heated breath against his face, caused a fleeting curve of his mouth. Damn her tart tongue. How he wished for another taste, her kiss sweeter than sugared orange peels.

"What do you think you're doing?" Righteous indignation laced her question.

"Your fidgeting will bring about our discovery. Stand still and pretend you're invisible." Ahh, if only he could do the same. He wanted her in the basest manner and every way in between. To take her, taste her, and claim her as his. He shook away the realization. By her own hellion protestations, she was scared of a life spent with a man she did not love, or worse, who did not love her in return. His future looked bleak, his chest as empty as an abandoned vault.

Or so he believed. For a decade he'd ignored his heart, buried it in hopes it would shrivel and starve, but now it lurched to life, eager and anxious, pounding an insistent beat in his chest.

"Have you lost your mind?" Her harsh whisper was accompanied by a swish of fabric. "Outside this door, my future may be decided, while I hide like a coward. It takes all my courage and self-possession not to open this door and demand Matthew explain himself," she finished in a threatening tone.

"You'll do no such thing." He kept his voice even, though his displeasure steeped. "The last thing you desire is to be married to a social outcast." He was a lesser level, actually. *A murderer and a fool.* He tempered his words. "And that's the first thing you'll accomplish if you open the damn door."

She stood silent for several minutes and then her breathing hitched as if he'd upset her. She moved closer and again he begged his feet to take a reluctant step as his instincts stirred with warning.

"I'm sorry, Lunden."

Her soft-spoken apology delved to the center of his soul, although it remained unclear for what she apologized. Was it his fall from society that brought her sorrow or disreputable status as a bridegroom? He could not know. His chest grew tight with uncertainty.

Her hand curled around his cheek and he wanted to turn into the warmth she offered, kiss her palm, and run his tongue along the seams of her fingers. He grimaced in frustration. If he possessed a modicum of respect for a gentleman's code of behavior, he'd stop this madness now. Guilt, disloyalty, he nudged the emotions aside. Nay, he shoved them. With both hands. Then he reached for her.

She fell into his embrace with a soft sigh of agreement. "Troublemaker."

He waited for her objection.

Instead, her full, delicious mouth pressed hot onto his and a wild, desperate need scratched at his skin from the inside out. She might be a hellion, but she kissed like an angel, and any feeble objection he meant to initiate evaporated. She tasted like her words, bittersweet and invigorating; as habit forming as opium.

He immediately became dependent.

The revelation shook him to the core. He was a man of intense emotion, when he allowed it. Romantic entanglement was out of the question.

Still, her tentative kiss, the sweet softness of her mouth upon his, would shatter his soul if he wasn't careful. She smoothed her palm against his cheek, a silken sweep, and some strange shadowy emotion, buried bone-deep and long hidden, sparked to life. He'd do best to extinguish the fledgling sentiment, yet instinct took over and he deepened the kiss, backing to the wall and taking her with him. She was wondrously warm and soft against his body, his remaining senses acutely aware of every nuance as they kissed in the dark: the flavor of her mouth, her light jasmine scent, the crush of her breasts against his coat, the sound of their breathing, heated and erratic.

His heart beat faster, harder, as his hands found the small of her waist, smoothing the fabric over her hips, the delicate silk as erotic as her petal-soft skin hidden under layers of cumbersome cloth. He splayed one hand at the small of her back, bringing her flush against him, and his breath caught when she made a pleasure noise in the back of her throat. He should stop. He really should. He needed to pull away.

She drew back the scarcest breadth. "Lunden."

Had she the strength he lacked? Her velvet whisper sent a wicked sensation spiraling through him. Possessiveness, raw and unforgiving, consumed him, and he wrapped his arms around her tighter. "Yes?"

Chapter Twelve

Nothing this exquisite could be a good decision, but logic failed her and Amelia pressed into Lunden's embrace, her heart hammering applause against his solid chest. From the morning she barged into the study and viewed him across the room, his whisky-warm eyes full of untold emotion, questions trembled on her lips. What did he hide, this man of unending challenge? Why did he live such a private existence? Keep such a tight rein on pleasure? He'd returned her kiss deliberately, as if she were a puzzle he needed to solve. Indeed, she yearned to unravel his secrets bit by bit, layer by layer, until she reached his heart.

Now, when he called her "Troublemaker" in his low tenor, intimacy took hold. A sensual shiver teased her senses while fire licked beneath her skin. Somehow the name on his tongue became an endearment, each syllable a caress. The opportunity to grow closer, to learn the mystery behind the man, was never more attainable or more enjoyable.

She imagined a flash of his charming smile and breathed deep, inordinately pleased they shared the same air. They may be closeted away, but he brought with him the scent of the weather. Crisp and fresh, warmed by the afternoon sun and very male. With belated awareness, she realized he waited for her to speak.

"I didn't mean to—"

A burst of congratulatory laughter interrupted her mid-sentence and she stilled, her attention drawn to the activity on the other side of the door. The noise faded as Matthew and Collins exited the study. If she held her breath, she could hear the mahogany grandfather clock striking seven in tune to the hour. They were expected for dinner though she'd rather stay wrapped in Lunden's strong arms. Impulsivity was a weakness, but something else drove her to lean into his mouth. As if controlled by an invisible force, some pull she could not name.

Awkwardness broke the mood and she withdrew from his loosened embrace. Channeling the energy that hummed in her veins, she twisted toward the door and placed her hand on the knob, surprised at how her palm slipped against the brass. With the door opened, she glanced over her shoulder and squinted, unaccustomed to the lantern light. Lunden stepped forward. When their gaze locked, she searched for some show of emotion, but his eyes were clear.

"I'll distract and stall while you change your gown."

How could he appear unaffected by their kiss? Hadn't he lost a piece of his soul, too?

"Thank you." She forced her mouth upward in makeshift appreciation.

His eyes softened to a smoky amber and he looked pensive, as if he meant to say more. When he didn't, Amelia fled the room.

Lunden entered the dining room no worse for the wear, his conflicted emotions smothered and full concentration on the task at hand. Matthew was up to something.

"Good evening." He greeted Lord Collins as Matthew acquainted the men.

"Scarsdale." Collins viewed him with a disapproving crease in his brow. "I had no idea you'd returned to London. Nasty business in your history. I thought this city would never hear from you again."

The stark honesty of Collins's statements rattled him. Focused on Amelia's plight more than his own concerns, he never expected a discussion of his past character from someone he'd never met before. "Life is full of unexpected circumstances." He managed an even tone.

"How very true." Matthew offered brandy as he interjected. "Consider your current situation, Collins. It's a fine example of unpredicted life change. Last month, I daresay you never suspected your brother and sister-in-law would pass and you'd become responsible for their brood of children."

Lunden took a long swallow of brandy and scrutinized Collins with new understanding. So this lay at the core of Matthew's matchmaking. What would be gained? With surety, the aged lord could not be Matthew's ideal match for Amelia. What coveted compensation did Collins offer?

"Agreed." Collins minced no words. "But you have offered me a gracious solution to my problem." He swerved his eyes to the door. "Where is your sister anyway? I believe punctuality to be a necessary quality in a wife. Obedience, congeniality, and docility as well. She will need a firm hand with the children and an anxious hand when they are put to bed."

Lunden coughed into his fist. "Her tardiness falls on my shoulders." He would shoot Matthew in the other leg before seeing Amelia married to this pompous fool. "Unforeseen circumstances detained her, although I believe she'll arrive shortly." He drained his glass and set it down with too much force.

"And here she is now." Matthew stepped forward and completed introductions.

They moved to dinner and as Matthew seated Collins beside Amelia, Lunden struggled to keep his temper in check. The two men had a collusive arrangement. They eyed each other often, as if the dinner conversation were part of a dubious game.

Want for calm, he studied Amelia across the table, breathtaking and beautiful in a gown of pale yellow silk. She played the part of compliant sister, although he held no doubt she perceived her brother's haphazard plan with ease. The vixen proved an expert at disguising displeasure when useful. He watched as she laughed at Collins's inane quip about the weather. Was that the best he could do? Discuss the rain and unseasonable temperature? Good Lord, his blood still simmered from Amelia's hot, erotic kiss, her mouth his problem. One glance and fierce desire wracked his body. And the tentative touch of her hand against his face. It was black as pitch inside that closet, yet he'd experienced her touch as if the stars burst in heaven. She'd reached inside him with the intimate gesture. That one, perfect kiss. He'd see hell freeze over before Amelia's lips lowered to Collins's corpulent jowls. He sliced into the roast beef and his knife clattered to the plate. All conversation ceased as three heads swiveled in his direction.

"Scarsdale, you're too quiet. How do you find London now that you've returned?"

"The same way I left it." He strove to remedy his surly tone, although his scowl stayed in place. "Full of disreputable gentlemen who seek to satisfy their own agenda, rather than serve the greater good."

Collins's eyes widened and he swung his attention to Matthew, who in turn skewered Lunden with a pointed stare meant to implore he not instigate disaster.

"I understand your bitterness considering the circumspect

incident of your brother's death, yet it seems unfair to categorize all polite society in the same shade of black." Collins's satisfied expression erased any sincerity in his commentary. "Gossip will out when no clear truth has been established. Either way you acquired the dukedom. You should enjoy the spoils of your title."

"My brother's death is a private matter." He wouldn't say more. Let Collins be damned for crossing all lines of etiquette with his insensitive remarks. From the corner of his eye he noted Amelia's look of distress. Matthew cleared his throat and motioned a footman forward to refill the wineglasses.

"No need to look toward the past when we have an eye on the future," Matthew gushed as he lifted his glass. "Now that dinner has completed, perhaps Amelia can show you through our garden, Collins. The pyramidal orchids have flourished this year."

The gentlemen stood and Lunden's severe glower trailed after Amelia's departing form, uncomfortable with Collins leading her through the garden unchaperoned. "Shouldn't Mary accompany them?"

"What has gotten into you?" Matthew charged with purpose, his limp a forgotten disadvantage. "I thought I had your allegiance in this matter."

"I never pledged to withstand ignorance. Collins is a bumptious snob who likely spends most of the day peering down his nose with indecision on how to serve his own purpose. I could never envision Amelia finding happiness with a man of his cut." Lunden blew a long breath and lowered his tone. "The field of bachelors cannot be that shallow. I'll make a more concerted effort." A twist of emotion accompanied the statement but he did his best to ignore the inner jab.

"Collins's title is unblemished and he has wealth to

spare. While he seems a forthright speaker, the trait has served him well as president of the Society for the Intellectually Advanced. I've not heard an unsavory word against him in the years I've belonged. He'll serve as ballast for Amelia's impetuous and often feckless behavior. My sister needs predictability and routine."

Lunden had wandered to the window, his eyes on the garden, but he whipped his head around upon hearing Matthew's last statement. "Do you not know your sister in the least? Amelia will wither and die if trapped in a mundane routine. Her rebellious behavior is an act of boredom—" *And fear.* He caught the words before they left his tongue. "Consider your choice with care."

"I do. Be assured of that." Matthew joined him near the window. "It's no easy feat to see my sister settled. At least Collins aligns with the list my mother comprised. I see no reason not to encourage the match."

"And what will you gain in return? I've known you long enough to understand the workings of this dinner arrangement." He raised a brow in dark skepticism.

Matthew reached to his cravat, the knot all at once too tight. "Your implication is disreputable. You suggest I have some personal motive. I'm insulted."

"You are not." Lunden encouraged a lighter tone. "Just don't do anything rash. If you're set on this courtship, allow Amelia time to adjust." *And me, more time to achieve her list of demands.*

"I thought you were in a hurry to rid this city."

"Make no mistake, I am. As soon as I resolve my business, I plan to leave. Forever. London holds memories I wish abandoned once and for all." He paused and a sense of loss enveloped his final words. "Nothing could keep me here."

For some reason, his mind returned to Amelia's kiss and he wondered for the hundredth time why she'd done it.

Why he'd allowed it. Ha, allowed it? Now that was a bit of voluntary self-deception. He'd savored every minute of it.

Marry Collins? Unthinkable. He'd see to each of her requests. That way, if Matthew did foist her off and pursue this insane courtship, she'd be able to shoot Collins and flee on horseback. A bubble of amusement percolated within his chest with the preposterous vision and he almost chuckled. If she committed the deed, he'd harbor the little refugee at Beckford Hall afterward.

Conversation wafted through the terrace doors and further discussion was abandoned. Amelia returned, no worse for the wear, although Collins's lascivious leer revealed he had more on his mind than pyramidal orchids.

The clock struck nine, reminding Lunden of his late-night appointment and eviscerating further deliberation. He politely withdrew. Best to get on with confronting the makeshift blackmailer so he'd be able to focus on smoothing every other wrinkle in his life.

Chapter Thirteen

As instructed, Lunden arrived at Rotten Row at the time indicated in the missive he'd accepted two days earlier. He opened the glass window and waited. Dangerous business, meeting during the night hours with little knowledge of the other participant, but he had no care for his safety. For years he'd wished himself dead instead of his brother. What difference would there be in the world if upon morning he turned up deceased? He'd leave behind no one to mourn, no one to fend for security. His bills were current, his staff nicely paid. He could be erased from this world with little consequence.

Time ticked at an infinitesimal pace and regret stole over him like an unwelcome shadow. Aware the heavy weight of despair would eventually crush his soul, he conjured images of Amelia, her green gaze brilliant with laughter, but the vision would not hold. Instead, from some murky corner of his mind, remembrances of the night his brother died resurrected with pristine clarity, the image of Douglas's moonlit corpse as vivid as a lethal nightmare.

A personal liaison was private and he'd had no right to intrude where Douglas chose to exclude him. His brother's reaction had been appropriate, albeit unnecessary. Had Douglas allowed him into his life, would he have accepted the circumstances? Hindsight shadowed the obvious answer with doubt. With certainty though, had a conversation ensued instead of a reckless chase on horseback in the middle of the night, his brother would still be alive. And Lunden had caused the chase. Unintentionally, but at fault nonetheless.

There was no solace in the thought. He didn't speak for weeks after his brother's death. Mute by choice. Safety in solitude. Now, he'd rejoined life as he'd once known it, and nothing had changed. The loose filaments that formed his caliginous memories remained interwoven in profound heartache.

He threaded his fingers through his hair in frustration. This foolish game of *what ifs* and *had onlys* claimed no winner. He accepted all blame years ago.

With a sigh of resignation, Lunden removed the suede pouch from his pocket and slid his brother's watch into the palm of his hand. The hour nearly matched the current time. The eerie observation served to snap his attention to the clatter of approaching horse hooves.

In less than two minutes, a carriage pulled adjacent to his, the windows aligned in neat unison. The glass opened and Lunden inclined his head, peering into the dark coach interior in an effort to discover the mysterious visitor's identity. He could see nothing, the stranger having extinguished the light.

"Thank you for keeping this appointment."

The voice was unfamiliar, a rich baritone. Lunden moved his lantern closer to the glass, in hope of a fortuitous glimpse inside the adjacent carriage.

"How could I not when it concerns Douglas? Your letter indicated it was of the utmost importance."

He could hear the shuffle of boots on the lancewood floor as if the occupant reordered his thoughts along with his position.

"Correct. I've learned you intend to sell the Lamb Street town house. I would like to make an offer of fair price for its purchase and conclude a private sale."

Stunned, Lunden inhaled a sharp breath. "Your letter was misleading. You implied you had information concerning the night of my brother's death. Was that a ploy to force me here and infuriate me? If so, you've accomplished your objective."

The stranger remained silent. When he spoke again, his voice held a softer edge as if he'd lowered his guard and realized the error of his ways. "I knew your brother well. I saw him the night of his death. Earlier that evening, actually."

When the stranger said no more, Lunden prodded, his temper barely contained. "That's all? You can't expect me to express gratitude for such useless information."

Again he heard shuffling from inside the stranger's carriage. Minutes ticked by. Lunden reached upward to rap on the carriage roof and indicate his desire to leave, when the inscrutable stranger spoke again.

"Douglas planned to meet someone that evening. When you interrupted their rendezvous, your brother panicked, setting off at breakneck speed. You followed. His horse stumbled and your brother was thrown. Behind, another gave chase, angered by the intrusion and worried on Douglas's behalf. You returned home with your brother's body under duress and gunfire. Someone was injured. Shot in the leg. You fell into mourning and the obligations of your newly acquired title with little happiness. You never returned to London nor learned who your brother entertained that evening, but you understood the circumstances. You've blamed yourself for his death ever since."

Blame well placed. A suffocating wave of regret consumed him and Lunden fought for breath.

"Rumors circulated concerning the volatile relationship between the two of you. There was the public argument witnessed only hours before Douglas's death. Society believed you snatched the duchy through fratricide. You fled London to keep your brother's memory unblemished and the gossip-mongers at bay."

Lunden forced calm. He paid a heavy price to have that secret kept and this stranger recalled the night's events as clearly as he knew them to be true. Had this man shared the information with anyone? The threat of injury to Douglas's reputation, his memory, and exposure of their history was more vulnerable than ever before and the knowledge he no longer solely harbored the truth, shook him to the core.

"I must go." A tone of impatience underscored the stranger's three words. "Consider my offer. Otherwise, no matter the degree of your discretion, word will spread. Everyone will be aware of your return within hours if I deem it so, and if that doesn't change your mind, I'll expose your private knowledge gratuitously."

"Wait." Lunden bit out the command through clenched teeth. "How do you know these things? When will we meet again?"

He watched as the glass closed and the carriage jolted forward, his connection with the past broken for the evening.

"I have so much news to share, I may burst." Amelia settled on the bench beside Charlotte, anxious to impart the details of last evening. "It seems forever since we've spoken and with my leaving for Lakeview I needed to see you this morning."

"I wondered at the hour. Even Dearing doesn't wake this early, and he is fastidious about keeping his daily schedule." Charlotte nodded in affirmation of the fact.

"I wish there was some way we changed his mind and you accompanied me today. It will be a terribly quiet trip with Mary in the coach."

"You can blame yourself for that." Charlotte offered a crooked smile, amused with her friend's antics. "But once you arrive, you'll have a splendid visit with your family. I will miss you most. I look forward to our daily jaunts, otherwise I rarely leave the town house. Dearing prefers I stay at home. . . ." Her voice trailed off in a despondent whisper.

"Another troubling stroke of the brush." Amelia clasped her hands together and huffed a frustrated breath. "He keeps you captive for no reason." With preoccupation to her own marriage plight, she'd neglected Charlotte's unhappiness, and now the weight of poor conscience crushed her enthusiasm flat. "I'll only be gone two days. When I return, we'll pursue this problem with vigor." She held her palm up when Charlotte opened her mouth to object. "Your future is as important as mine. While you worry on my behalf, and you should, for my brother is orchestrating a scheme I've yet to decipher, I'm determined to see us blissfully content."

"Why would Matthew instigate something devious? Are you sure you're not jumping to conclusions?"

The troubling note of despair in Charlotte's reply had Amelia wishing she'd never mentioned her suspicions.

"Perhaps, although the last few days have led me to believe differently. While I've known Father assigned him the task weeks ago, Matthew never seemed motivated to achieve my betrothal with persistence and I believed he would offer me more understanding in the matter. That being said, I would never have engaged Lunden's assistance if I knew Matthew secured a candidate and intended to proceed with intense determination." She paused, concern causing her words to soften in regard of the present state of affairs. "I walked with Lord Collins in the garden after dinner and he behaved as if a decision has been made, acknowledging my brother sought him out with an agreement. I'm puzzled to what my brother hopes to gain and disappointed at his callous decision making. I expected some degree of thoughtfulness from Matthew."

"Is Lord Collins so terrible? Do you see no way to be pleased with the union?"

"Charlotte, the man is almost as old as my father." She shot her friend a wide-eyed look of exaggeration. "And while he appears congenial, I suspect there's more to the story. Why would he wish to marry so quickly? He knows nothing of my personality other than what he's gleaned from idle gossip. It's hardly a firm foundation for a lifelong commitment. When I suggested we take time to get to know each other with a considerable courtship, he dismissed the idea and uttered he 'needed to get on with things.'"

Charlotte's aghast expression spoke volumes.

"Well, I'll have none of it." Amelia rose from the bench. "With Lunden's assistance I have already secured preemptive survival skills. No man will ever find me at a disadvantage. I intend to marry for love, not convenience." She paused and eyed Charlotte with a softer expression, although her words fortified her resolve. "As for your marriage, we've yet to discover the source of Lord Dearing's discontent. But we will. We may be women in a society which grants all the power to men, but we are intelligent women determined to find happiness."

By the end of her speech, empowerment echoed across

the courtyard and the ladies looped arms set to return home. Amelia had planned to regale Charlotte with every detail of her closeted adventure with Lunden, the scent of his skin, the heat of his body pressed against hers, and the magic of their kiss, but having reconsidered, remained pleased with the dual-purposed focus of their discussion.

Besides, kisses were best kept private. The tingling sensation coursing throughout her veins whenever she relived the moment assured she made the correct decision.

Returning home, she found her traveling bags packed, Mary in the hall, and the carriage set to depart. Upstairs, Matthew was in the study examining his puzzle, his face a mask of concentration. Scooping Pandora into her arms she strode to the window, but not before she spared a glance toward the closet, an amused smile curling her lips.

"You seem a little anxious to be rid of me. Mary already waits in the hall."

"Take no offense, dear sister. I merely want you on your way before the hour grows late. I've assigned additional tigers to the coach, but I reserve misgivings seeing you off without a more suitable chaperone. Had I the opportunity, I'd accompany you, but the society is holding an important meeting and I can't be absent. With your insistence to visit Father today, you leave me few options."

"I'll be fine." She reached forward and shifted a puzzle piece with her forefinger, clutching Pandora in a secure hold as the cat wriggled with impatience. "Your misgivings would have been more appropriately placed when you sent me into the garden with Lord Collins."

"Was he not to your liking then?" Matthew stalled in his activity and offered her a sidelong glance.

"You aren't serious?" Amelia captured her laughter before it broke free.

He returned his attention to the work before him and

dismissed the question with a derisive snort. "He's a well-respected peer with accomplished academic success and financial security. I fail to see your objection."

"He's as old as Father." She shuddered as her mind conjured an image of the man. Pandora meowed in objection.

"That's a gross exaggeration." Matthew's matter-of-fact tone revealed he was more interested in the pieces he placed near the Aegean Sea than her discontent.

"Not through my eyes." Amelia cuddled her cat closer to her heart, lost in the comfort of soft fur.

"Perhaps we both need a new perspective." He shifted to the corner of the table and examined his puzzle. "No matter how I attempt to assemble this portion, it will not match. It's as if the pieces are missing. I can't make heads or tails of it." His face pinched with displeasure and his brow pleated when he looked to her.

Her world was far more important than his. "And what of the situation Collins will soon acquire? Do you know of his familial circumstances?"

"Life is compromise." Matthew stepped away from the table and advanced with a stern tone. "Do you think when I was a lad running through the fields at Lakeview I imagined my future as an invalid with the limitations imposed by my limp? My friends are married and settled, supporting a family of sons and daughters who bring pleasure and pride. I learned quickly that women enjoy picnics and dancing, and when they seek a husband they wish for a complete man, not one who barely manages the stairs on a rainy day. So I aspire to make my mark as a scholar and find happiness in other pursuits. As a male, I have the luxury of time to choose my future and produce an heir, but you do not. Nevertheless, I have compromised. I suggest you do the same."

A rush of emotion humbled her usual rebuttal. Matthew's

wistful confession tugged at her heart. She touched his sleeve, but he shrugged off the gesture and returned his attention to the puzzle. The thought of marrying Collins was no less repulsive, but perhaps she needed to consider her choices with enlightened importance.

Still, her intent with Father to convince him to allow her to choose her own spouse, remained steadfast. And the sooner she arrived at Lakeview, the better. Firm in purpose, she straightened her shoulders and drew a deep breath.

"Shall I tell Mother you'll visit soon? She worries for you." She met his eyes squarely, determined not to belabor the subject. Matthew detested the attention.

"Yes. I'll plan a trip." Distracted by the pieces on the table, his answer was half platitude. "Once everything is resolved at the society, I'll have more time. Assure Mother I will visit within a fortnight."

"I'll be leaving then." She turned, hesitation in her step. "Have you seen Lunden? Do you know where he is this morning?"

The question garnered Matthew's attention and he pierced her with a glare. "What is this strange fascination with Scarsdale? His whereabouts are no concern of yours. I've warned you, Troublemaker, to stifle your curiosity. His arrival in London is not to be shared."

Disregarding his brusque tone, she tutted her disapproval and carried Pandora from the room, annoyed with her brother's misplaced admonishment.

Safely nestled in the carriage with her sleeping maid, Amelia stroked Pandora's coat and considered which tactic would convince her father she deserved to choose her own husband, despite stalling through several Seasons. Eventually, her thoughts alternated to Charlotte's situation and her hopeless feelings in assistance to her friend. What was wrong with Lord Dearing? Did he not realize he'd married one of the kindest, gentlest women in all England? Or was there something in Dearing's countenance that he feared revealing to Charlotte? Through her friend's insecurities and society's natural inclination, they'd come to place the blame at Charlotte's feet, but without a doubt the same could be suspected of Dearing. She'd need to ask more questions to truly solidify if her suspicions were correct. With new determination, Amelia vowed to secure Charlotte a better future, even if she had little control over her own.

The carriage rolled to an abrupt stop and Pandora leapt from her lap and settled in a corner below the far banquette. Concerned, Amelia swept the curtain to the side and peered through the window, curious why the coachman would rein in the team when they'd only traveled a short distance.

"Milady?" An outrider came to the square window. Sincere distress marred his young face.

Amelia opened the glass and waited for his explanation.

"Barley has gone lame." He indicated the tawny mare aside the chestnut with a curt wave of his hand. "She can't continue. Should I ride home and return with a fresh team? We haven't traveled very far."

The sun remained high. It couldn't be past noon, yet they'd never reach Lakeview before nightfall if she didn't have a strong team. Best spend a short time waiting beside the road than risk traveling into the night hours. It wouldn't take long for one of the outriders to return with new horses.

"Yes, please do so. Have the driver lead us to the side, there near that meadow, and we'll await your return." Amelia's eyes passed over Mary fast asleep in the corner, blissfully unaware how their plans had altered. "Thank you."

The servant nodded his head and disappeared toward the front. Amelia closed the window, although she heard their conversation resound through the carriage roof. After the coach pulled to the side, the jangle of the harness signaled the team was unhooked before the thunder of hooves marked the outrider's departure astride the chestnut.

"I do hope he hurries." Muttering her concern, Amelia pulled her knees under her skirt and settled in to wait.

Chapter Fourteen

Lunden bridled Hades and reached for the saddle. The horse snorted and pulled at the bonds holding him hostage, anxious to be free of the stable. At Beckford Hall, the horse roamed the acreage, strong and obedient, as fast as a secret unleashed. Riding served as one of the few pleasures Lunden allowed himself, the wind in his ears instead of the cynical voice of regret. Now, Hades whinnied and shook his mane; a flick of his tail signaled his impatience. Lunden spoke to him in a low soothing tone as he tightened the buckles and secured the leather straps.

"Coming in!"

An outrider entered atop one of the estate's chestnuts, his cap askew from his wild entry. Hades pawed at the ground in restless agitation.

"Excuse me, milord." The boy slid from the saddle and spared no time to tether the reins, instead charging with the straps secured in his fist, his words spilling forth with the same expedience as his entry. "Lady Amelia's coach. We've lost a horse and she awaits my return with a fresh team."

"You left her alone on the side of the road?" Lunden mounted Hades before he finished the sentence. "Tell me her whereabouts and have Spencer send a message to Whittingham informing him of the circumstances. I'll need two stallions to follow. Make haste, young man. Your head depends on it."

The lad nodded, dispersing the necessary information before darting toward the house.

Lunden kicked Hades into a gallop and tore down the gravel driveway onto the main road. Without a care for safety, he maneuvered the afternoon traffic, thick and congested, as carriages vied for parking along the shop-lined avenues. Within minutes he'd accomplished the worst, steering toward the outskirts of town where he prodded the horse to top speed. He'd traveled no less than forty-five minutes when he spotted the Whittingham coach near the edge of the thoroughfare. The sharp sting of air braced his face as he urged Hades on, but he found the conveyance empty, the lame mare at a distance, tethered to a nearby elm. Someone, an acquaintance or passerby, must have offered Amelia help. He clenched his teeth in frustration. How far had they gone?

With a curse into the wind, Lunden yanked at the reins, pulling Hades to attention with a simultaneous kick of his heels, but the horse resisted, a rebellious whinny slicing the air. Dead center of the narrow roadway, a black snake reared and hissed, his head raised in a threatening pose, his long, lithe body poised to strike.

Black snake. Bad omen. And bloody lethal.

Hades snorted, unsettled and anxious to break leather. With a soft click of reassurance, Lunden eased them backward, one hand tight on the straps as the other stroked the horse's neck, soothing the animal into obedience and guiding him from immediate peril. He flicked his eyes to the coachman's perch atop the abandoned carriage. With a precarious reach, he snatched the whip from the bench, angled Hades forward, and with an abrupt snap of his wrist, lashed the snake in two.

Sparing not another glance, he forged down the roadway, the thunder of hooves an echo of his dark considerations. Had Amelia met with trouble? Highwaymen liked nothing better than to snatch the spoils of the rich. It would take little to subdue her and her makeshift maid, although the carriage showed no signs of struggle. He dismissed the notion as another took hold. Had she decided to take fresh air while waiting, Amelia would have encountered the deadly snake. Some odd emotion worked its way up from deep within his chest and he kicked Hades harder.

At last, he spied a coach in the distance. It wasn't until he'd neared the conveyance that he deciphered the emblazoned seal on the door. *Nilworth.* A black snake of another kind and a smirch on polite society. Temper heated his blood. Nilworth may be the heir to an earldom, but that did little to excuse his insolent personality. The man was a cur. Amelia had best not be inside that carriage.

He raced past, skirting the rushing wheels with speed and precision, to place Hades in the middle of the road. His interference caused the coachman to stop in much the same manner a highwayman would waylay his victim. Nilworth's head emerged from the window, impertinence riddling his face. Lunden took satisfaction from the man's obvious anger.

"What's the meaning of this?" Nilworth shifted his position, twisting his neck from the coachman's perch to the obstruction in his path. Realization lit his eyes and his grimace transformed into a brief show of surprise before it reclaimed an expression of haughty disdain.

Lunden remained motionless. Did he hear a female voice above Nilworth's sharp objection? He managed the man's name through clenched teeth. "Nilworth."

"Scarsdale." The earl spat his return.

Lunden definitely heard Amelia's voice now. What trouble had the hellion found this time?

"Go around him. We have no business here," Nilworth ordered his coachman and withdrew into the interior.

"No. Wait."

A discussion, perhaps a scuffle followed, then the carriage door opened and Amelia pushed her way out before the steps could be extended.

"Your Grace." Her lips curled in an impish grin, as if she were happy to see him, although she offered the same benevolence to Nilworth as he exited behind her. "What are you doing here?" She hurried to stand beside his horse, her brilliant green gaze shining upward.

He lowered his voice excluding others from their exchange. "I could ask the same of you, although I surmise Nilworth offered assistance and you accepted, desperate to be off the roadway and traveling toward Lakeview."

She nodded with vigor and glanced in the earl's direction. Her smile of appreciation soured his stomach and in a work of distraction, he averted his eyes to the coach where Mary's petite head poked from the window.

"Are you all right?" He prodded Hades to sidestep, his assessment noting every aspect of her appearance. How dare she accept refuge from Nilworth. The man fueled the most vicious gossip surrounding Douglas's death, expounding upon untruths and perpetuating the *ton*'s speculation long after time buried the accident. Nilworth had been present when he'd argued with his brother earlier that evening. He'd latched on to the smallest snippets of conversation, created mistruths to bind the missing pieces together, and manufactured a tail of vindictive fratricide the gossips accepted with relish. As time passed, whenever another shame arose, powerful enough to erase the Scarsdale tragedy from the *ton*'s memory, Nilworth worked with assiduous fervor to revive the well-preserved scandal.

He speared the man with a glare of vicious malevolence. "Lunden?"

Amelia's inquiry broke free the bitter memory and he dropped his gaze, pleased to hear she'd returned to the intimacy of his Christian name. A light breeze ruffled the dark curls near her cheek and disarmed by her beauty, his expression softened. "Has this man done anything untoward? Should I disembowel him on your behalf?"

"Of course not." She raised her eyes to his and her pouty grin fueled, more than assuaged, his temper. "He's behaved kindly."

A bitter retort stalled on his tongue.

"You're the last person I expected to encounter this afternoon." Nilworth invaded their private conversation, disgruntled at having been excluded so effectively.

Lunden looked down at him and leveled a stare meant to announce he resented the intrusion. "I'm no more pleased by the occurrence, although Lady Amelia's safety remains my main concern." An awkward silence took hold. "On horseback, I'm unable to escort the lady and her maid, so we find ourselves dependent upon your courtesy." His voice lowered to a deadly tone. "I'll travel behind your carriage until the journey to Lakeview is complete."

He spared a glance to Amelia who glowed with admiration. Could she possibly be enamored with the lout? Jealousy, hot and immediate, spiked through him and he pushed hard against the emotion. Some might consider the man acceptable, having a title and a modicum of style, but it would be over several dead bodies before Lunden saw Amelia matched with the likes of the scourge.

Logic forced him to reason. She could not know the misery Nilworth caused or the heartache he perpetuated with his vicious lies and exaggerations. Nor did she understand what was at stake. It would be unfair of him to jump to conclusions, yet with Matthew's insistence she marry Collins, one could not know the extent of Amelia's rebellion.

"What do you fear, Scarsdale? The lady appears pleased

with my company. You should ride off the way you've come. Return to the dark recesses of your past." Acrimony blazed in Nilworth's eyes and he motioned in the direction of the roadway with blithe dismissal.

Hades whinnied and Lunden realized he'd pressed his heels, his muscles tight at the bold provocation. He watched Amelia's smile falter at Nilworth's reply before a pensive, questioning expression took hold.

She had no idea of his past, too young to be included in the details connected to Douglas's death and removed from the city's bitter rumor mill. Still, she resisted marriage, courtship, at every turn. Nilworth was worse than Collins in every respect. How could she consider him worthy when she'd met the man less than an hour ago? Or for some unexplainable reason, did he jump to conclusions too rapidly?

"It seems the sensible thing to do," Amelia asserted, not willing to be absent from the decision making, and perhaps perceiving the animosity.

"I agree." Nilworth offered Amelia his arm in a bald show of triumph. The two began their return walk to the carriage although Nilworth's voice rang clear. "I hesitate to make mention of this, but your brother has kept poor company. Scarsdale possesses a high degree of anger. Some consider him volatile."

"I've never found him so. Whatsoever do you mean?" Amelia's eyes, heavy with curiosity, moved from one man to the other.

Lunden clamped down his temper, unable to react or he'd prove Nilworth's claim as truth. The last thing he desired was for his past to be discussed within the carriage while he rode outside, unable to define the truth.

"Perhaps I'll expound once we're under way." Nilworth handed Amelia into the coach, his eyes fixed behind him. "Lunden has an interesting history."

Chapter Fifteen

Lunden led Hades in a canter behind the carriage. His memory, razor-sharp, needed no encouragement to resurrect the past hurt of his brother's death with pristine clarity.

It was his fifteenth birthday and, daring manhood, he'd schemed a jaunt to a disreputable tavern near the edge of St. James. Matthew joined him in celebration at The Backward Ram, equally enthralled with their plan of rebellious behavior. They'd only finished one tankard of ale when Douglas arrived, angered to have traveled to an undesirable part of the city in search of a brother who rarely made the right decisions and often landed on the left side of trouble. *At least in his eyes*. Their discussion turned to disagreement in less than a few words, and the other patrons, both peers and pedestrians, took notice of the duke and his younger brother as a heated altercation ensued.

As with many arguments, things are oft said in anger, without thought and consideration. How Lunden wished he could retract the ale-induced words he spewed with vehemence as Douglas left the tavern.

Life would be much better with you dead.

But there was no turning back the clock, no way to repair the damage.

He'd then ordered another round of alcohol and celebrated his ill-begotten victory, even though his conscience gnawed at his heart, aware he'd cleaved a bigger chasm in their tenable relationship.

Hours later, when Matthew with his usual instigation of unconcerned mischief, dared him to discover the guarded secret where Douglas oft spent his evenings, Lunden clamped on to the idea with the foolish belief it provided a means to make amends. He would apologize to his brother and set things to rights, retract his foolish words in the tavern, erase the argument, and start anew. Perhaps he could better understand his brother and learn a scrap to explain Douglas's distant nature.

In retrospect, Lunden saw the errors in his conclusion, how emotion had eclipsed rational judgment, but ten years ago he'd spent no time in deliberation of the plan and forged headstrong into the night.

Amelia settled in the corner of the carriage as Lord Nilworth forced small conversation. Questions concerning Lunden's past tumbled one over another in her mind. Whatever existed between the two men remained connected to that evening long ago. The origin of Lunden's unhappiness, not just Douglas's death, but the consequences of that evening, her brother's injury, and Lunden's suffocating regret, were intertwined in details a decade spent. A secret so private and imperative, her brother took a bullet and still claimed Lunden as his friend. Something inside her tightened. She yearned to ease Lunden's turmoil. Perhaps she could ease his pain, prompt him to smile, if she understood his past.

She skimmed her eyes over the man seated across the carriage, so engrossed in his idle conversation, he didn't notice her inspection. Nilworth might be labeled attractive by some, although gray tinged his narrow sideburns. His nose, as sharp as his tongue, did not ruin his features as much as his pervasive personality and protuberant eyes. He spewed a wealth of tawdry information proving he possessed a distasteful proclivity for hearsay. To encourage Nilworth was unthinkable. She'd assumed him a respectable gentleman, his arrival fortuitous and his offer of transportation generous, but perhaps she'd been too quick to judge. Lunden would loathe conversation concerning his past while he rode in protection of her honor, paces behind the carriage. And she could not betray him, no matter the incessant desire to learn the driving force behind his solitude and despair.

It was more than idle inquisitiveness. Something pulled her toward Lunden. Something intangible, and powerful. A force stronger than any emotion she'd experienced. His kiss haunted her every daydream. His touch lived as if a constant energy within her heart.

A visceral ache swelled in her bosom at the realization their paths did not converge. He meant to solve his problems and depart with haste while she entered into an unwelcomed union. Neither Lunden nor she wanted the future that waited, yet fate had stolen their choices, pushed aside any desire aimed at happiness, and instead laid plans for years of loneliness and sadness. She could not allow it.

Their kiss had been magical. When their lips touched, the world dissolved, leaving only the incredible sensation of desire, and something deeper, a connection so powerful, she trembled still from the remembrance.

Determination replaced the burden of hopelessness blanketing her heart and she straightened in her seat. The coach rattled over a rut and the unexpected vibration snapped her attention to the present, unaware she'd lost track of the conversation minutes before.

"Your brother holds a weakness for Scarsdale, unable to

sever relations no matter the cost. It's my hope you don't suffer from the same poor judgment. Their odd association causes me to wonder what's kept them connected all these years. Scarsdale abandoned this city and any friendships to be salvaged after the inauspicious circumstances surrounding his brother's death. Do you know what prompted him to break a decade of solitude?"

Amelia shifted uncomfortably under Nilworth's scrutiny. While he smiled in a façade of congenial conversation, his probing gaze sent a shiver to her core.

"I'm sure I don't know. His Grace is a private man." She hid her disapproval with a glance out the window.

"As well I believe. Even now, over ten years past, no one has uncovered the truth of what occurred that evening, although I suppose your brother has a better understanding than most. I witnessed the argument at The Backward Ram. One must surmise Lunden made true on the threat he issued that evening."

"I'm afraid I don't understand." Amelia swallowed a note of trepidation, aware she walked a fine line between curiosity and betrayal. "Are you saying you know these facts with surety?" Her heart rebelled. Lunden was no murderer and anyone in society who believed such a far-fetched tale born of misconstrued, distorted rubbish didn't deserve the truth.

Nilworth's prompt hesitation to her question caused a vague uneasiness. Perhaps a change in subject was best, but he formulated his response before she could suggest a more suitable topic.

"I sat not three tables away from where they argued. I heard the threat. We all did. And then the duke was announced dead the next morning. One need not be an intellectual to put the pieces together."

A note of agitation accompanied his reply and Amelia eyed Nilworth with interest, perturbed by his avid obsession in an event more than a decade past. Something akin to embarrassment, or perhaps vulnerability, flashed through his eyes whenever he mentioned the late duke's name.

"My brother would never align with Scarsdale were he capable of what you propose." She stumbled over the words, unsure of perpetuating the conversation. If she focused, she could hear the steady drum of Hades cantering behind the carriage and it unhinged her emotions as much as betrayal pricked her conscience.

"Unless he too had something to hide."

The words hung in the air unanswered.

Nilworth's comments were distasteful. She strove to change the subject with aplomb. "We should arrive at Lakeview soon. The fine weather has kept the roads passable."

Nilworth nodded in return. "It's smart of you to steer our conversation from the unsavory, Lady Amelia. You have proven to be a most pleasant traveling companion. May I call upon you when I return to London? I'm of an age when I need to consider family. I have heirs to produce and a future earldom to cultivate. I understand you're in the market for a husband."

Mary straightened in her seat, the stark statements breaching all language barriers. Amelia wondered how far Nilworth would encroach if given the latitude.

"One mustn't believe every word uttered in the *ton,* although my brother feels a strong insistence to see me settled." Her words, spoken with crisp finality, implied she wouldn't elaborate. Let Nilworth and his jaded gossip drop to the devil.

"One mustn't waste precious time. Most especially when one has finite opportunity to find a husband." He leaned forward as if imparting innocuous advice.

Everything in her shuddered. The man proved vile. Lunden was correct. How could she have perceived him as intelligent and kind? Would the conversation have advanced to the same point regardless of Lunden's appearance? She'd never know although something inside told her Nilworth cared little for others' feelings and would have pursued the same line of questioning no matter the circumstances.

The coach veered to the right and bowled down the twisting drive. She dared a fleeting look out the window, relief taking hold as she recognized the stone gateposts and tree-lined avenue marking the approach to Lakeview.

Settled in the parlor with a fresh cup of tea, Amelia relished the comfort of her childhood home and took her father's hand in an affectionate stroke. She loved her father dearly and her heart warmed to be together again. He seemed thrilled in equal measure for her visit, his health somewhat improved. He'd hardly coughed since she'd arrived, and while his complexion remained pale, the twinkle had returned to his eyes. In London, his pallor verged on ashen, but now he appeared healthier than she remembered and the observation nudged a bubble of hope high in her chest. Perhaps he'd relinquish a bit of control concerning the rush to the altar. "You're feeling better, Father." Green eyes met blue and he returned her attention, his joy at having her visit evident.

"Yes. Today I feel quite well. Horrid business, having you travel with Nilworth. I must speak to your brother concerning his inferior choice in horseflesh. It's a good thing Scarsdale proved valiant and oversaw your passage." He coughed into his handkerchief, but the conversation did not waver. "I never thought I'd see the man again. Sequestered at his country estate. This visit will do him good, as much as your pleasant company."

Her father gave her hand a loving squeeze, his strength another sign of encouragement for her impending plea.

"Now tell me, Amelia. Has your brother found you a husband? Are you here to share optimistic news?"

The abrupt change of subject took her by surprise. Thank heavens Lunden had excused himself after greeting her parents. Before he took his leave she'd searched his face for some clue, but an expression of incomprehensibility masked his true emotions. She'd executed her best attempt at eavesdropping during his conversation with the housekeeper, but failed to ascertain which guest room he'd been assigned. She'd need to discover that later and speak to him concerning Nilworth's intrusive attitude. What if the man contacted Matthew for permission to court her? Wasn't Collins enough of a burden to bear?

The throaty rattle of her father's cough jarred her from these concerns. "No news of yet." She tried for a tone of sincerity, though vivid images of throttling Matthew's neck flickered through her mind. How could her brother suggest Collins as an ideal suitor? "Perhaps Matthew would appreciate my help. Would it not make sense for me to have a hand in the process?"

"But you've had several Seasons to do so." Her mother's admonishing voice rang across the parlor as she approached. "And you've done nothing but drag your feet. With your father's health condition, we need to see you married and settled. A simple request for a daughter who believes she can always do as she pleases."

"Simple request?" Amelia released her father's hand and rose to face her mother. "We're discussing the rest of my life, not my choice of new slippers. My entire future is wrapped up in one decision. I've tried to find someone who catches my interest. I've attended balls, danced waltzes, and conversed with handsome gentlemen, but while pleasant, no one has made me feel special. Their attention didn't cause my heart to pound or fill my head with dizzy daydreams. And I don't wish to settle for someone who doesn't touch my heart." She paused, an answer she couldn't voice alive within her. "If Matthew chooses incorrectly, what will my future be? Naught but unhappiness. Would you have that, Father?" In a swirl of skirts Amelia resettled and clasped her father's hands in a tight embrace. "Grant me the opportunity to find my own husband. I promise to have it done this Season. I know I've wasted time and I regret not pursuing the matter with earnest." She inhaled deeply to disperse lingering doubt and evoke fortitude. Charlotte's unhappy marriage, fear and ambivalence, all combined to work against her plea. "I worry about Matthew's judgment. What does he know about gentleman suitors? He hasn't escorted a lady anywhere since his leg healed. Hasn't set foot in a ballroom since—"

"Amelia. That's quite enough. After what your brother endured, we see no reason to press. He'll produce an heir in due time."

The prickly tone of her mother's reprimand stalled her tongue.

"Your brother isn't the issue here and it will do little good to charm your father. If your happiness wasn't important to us, we would never have granted you Season after Season to find a suitor. We mean to see you married, the sooner the better. Matthew wants the best for you."

"I doubt that." She leaned in, her nose nearly touching her father's as she whispered, "You should see the man he favors. Lord Collins could hardly manage our wedding waltz. He is dreadful, Father."

"You exaggerate, dear." He chuckled low, his expression amused. "You've always possessed a penchant for the extreme. Your brother wouldn't turn a wrong and I need to see you settled in case my health declines."

He squeezed her hand again; whether in gravity of his last statement or to soften the blow of his impending words, she did not know.

"You need to take a husband. I must know you'll be

provided for beyond my security. Surely you desire a family of your own."

"Yes, of course I do." She released her tight hold on his hands and reclined against the velvet settee. "I also desire a say in the matter." She shot a glance to her mother where she stood near the window arranging flowers in a vase. "Had I known you'd both react with haste I'd have approached the past Seasons with more deliberate purpose. I never anticipated the current state of things, and it's not as though gentlemen are vying for my attention." She finished on a deprecating note. She wasn't sure her father noticed.

"That's ridiculous. Only a man with impervious constitution could resist your charms." He used a soothing tone, and wrapped his fingers around her arm in an insistent clasp to pull her closer. "Let's see where life takes us before we make any more decisions. Love can be capricious."

Her father eyed her mother over her head and the two shared a smile meant to communicate more than simple affection. Still, the daunting shadow of impending doom hung heavy in the air and Amelia couldn't shake the feeling the illusion of control was meant to placate her more than solve her problem.

Chapter Sixteen

Abovestairs, Lunden paced a hard line at the foot of the bed. The guest room was huge, but he made no more than five strides before he pivoted, intent on reducing his temper and releasing the tension that knotted his stomach as tightly as his cravat. Nilworth. Anger smothered him in a deluge of stark desolation. He wrapped his fingers in the knot of his neckcloth and pulled it free. Before his return, he'd held little faith in keeping his appearance secret for very long. Optimism did not come to him easily, but meeting Nilworth on the road to Lakeview was an unfortunate encounter he'd never anticipated.

Society would know of his return before sunset. Worse, every snippet of gossip would be exhumed; theories composed of assumption and speculation would be resurrected. He thrust the linen cravat onto the counterpane, wishing to discard the burden of his past in the same fashion.

Painful memories bombarded his mind with an intensity no less devastating than the last time he dared allow them to the surface. Douglas was never much of an out-and-outer, his friendships and societal ties discreet. Upon his death, suspicion led to unfounded accusation with nothing but stony silence from Lunden. Dealing with the tragic result of his foolish endeavor at such a young age left him ill equipped to face the barrage of questions foisted in his direction. He could never reveal the truth, yet locked firmly in boyhood he lacked the skills, charm, and credibility to supply sufficient lies to reason away his brother's untimely death and feed the *ton*'s insatiable appetite for the latest *on dit*.

Soon after, the duchy was labeled tarnished, the family name marred. Club memberships that had existed for decades were rescinded, invitations ceased, reserved luxuries terminated. Even his father's most revered comrades evaporated, severing all ties once it became clear Lunden refused to speak on the matter of his brother's death. In one snap decision, foolish as it may have been, he'd destroyed the world he'd lived in.

He would never subject Amelia to the same harsh treatment. She deserved more. She deserved abundance.

So much for his judicious investigation into Douglas's final act of business.

He shed his waistcoat and paused to remove Amelia's list from his breast pocket, skimming his eyes over her feminine script. One commitment remained. One more tether to a city that showed him no mercy.

A light knock sounded on his bedchamber door and he moved without thinking, swinging the panel wide. Amelia stood in the hallway as if conjured by his thoughts, her hair as unruly as her temperament, her beauty as insistent. She'd changed gowns from her traveling habit, this new gown soft pink perfection. Her skin shone with a warm flush to create a paradox of innocence and temptress. His breath caught.

"Lunden. I need to speak with you." Her eyes searched his face as if beseeching his agreement. "Please."

Her final word caused his immediate objection to evaporate. He stepped aside and allowed her entry, his ardor engraving an invitation while his better sense rebelled. He withdrew to the other side of the room if for no other reason than to steady his conflicted emotions.

The lamp waned low, its flickering light in competition with the fading flames in the hearth. A foreboding shroud of shadows, black as his past, danced on the wall overhead and he raised his hand as if to chase them away. Then he moved with purpose to the fireplace and added more wood, the heat on his skin a welcome reminder of how easily one might get burned.

"I need you."

Her silken whisper reached for him, and a thread of irrepressible wickedness prompted him to act on the temptation.

Damn it all, he wanted her.

Silence lay heavy in the room. She licked her lips. He refused to notice.

"Will you help me?"

He cut her a dry look and forced his attention to the conversation. "I already have."

Their kiss from the closet drenched his memory in lush remembrance. It was wrong—he knew that well—but it was also the one source of peace he'd experienced since leaving his country estate. What was it about Amelia? One look into her crystalline eyes and all heartache evaporated, his misery calmed.

She stood within arm's reach, and the desire to pull her into his embrace caused his hands to tremble. He clenched his fists to deny the yearning. She was not his. Not for him. She deserved a life of happiness no matter her brother's intent or her parents' wish. He could offer her nothing but despair and disappointment. He shook his head as if to banish the troublesome reality.

"Yes, you have, and I thank you for your help." She wrung her hands while she spoke.

Where was the headstrong hellion? He enjoyed that side of her more than he'd ever admit.

"I came here to convince my father his intent is ill-planned. I can find my own spouse . . . with haste if necessary."

Her words faded near the end and sympathy welled for the woman before him. *Forced into an uncompromising situation because of society's dictates.* They were not so different, both trapped, their freedom stolen for circumstances beyond their control.

"And what is your intent? To latch on to some codswallop, manipulated with ease to do your bidding or you'll exercise your plan of escape." He motioned toward her list, left on the counterpane aside his abandoned neckcloth.

"Something like that."

Lord, she sounded pleased with herself. But that path didn't lead to the happiness she deserved.

"You're a coward." He flung the words across the room, annoyed she would sacrifice her spirit and condemn herself to a half life, unwilling to face the challenge of offering love to another. A whisper of conscience labeled him a hypocrite.

"That's untrue."

Her hands clasped tightly against her skirts, she gave away her lie with every move. Lunden watched the facade of confidence, her objection chased by trepidation, not a hoyden but a delicate, frightened woman.

She followed the path of his stare and dropped her hands, unsure in her movements until she crossed her arms under her breasts and took a deep breath, the action calling attention to her delicious bodice where the silky soft fabric pulled taut with the motion.

His heart raced and his eyes returned to the bed. To lay her down, taste her skin . . . to find peace in the beauty of her soul.

"My list." She strode forward and snatched it from the coverlet. "We must complete the third request. Tomorrow morning. We can meet at dawn. I doubt anyone here keeps country hours."

"Yes, one should never forget your demands." He let out a breath with frustrated delight. In her convoluted female perception, these skills represented freedom.

"We have an agreement. I trust your honor." The words were said with fragile sincerity although their meaning skewered his heart.

He took the stride needed to bring them together and emotion flickered bright in her eyes. What did she see on his face? Could she tell he ached to hold her, to lose himself in her comfort?

"That could prove unwise." He meant to tease, but the words sounded heartfelt despite the effort. He caught the scent of jasmine and inhaled deeply.

"I'll take my chances." Her smile flashed wide.

A palpable silence stretched as sensual tension thickened the air. Did she recall their kiss in the dark confines of the closet? Had it affected her with the same intensity?

"I should return to my rooms."

The words were breathless, forced past her lips, as faded as her smile.

Her rooms. He wanted to put her to bed and tuck her in with kisses . . . after they'd laid bare their passion on the sheets. A thread of integrity clawed its way to the surface. He should urge her to leave. He needed her out. The memory of her standing near his bed, a vivacious temptress, her hair a wanton tangle of mystery and seduction, would prove torture enough. He could not endure her spirit haunting his rooms once night fell.

It took every ounce of effort for him to obey better sense. "Yes." He stepped back, creating a hopeless void between them. "You need to leave."

She hesitated for a breath, the click of the door latch

the only sound as a familiar shadow of loneliness stole over him.

The next morning proved fair as Amelia rose at the cusp of dawn, anxious to meet Lunden for her final lesson. Having a maid who spoke little English proved a glory. No explanations or inane niceties were necessary as she donned a simple day gown and instructed Mary to plait her hair. A few curls rebelled as always, but Amelia didn't fuss. She moved to the window as Mary gathered her nightclothes and left the room. Sunlight permeated the sky in rays of golden yellow. Beyond the fruit trees, mist danced on the surface of the lake. The water would be cold, but her desire to learn how to swim could conquer the challenge. Then her list would be completed.

A sliver of sadness accompanied the latter realization. Where would Lunden go once he'd finished his business in the city? Would he resume his life of solitude at Beckford Hall or find the strength to embark on a new adventure? Would she ever see him again? Her heart thumped a heavy beat. Every fiber of her being had been tested last night in his bedchamber. How she yearned to fall into his embrace, to touch her lips to the tanned vee of skin exposed by his lack of cravat, to feel the warmth of hard muscle through his fine lawn shirt. Pity, he viewed her as no more than a nuisance, an obligation to be fulfilled.

After their kiss in the closet, she'd foolishly believed he'd experienced the same enigmatic pull, their lives connected by some unexplainable thread. But no, he'd never mentioned their embrace, and his words last night were spoken in a dismissive manner, his body language tense and uncomfortable, as if he could not wait for her to leave his bedchamber. Disappointment pressed up her throat. She could easily lose her heart to his golden-brown gaze, the husky deep tenor of his voice. Her pulse hitched another notch, no matter her intelligence marked the proposition an exercise in futility.

She turned from the window and made her way through the house with silent steps. Nary a servant was awake, their services not needed until later, and she slipped out the terrace doors undetected, careful on the slick, dew-covered slates that led through the rose garden and beyond, to the lake at the rear of the estate property.

She arrived first and leaned against the trunk of a sturdy willow to remove her slippers and stockings, tossing them with abandon into the grass next to the towel she'd carried. Visions of her childhood flooded back in vivid color, reckless adventures of wading and hiking. How she enjoyed those days, when responsibility meant nothing more than returning for lunch with her dress kept clean.

The lake glistened in invitation. Barely a ripple stirred the surface, bathed in new sunlight, as peaceful as a young girl's dream. Cattails lined the water's edge and tall reeds created a barrier toward the left side. An ambitious dragonfly lighted atop the highest stem with tentative poise before it flitted away in freedom, lost in a cluster of low branches, their leaves teasing the still surface. Amelia stepped down the sandy bank and into the cool water, her bare toes welcoming the squish of earth beneath her feet.

Carefree days seemed far in the past. She fought against her mounting trepidation. Deep water frightened her. *But not as much as an unhappy marriage*. To ask Lunden to teach her to swim was unthinkable. She'd be ruined were anyone to discover her proposition. Yet, she stood strong, unwilling to enter marriage helpless and dependent. Knowledge brought power and security more than any dowry provided. Knowledge ensured her a future, no matter how her family manipulated fate.

Across the lake, something broke the water. Circles of

wake rippled over her feet, lapping up her shins in a cold shivered response. She scanned the surface, her heart thrumming as she spied Lunden at the center, his hair slicked back, his eyes focused on her alone. *He looked magnificent.* Droplets rolled from his bare shoulders, kissed by the soft rays of the dawning sun, his body glorious, as if newly made, naked and vulnerable, gifted from nature. Her heart skipped a beat. What had she expected? He couldn't swim fully clothed. But what did he wear otherwise? Her stomach tumbled over in a cacophony of emotion.

"You can't learn to swim from the bank." His voice over-rode a meadowlark's call.

She dared him a slight smile, then returned to the large willow amidst the center of overgrown limbs where the leaves formed a lazy curtain of privacy. She removed her gown, folding it with care as her mind worked methodically to determine which undergarments to remove. With belated awareness, she amended her plan. She'd never learn to swim encumbered by too much clothing. Stripped to her chemise and pantalets, she emerged from cover.

She crossed her arms over her chest at Lunden's odd expression. He appeared angry, or at least disgruntled, and she waded to her hips, the chilly water sending a shiver straight up her spine. She'd never gone farther, even as a child, and now her desire to accomplish her fear and learn to swim forced her feet forward until the waterline wet the bottom of her breasts. Lunden remained a distance away and she wondered at his silence. Did her eyes reveal the frantic beat of her heart and paint the portrait of a coward?

"I'm not frightened." The words meant to banish any doubt he harbored at her dedication to the task and fortify her effort to continue.

At last he spoke, his voice gruff. "I would never sug-gest it."

He swam closer. Each stroke of his muscular arms sliced

through the water with a precision that barely disturbed the surface. He stopped within a few feet and narrowed his eyes as if he considered her with great deliberation. When she dropped her arms, he averted his gaze. Confused by his regard, she bent her knees, lowering her body until the water brushed her chin, although she ventured no deeper.

"Give me your hand." He sounded furious, the angles of his jaw hard and unforgiving.

He extended his reach forward and droplets of water raced down his firm muscles, the tanned skin reflecting the sheen of the morning sun. Amelia wanted to touch him. To run her palms along the lines of his biceps, trace the outline with her fingertips, feel the warm skin beneath the cool water.

She reached for his hand, but he needed to lean closer before their fingers twined and locked. Then he yanked her forward, off the muddy bottom and into deeper water. Her pulse beat triple time and her breath caught as she fluttered her feet to regain footing.

Nothing was there.

Frantic, she grabbed his shoulders with unexpected panic. His muscles tensed at her touch and she shot her eyes to his face, curious to his reaction. She swore one side of his mouth hitched in an approximation of a smile. It would be a first.

"We should begin this lesson in shallow water." She pointed out his error with hope he'd return her to the shore and solid security.

"We don't have all day and you've hardly dipped your toes in this puddle. We need to begin."

His deep commanding rasp sent a shudder of pleasure straight through her. How would she view him in the parlor, dressed in finery, after experiencing his smooth skin, the flex of every movement now inscribed on her memory?

She'd never forget until she scrubbed her brain clean of the image.

Water dripped from his hair to her forearms where she clasped him tight around the shoulders. She yearned to thread her fingers through the damp waves, push them out of the way in a familiar gesture, but she remained silent and still. She'd never touched a man with such intimacy. No matter the kisses or embraces she'd experienced in her years, never once had she been so close to a barely clothed male.

And Lunden looked magnificent.

In wait of his next instruction, she held him tighter.

Chapter Seventeen

Bloody hell and blazes. What devil prompted his agreement to this torture? Shouldn't cold water decimate his arousal? Instead, the sight of Amelia's erect nipples visible through the flimsy cotton of her chemise caused his cock to tighten and strain inside his smalls, no matter the temperature of the lake.

He needn't lie. He was lost as soon as he spied her wading at the water's edge, as mystical as a wood sprite. He'd watched her from afar, an enchantress in the violet dawn, her dark hair and green eyes all lovely, wild beauty, and he'd grown hard as stone.

Now as he steeled himself to her touch, the effort proved useless. Cold water did nothing to soothe his condition, and the tentative stroke of her fingers combined with the trusting clasp of her palms against his shoulders made him ache with misplaced desire. How he would teach her to swim and also maintain dignity confounded him.

And she spoke the truth. They needed to return to shallow depths so he could instruct her on proper form, but his own foolishness had taken control, wanting to hold her close and simultaneously conceal her delicious body, all softness and curves beneath the flimsy cotton garment.

He could only imagine how she'd appear now, the fabric, wet and transparent, outlining her full breasts, the tips rosy pink and hardened beneath the sheer veil. Lust-filled images of Amelia rising from the lake, nude as a goddess, inviting him to taste, touch, indulge, bombarded his mind and demanded attention. He swallowed hard and pulled his body farther from hers, his current problem increasing with each passing breath.

Amelia fluttered forward, anxious in the deep water, and misreading his movement as abandonment. He needed to begin the lesson. Now. Before his body imploded.

"Have you mastered floating?"

She startled at his sudden question. Then she tilted her head, offering a flick of emerald-eyed torture, though she did not answer.

"On your back? As a child? Were you able to relax and float atop the water's surface?" He blew out a breath and mustered a tolerant grimace. Conversation eased the ache of his arousal and he willed his body into compliance. What would he do when he needed to exit the lake if he could not control his absurd reaction, as raw as a boy fresh from boarding school?

"No. Never." She shook her head in the negative and a few rebellious curls fell across her brow.

He watched as she struggled with the circumstances, unwilling to release his shoulders to clear her line of vision. She tossed her head twice, and a third curl joined the others. He fought amusement. In no hurry, he lifted his hand from the lake and shook free the dripping water, before he gathered the silken curls in his fingers and tucked them neatly behind her right ear. His hand paused, his palm pressed against her cheek as their eyes locked. Her lips parted as if she wanted to say something and he was struck with the impulse to lean in to her lush mouth, lick her lips, taste her tongue. A shot of erotic fantasy tightened his groin, but his brain interrupted. What was he thinking? Amelia was the sister of his closest friend. He needed to begin the lesson, his misplaced desire be damned.

"We best get on with it then." He treaded water with ease and towed them to a shallower depth.

Her smile lit the sky as she regained her footing in the waist-deep water. She released his shoulders and the small action left him bereft. He dropped his eyes and groaned. His earlier fantasy, Amelia wrapped in the gauzy outline of her chemise, materialized with more impact than his imagination conjured. In a desperate scramble, he summoned thoughts of poverty and hardship, the anguish of his brother's death, but nothing could replace the erotic display before him.

The realization she was untouchable, the sister of his most loyal friend, evaporated. With truth he hadn't considered it with sincerity in a long time. It had grown cold from abandonment and ceased to exist in nothing more than an obligatory, fleeting notion. Now his yearning intensified, white hot and urgent.

"Amelia."

"Yes?" Her skin caught a soft sheen in the delicate rays of the rising sun.

"I cannot teach you to swim." He paused to gauge her reaction.

"But you promised. How else will you be rid of me? We have an agreement, do we not?" Her bottom lip protruded in a slight pout, but her eyes flashed fire.

"I . . ."

"I will do better. I'm determined. Don't misconstrue my slight panic for anything more than initial hesitation. I'm ready to learn." She edged past him and ventured into the deeper water, resolute to prove she was a willing participant in the lesson. "I'm not afraid. I—"

She lost her footing on the moss-covered bottom and he

vaulted to save her before she slipped under. He captured her in a tight hold and dragged her into the shelter of his chest, her braid whipping against his shoulder in the process, her eyes wide with fear. She clung to him with a ferocity she would regret later. He was sure of it. But he would not object now, her breasts pressed flush against his chest. He wrapped his arms firm and brought her closer as the rub of her silky body stroked his ardor, her mouth no more than a whisper away.

"Lunden."

She said his name, dulcet and reverent, and the last thread of control snapped. He looked into her eyes and like quicksand he sank deeper, unable to save himself no matter how he fought against delicious temptation.

Bloody hell and damnation.

Devil deuce it.

He captured her mouth, crushing his lips to hers, and letting loose the undeniable urgency of passion scorching his blood, fever-fierce.

Amelia.

He was doing something he knew he mustn't, but the knowledge fueled his desire more. He cupped her bottom and pulled her against his arousal, their bodies separated by nothing more than the thin barrier of wet cloth.

A small sound escaped her throat, neither plea nor objection, and he answered with a low rumble of appreciation, his mouth slanting to take hers more fully. She returned his eager petition.

Her kiss was tart with spirit, sweet with femininity. Not the angry defiance during their shooting lesson or the seductive entreaty in the closet. This kiss aimed at spilling his soul's secrets. It shot straight through his heart. How she managed to find the damned thing, he'd never know; still her affection sliced the lost organ to ribbons.

Heat pumped through his veins, settling in his lower half. He gripped her waist, cool under the water, his touch a brand upon her skin. He wanted her with a blind madness he'd never experienced. He was a fool, but he wouldn't stop. Just this once. Here. Now. One memory to assuage him for all the long, lonely days of his future.

His kiss grew hungrier and she answered him with wild abandon, her tongue anxious to stroke, eager to compete, holding back nothing in the rebellious behavior she flaunted. A leap before she looked.

He wouldn't consider the consequences. Lost in her, he abandoned logic. She slid her hands across his shoulders, skimming the water from his skin in a slick, smooth glide. Her fingers pushed into the hair at the nape of his neck to grasp his head and hold their kiss firm. She wanted this. The awareness fed his greedy possession.

With care he coaxed her to the left side of the lake where reeds and cattails shrouded them from view, her legs fluttering behind as he swam through the water. She could stand with no effort, but Amelia melted against him, her body pressed tight, the tips of her breasts an erotic reminder of all she offered as their kiss continued, each delicious stroke of her tongue against his delivering a jolt of sensation straight to his groin.

He tore his mouth away, coasting persistent kisses across her cheek, farther to her neck and down her shoulder, his mouth hot against her water-cooled skin. The ribbon of her chemise fell open by the determined nip of his teeth and he moved his lips to the slope of her breast, the rise and fall of her hurried breathing an erotic aphrodisiac. She clung to him, her embrace a balm to long-lost emotions buried deep under recrimination and regret. He ignored their awakening and kissed her again.

* * *

Amelia gasped against his mouth, her body a mad rush of delicious sensitivity. His intense passion drowned her in sweet pleasure, and she wanted no rescue. Everything was new, an exotic adventure, and the heat flooding her veins reminded it was real, hers for the taking. She splayed her fingers against Lunden's back, anxious to explore the strong contours of his skin, discover the sharp angles of his shoulder blades, the male body a mystery. His muscles jerked beneath her touch and he groaned, the deep growl an encouragement to continue.

He dragged his mouth from hers and traced her collarbone to the pulse at the base of her neck, where he flicked his tongue and licked the indentation. She shivered with the intimate caress.

"You're not cold." He breathed the words into her ear and she shivered again.

"Not at all," she whispered, although he posed no question.

He lowered his lips to her breast covered by only a thin layer of cotton and the heat of his exhale against her skin heightened the anticipation of his touch. His kiss, gentle at first, then persistent, lingered near the edge of her chemise, and she wondered at his sudden hesitation. She threaded her fingers through his hair, and brought him closer, granting permission. The briefest quirk of his lips against her bare skin confirmed his pleasure.

He hooked his finger in the neckline of her shift and lowered the wet cloth, his hand at her back bringing her to his mouth in a rush of water and desire. She nearly cried out with pleasure.

He took her more fully, his lips holding her breast in velvety heat while his tongue, rough and persistent against the sensitive tip, stroked and caressed with divine pleasure. Like a maddening miracle, the cool water combined with his hot mouth awakened every pinnacle of sensation. Her heart hammered in a frenzied beat. He touched her with reverence but the effect radiated through her body with pulsating urgency. She gave a little unwilling cry, unsure how much more she could endure, while her heart begged he never stop.

Gunshots echoed across the lake and broke through their romantic haze.

Lunden whipped his head up, clutching her to his chest as he swam backward into the reeds, his arms tightening in a fierce embrace that crushed her body to his, a shield from danger. She twisted her neck, chancing a glance at his expression. His eyes were hooded, his mouth pressed in a tight line, and whatever pleasure he'd experienced moments before, ceased to exist.

"Lunden?"

"Stay silent, Amelia." His eyes met hers with dark severity. "Obey me in this."

"But I mean to—"

He scowled, but she would not allow him control. She pushed against the wall of his chest, righted her chemise, and placed a hand on his cheek to gain his attention.

"Father is trapshooting. There's no need for concern."

He stared at her for several breaths as a series of conflicted emotions flashed across his face. Then slowly, a change took hold. His eyes, warm whisky brown as he'd embraced her, transformed from stark vulnerability to the depths of secrets he didn't wish to share.

A series of reports rent the air and the enchantment that once held them hostage faded with the sound.

"You'll catch a chill." He drew away. "You should return to the house."

"But my lesson. We haven't finished."

He motioned toward the far shore with a nod of his chin. "Yes, we have."

A trickle of dread chased his words. She'd like nothing more than to ask him to elaborate but he'd already dismissed her, his posture guarded, his expression impenetrable.

She waited another minute before wading to shore. By the time she'd toweled off and dressed, Lunden was gone.

Chapter Eighteen

Lunden stormed into Bolster Hamm's office, dust on his boots and fury in his eyes. If the solicitor had no further information concerning Douglas's town house, he would visit the residence this evening to question the tenant and dismantle the matter. He needed to rid the city, the sooner, the better, and flexing muscle in the process held definite appeal.

The return ride from Lakeview had been tainted by his struggle between erotic fantasy and self-recrimination, the latter claiming victory. Visions of Amelia, scantily clad, ignited his blood with a fever that would not extinguish, and her sigh, a breathless pulse against his mouth, lived in him, no matter how he struggled to blot out the sweet pleasure of her touch.

Still the fact existed she was Matthew's sister and far too good to be brought down by a man responsible for his brother's death and destined for a bleak future. He wouldn't be tempted again.

He rushed past the reception area and twisted the brass knob leading to Hamm's private office. His sudden entry startled the older man, only warned by his thunderous

approach and the harried objection of a secretary who
trailed behind in helpless fluster.

"It's all right, Fullerton. I'll see His Grace now." The
solicitor waved away his employee and motioned to the
upholstered wing chair to the right of his desk. "Good
evening. I'd riddle you with questions as to your unexpected
visit, but by the look in your eyes, I suspect you desire answers more than interrogation."

Lunden sat in the indicated chair, then rose and paced
away from the desk. He pivoted back, too frustrated to relax
and converse as if everything could be squared away in a
neat discussion. So many unknowns existed, his life a
bigger void now than when he first traveled to this wretched
city. Some unnamed emotion clawed at his repose from the
inside out and he could only associate it with the unsettled
legal matter. His brother's unresolved testament must be
the ill ease disrupting the silent existence of his soul. He
wouldn't consider other options.

Hamm perceived his impatient repose and waited no
longer. "I've failed to discover anyone responsible for the
letter you received regarding your brother's town house. The
current occupant has been living there for over a decade. He
pays his rent in advance and never causes a bit of trouble.
I presume he'll be overset when he learns you mean to sell.
That is, if we can find a legal path through your brother's
contingency." He cleared his throat and continued. "I can
offer my services and accompany you to meet this illusive
letter writer, but other than a complete investigation into
your brother's past, I doubt I'll uncover the information
you seek."

"Another dead end." The bitter words escaped before
Lunden could think better of them. He'd let too much time
lapse, unwilling to regard the painful necessity of settling
Douglas's will, and the selfish choice had created an additional knot of difficulty. "I understand. That won't be

necessary. The letter could be no other than the work of a gossip-hungry villain." He blew out a long breath of frustration. "Is there no way around the will's stipulation?"

"None that I've discovered." Hamm leaned back in his leather chair, seemingly relieved their conversation had evolved into something more manageable. "The document states you are to allow the tenant full residence of the town house for as long as he wishes to live there. Under no circumstances is he to be evicted. Therefore, the property cannot be sold, only transferred when it is vacant. I foresee the tenant, Russell Scotts, would not react favorably to any attempted change in the agreement."

"I have to wait for him to die, otherwise remain the landlord of a property I no longer wish to own?" He should have tended to the matter years ago, but the action had been beyond him then. His feelings had been too raw, the remembrance of that night resurrected whenever he dared consider dealing with the mess. Selling Douglas's town house finalized his death. Ridiculous, to imagine one could preserve the memory of a man in nothing more than brick and mortar. He knew better now. "Lord Scotts? I don't recognize the name. Does he hold a seat in Parliament?" Frustration clouded his memory as he struggled to decipher any familiarity.

"Have you read nothing I've sent from this office over the past ten years, Your Grace?" Hamm rose from his desk and turned to glance out the window, a disgruntled grimace displayed on his face. "Russell Scotts is no member of the realm. You won't find his name on any peerage list as he's not gentry. I wrote you of my concerns years ago, but your initial responses foisted responsibility in my direction, urging me to let matters rest and perpetuate the status quo. As years passed, whenever I pursued the peculiarity in your best interest, you answered with an exacting message to leave you alone. Thereby we find this troubling predicament

ten years older and Scotts's resolve that much stronger."
The solicitor pinned him with a stare meant to hackle a
response.

Lunden matched Hamm's eyes, though his murmur was
barely heard. "I see." He bit out the words, the most he
could manage, his mind at war with his increased regret,
layer upon layer, year after year. Now, emotion no longer
mattered. He wished to sever all remaining ties to London
once and for all. "I'd dismiss the whole situation if I could
live with myself afterward, but the unfinished business
would haunt me and I'd live in dread of the day I'd be called
back to this infernal city to remedy what I've already disregarded overlong."

"Have you spoken with the man? Considered his relationship with your brother? Surely he must have known the
late duke well to warrant this unorthodox condition upon
your brother's death." The solicitor resettled behind his desk
and leaned forward, his elbows propped near the edge of his
blotter as if contemplating the matter with great diligence.

"I haven't." Lunden rose. He brushed his palms down the
sleeves of his waistcoat and readied to leave. "Perhaps that
presents the most logical solution." Although he couldn't
imagine any tenant who'd volunteer to vacate a nearly rent-
free residence. He never considered it before, but the minis-
cule monthly payment paid by Scotts presented another
curious aspect of the arrangement. Perhaps his brother owed
the man a debt. Not monetary in nature—the duchy was
financially sound—but in some other facet. It was worth
deliberation. He stepped to the door, deep in thought, and
nodded to Hamm as he took his leave. "I'll be in touch."

He returned to Cleveland Row directly, his thoughts scattered, crammed with disharmony of regret, obligation, and
unfulfilled curiosity. Worse, his desire to see Amelia simmered under the surface and demanded attention. He vowed
to ignore the persistent longing, grateful she remained in the

country, powerless to revive the feelings he worked diligently to bludgeon, although the relentless image of her rising from the water burned his memory with a fire-hot ache. Damn it to hell, he couldn't think straight.

Intent on speaking with Matthew, he bounded up the stoop, past Spencer who startled with his sudden entry, and on to the second-floor study.

One goal plagued him.

Something had to be done about Amelia.

He found his friend in the usual pose, hunched over a half-completed puzzle, locked in concentration. At the sound of footsteps, Matthew threw a glance over his shoulder, his mouth quirked in a grin before his attention fell to the challenge on the tabletop.

"There you are. Returned from Lakeview already? Are my parents well? They must have been pleased to see you."

"Then you've received my message. Very good." Lunden slowed his steps and joined Matthew near the window. "Your parents were a delight as always. Your sister, well there's another issue." He strove to conceal all emotion with the comment though a stab of conscience pierced his sternum and lanced his heart.

"Aaah, so you've had your fill of Amelia's charms." Matthew coughed to stifle his laughter. "Don't worry. I've the situation well in hand. You can dismiss any notion of finding the she-devil a suitable husband. The paperwork is drawn for her betrothal to Collins." He flashed a cocky smirk. "As a bonus, the man aligns with every item on my mother's list."

"Collins? You can't be serious?" His pulse seized for the length of a breath before fierce possessiveness took hold, pumping his blood in an unruly rush of objection. "The man's as bland as a glass of milk and old enough to be her father. He'll never be able to handle your sister's unbridled spirit." The final words snapped out, harsh and argumentative.

Nor her tart tongue, her mischievous shenanigans, her untamed passion.

"Tut, tut. Don't be fooled by the man's docility. I have no doubt he'll manage Amelia." Matthew laughed with no attempt to disguise the sound this time. "He's to inherit his brother's family. Amelia will be too busy with a brood of six children to make mischief and cause mayhem." He fitted a few pieces, focused on the puzzle, unaware of Lunden's lethal stare.

"I've never known you to be a cruel man. What brings about this decision?" Lunden struggled to keep his tone even, although an unexplainable tension coiled tight in his chest.

Matthew tilted his head up, his expression grave. "Not at all. The arrangement is beneficial. Amelia needs responsibility. Every time I turn around she's at the center of another problem to be handled. Soon no one will want her, a pariah among society, and she will be crushed, unable to retract all the time and opportunity she's squandered Season after Season. I protect her with this betrothal. Do not think otherwise."

Lunden winced at Matthew's blunt assessment. "A convincing argument." He turned away from the window and his eyes settled on the closet door. His blood ran akin to his heated temper and he flicked his gaze away. Damn it all to hell. Every time he attempted to rid her image from his mind's eye, a vision of thick, lush curls rich with the sheen of morning light interfered and obliterated his best effort. He had no right kissing her, touching her, imagining making sweet love to her. He did not seek permanence, yet somehow she'd gotten hold of a large piece of his heart.

"Either way, it's no longer your concern. I should never have asked such a preposterous favor of you in the first place. And you've taken my request to heart. You needn't trouble any longer. Consider yourself released from duty. Forget Amelia and carry on."

A weighty silence overtook the room. Lunden walked to the hearth and stared at the fire. With deliberation, he extracted the list kept in his right pocket and tossed the parchment amid the flames. His obligation to Amelia was satisfied, her role in their agreement moot with Matthew's departed news. The fire cracked and popped in agreement. Still, something urged him to linger when he should resolve Douglas's will and rid the city with haste. He glanced over his shoulder. "Does her happiness matter so little?"

"I'm curious why it matters so much." A perplexed frown filled Matthew's eyes and he absently rubbed his leg before limping to his cane hinged on the corner of the desk. "Has she bargained with the devil and claimed your loyalty? If so, she's engaged you in a worthless endeavor. Nothing will sway me in this. She'll be married to Collins and the matter settled."

Lunden's mouth tightened in mute reproach and he swallowed his immediate rebuttal, the tenuous balance of reining his temper and choosing the correct words, occupation enough. This was the reason he lived alone, secluded on a country estate and far away from society, safe from complicated emotions and anyone who might ask him a favor or request his advice. Emotions were a tangled knot better left unexplored. When he spoke, his reply possessed a sharp edge. "Consider your choices. Your sister will never forgive you."

"My sister enjoys being contrary. It's her special talent." Matthew forced a laugh, dismissing the gravity of their conversation out of hand.

Could it be he didn't wish to see the truth of things, latching on to a blithe dismissal of Amelia's resistance and mistaking her reticence as disagreeability when it was clear to Lunden much more lie at stake? Her bleak outlook on marriage bespoke of a deeper reluctance, her comments barely scratching the surface. He may have confronted the situation only weeks before, but when he looked into her green eyes he saw intelligence, humor, and a great degree of courage. He remained sure the attributes camouflaged others. Fear, of that he was certain. Vulnerability, perhaps.

"She'll come to see the logic in my decision." Matthew averted his eyes and Lunden detected a bit of polish lost from his confident veneer.

"It's a mistake."

The longcase clock marked several minutes before either man spoke again.

"Is that what this is about? You wish to shield me from another mistake?" Matthew favored his right leg as he took the few steps necessary to close the distance between them, his voice dropped low. "Our actions that night were poorly planned. We were young and foolish, and true, there's no way to alter the pain caused that evening, but we can't live in fear of erroneous judgment. One makes the best decisions based on the facts presented at the time." Matthew glanced to his leg, his limp a physical reminder of the heavy price paid for his involvement. "Do not doubt I harbor regret, but too much deliberation in the past will naught guarantee a happy future. At least now I understand your passion for the subject. It explains your foul mood." He tapped his cane against his boot, his expression solemn. "You could come back, you know. Rebuild a life here in the city. Reestablish a presence."

"To what end?" The conversation made a perilous tilt toward emotion, a subject Lunden avoided at all costs.

"To be among the living. Hiding in the country smacks of cowardice and allows the gossips to relish victory. You could reenter society. I would stand beside you."

"To rub elbows with the same prejudiced snobs who accused me of murdering my brother before passing their gossip from tongue to ear with fierce promptitude? No, thank you." He wasn't hiding. He thought to mention the fact, but did not wish to prolong the conversation.

"Forgive yourself, Lunden. Begin to live life again. Take your mind on holiday tonight. Visit a theater or a brothel, whichever you fancy. Create a new memory to erase the pain of the past."

"If it was that easy . . ." He paused, his annoyance reduced. The one woman who piqued his interest was definitely off-limits, more trouble than the underworld, and his best friend's sister. The final fact sealed his fate. He could never dishonor Matthew and destroy their unspoken trust. Not for a handful of kisses and unexplainable misplaced lust. "I ask only that you consider Amelia's future with care."

"In this, I make no mistake. The results benefit us all."

"Time will tell." He dropped a sharp glance to his left breast pocket. He fit but one of the qualities on the husband list. Why he'd consider that fact proved foolish beyond comprehension. Matthew's advice was best taken. He should distance himself from Amelia's green-eyed beguilement.

The conclusion brought with it a dampening of spirit. He knew loneliness well. A few more decades of the emotion shouldn't prove difficult. "Perhaps you're right. While I know the price paid for poor decisions made, I've no right to interfere in your familial decisions. I should consider your suggestions, resolve all legalities, and move on with life."

Matthew's expression softened. "I've already heard low murmurings of disrespectful inquiry at the club. Word travels faster than lightning in this city. Best get on with your business, if that's your intent."

Nothing was said for a long-drawn moment, then Lunden quit the study and made his way downstairs where Spencer waited in the hall. "A letter arrived for you this morning. Shall I have it brought to your bedchamber?" Spencer extended a white folded note in his direction, the scrawled handwriting recognizable, and Lunden's temper reignited.

"I'll read it here, thank you." He waited until the servant left and then tore into the message, his eyes scanning the three lines of script.

Chapter Nineteen

"I wish you'd accompanied me to Lakeview. While the visit proved pleasant, it would have been all the more so had you shared it." Having returned last evening, Amelia wasted no time in sending Charlotte a message to confirm their early-morning constitutional. So much needed to be said, her brain overflowed, and she began with the choicest details of her time spent away as soon as their feet hit the pavement.

"It's disconcerting your father remains so determined to see you married and entrusts Matthew with the decision, but at least you've made known your displeasure. Did anything else happen? Anything that would explain your jubilant glow, no matter how you struggle with desperation to conceal your secret?" Charlotte settled on the bench and angled her head in question.

Amelia fought hard against a grin. She'd omitted the intricacies of her swim lesson, *and Lunden's cataclysmic kiss*. She'd practiced liberal editing and glossed over the interlude with careless aplomb in the retelling, yet her friend displayed an arched brow, her lips turned in a suspicious twist. Amelia strove for seriousness. Charlotte knew her too well.

"Scarsdale kissed you, didn't he? I can tell by the gleam

in your eye." Charlotte squeezed Amelia's hand in an urgent plea for more information. "I can't believe everything that has occurred in the course of two days. By comparison, my life is exceedingly dull."

"Don't be silly. The past two days have been unusual, that's all."

"Perhaps. Although I was terribly lonely while you were gone. Lord Dearing declined every invitation and claimed a megrim, shutting up in his study and demanding quiet. I spent most of my day reading, and while my mother and sister visited for tea on Sunday, I truly missed our time spent together." She ended on a melancholic note before she roused a bit of cheer and continued. "Now, tell me about your kiss. Was it magical?"

"I wouldn't say that." *Magical was an inadequate descriptor that barely scratched the surface.* "You're a married woman. The mention of a kiss, albeit a wonderful, breath-taking, soul-searing kiss, should not set you all atwitter."

The two burst into a bout of laughter, their smiles wide. When they managed to calm, Charlotte continued to pepper her with questions.

"What does this kiss mean? Is your list complete? Will Scarsdale leave London now?"

"Give me a moment, please." Amelia spent the carriage ride home from Lakeview deliberating the same inquiries. What could she construe from their shared intimacy? Was she a convenient distraction or did Lunden possess genuine affection for her? The man was inscrutable under the best of circumstances and he'd left that same day, without so much as a good-bye to lend her a shred of understanding to their interlude. His actions, never mind emotions, were consistently shrouded in secrecy.

After their kiss in the closet, she'd kindled the tiniest flicker of hope he cared for her as a woman and not as an obligation to be fulfilled, the sister of his closest friend. His abrupt departure confirmed the irritating suspicion that the worst may be true, and her stomach roiled as she forced herself to abandon the dismal conclusion. "I don't know, Charlotte. For the life of me, as wondrous as our time together, I'm not sure why he kissed me. His actions confound me. One day he's agreeable and kind, the next, surly and ill-tempered. It's as if he doesn't know his own mind."

"Or his own heart."

Amelia's chest tightened with her friend's whispered comment, but she had no time to dwell on the stark reaction as the sound of approaching boots drove her attention to the cobblestone path.

"Good morning, ladies."

A chilling shadow fell across the bench and Amelia quelled a shiver. She rose at the sound of Lord Nilworth's greeting, unwilling to allow his arrogant regard from above, and tugged Charlotte to her feet in the process.

"Lord Nilworth. This is unexpected." Amelia's expression lost all joy. No doubt the man ferreted out the information she shared a daily walk to St. James. This was no coincidence.

"And who is this delightful flower? Introduce us please, Lady Amelia." Nilworth inclined his head in Charlotte's direction, her expression cautiously polite.

Amelia did as she was told, although the uneasy feeling that slithered to the pit of her stomach reminded it best to detach from Nilworth with expedience.

"Allow me to stroll with you. I find it healthy to take the morning air. You would not mind."

Amelia glanced down the lane to where Nilworth's carriage waited. She held no doubt he'd orchestrated their chance meeting. But for what reason? He couldn't possibly make true his feigned interest in courtship. She drew in a deeper breath as Charlotte shot a desperate glare in her direction. Etiquette demanded she not decline Nilworth's invitation without a plausible excuse. They'd been laughing when he'd approached. It would be difficult to claim illness now.

"Of course." Amelia motioned to the maids seated several yards away and the trio stepped onto the cobblestone path leading from the square to the street beyond. Their maids trailed at a polite distance.

"How very fortuitous to have you placed in my path once again, Lady Amelia."

"Truly uncanny." Amelia held no desire to disguise her displeasure despite Charlotte poking her hard between her ribs on the left side. "Imagine my gratitude for such good fortune."

"With two lovely ladies to escort." Nilworth eyed Charlotte then returned his probing stare to Amelia. "What gentleman would feel luckier?"

Amelia quickened her stride. The sooner she returned Charlotte home and continued to Cleveland Row, the better. Nilworth pursued something and while she couldn't decipher his goal, the man was not one to be trifled with for long.

"Did you enjoy the time spent with your parents at Lakeview? It was my pleasure to assist you when your carriage became disabled. A favor well spent, if I may."

A sudden awareness, that Nilworth meant to elicit repayment for his favor, provoked her brain, and she scrambled for a polite response while mentally considering his motives.

"My parents are well, thank you. Perhaps Lady Dearing will accompany me the next time I visit." Ill ease made her reply sharp.

Lord Nilworth snickered. "Lord Dearing will have none of that."

The bald comment struck both women by surprise. Amelia shot her eyes to Charlotte who appeared mystified by the startling response. For half a block the trio walked in silence, their combined footsteps with Nilworth's cane against the pavement a lonely noise to disrupt the morning air. They turned at the corner adjacent to Rotten Row and the activity of the awakening thoroughfare prompted a renewal of conversation.

"Has your houseguest settled? Scarsdale's homecoming has set the tongues to wag. I admit my curiosity is pricked. Considering the conditions of his departure, I'd wager an event of significance provokes his return, although you may well tell me the opposite."

Amelia bit her bottom lip, her pointed replies to his unseemly comments anxious to be heard, but she would not allow him to goad an answer. How dare Nilworth speculate on Lunden's cause for visit, no matter the revival of talk amongst the gossipmongers. "I assure you, all is well. Aside from my brother's preoccupation with my unmarried status, life at home remains unremarkable. Respect for one's privacy is a Whittingham code of honor." Again Charlotte jabbed her side, and Amelia gave an abrupt jerk, the swivel of her head in line with the action.

They'd reached Dearing House and with Charlotte tucked safely inside, Amelia continued a brisk stride along the sidewalk with Lord Nilworth at her side. She appreciated her friend's reluctance in leaving, the reason more than obvious, but Amelia intended to reach home and scurry inside before Nilworth continued his invidious questioning.

"It would be ghastly to have all the old rumors exhumed and made fodder for the ballroom. Scarsdale must have intended to keep his visit private or run the risk of censure, reliving his past all over again. A true friend would advise him to take his leave with haste." His voice dropped to a confidential tone. "Of course, no one truly knows what transpired that evening, except Scarsdale, your brother, and the late duke."

Amelia stalled. She whipped her head around to face the man beside her, a bitter retort on the tip of her tongue, but as if Nilworth anticipated her set down, he stepped away, inclined a curt nod, and let the enveloping crowd on the street swallow his retreating form. Without pause, she scampered up the steps into the safety of her home.

In habit, she shot up the hall steps intent on speaking to Matthew and uncovering the intricacies of Lunden's past. Only then could she decipher Nilworth's interest and understand Lunden's heart. This time she would not allow her brother to shove her feelings aside and dismiss her inquiries as those of a gossip-minded ninny. Nilworth intended to interrupt her morning walk and deliver his cloaked message. His actions overflowed into her life now. Matthew could ignore her questions no longer.

But things were not as she expected when she burst through the study doors without knocking. Her brother did not brood over his tiled puzzle. Instead he stood near the brandy decanter, his glass raised in a toast with Lord Collins. Her eyes shot to his desktop where a quill lay atop a long sheet of white paper, the inkwell nearby. Her breath caught with the conclusion the men had signed the marriage contract only moments before. Had Nilworth not stalled her, she might have interrupted their agreement and put a stop to the license.

A sudden flash of panic clouded her vision and she clung to the brass doorknob as dizziness swamped her from head to toe. No one would steal her freedom, lock her into a cage by marriage of poor choice, and drive her to execute some plan of escape. Her knees threatened weakness. She steeled her resolve and forced her heart to a normal rhythm. She was no shrinking violet. She would not swoon, nor would she fail.

"Amelia. For once you show perfect timing."

The words spurred Collins to remove his pocket watch.

He glanced at it briefly and tucked it away. Only then did he raise his eyes in her direction, his expression satisfied.

She chose her words with precision, her solitary goal to extricate herself from the room and retreat to her bedchamber to reassemble her plans. "Matthew, Lord Collins. I did not mean to interrupt your business."

"Come in and close the door behind you. I have news to share."

The men stared at her with intent, her brother's grin larger than Lord Collins's, but both pleased nonetheless.

Her eyes darted to the desk where her future lay deceased in a mixture of ink and sand, then back again, to the satisfied gentlemen enjoying their celebratory brandy. "I'm afraid I cannot stay. I'm feeling unwell. It's the reason I returned from my walk with Charlotte so quickly. Please excuse me." She backed out of the room and closed the double doors behind her. The only thing quicker than the anxious tattoo of her heart was her feet on the carpet as she hurried away.

Chapter Twenty

Steeling his composure, Lunden led Hades down Lamb Street toward his brother's private residence, the town house unbeknownst to him until the fated night when his life shifted from boy, notoriously undisciplined and bent on distraction, to man, ensconced in obligation and duty. He should never have accepted Matthew's callow challenge to follow Douglas and discover the unforgiving truth. Truth was dangerous, sometimes more so than a lie. Truth proved the catalyst to the chain of events instigating the destruction that ended both their futures.

He'd give his life to retract his youthful foolishness and alter the course of events, but eerie whispers chanted a litany of guilt to remind no solace for impudence existed.

He reined his horse to a slow canter while his eyes skimmed the neatly lined buildings, one after another, a life and story tucked within each. Due to the late hour, neither hackney nor lamplighter haunted the street, the private community as quiet as an abandoned church, and his solitary existence comforted in the evening dark. He'd waited until calling hours concluded, ensuring the best opportunity to find Russell Scotts in house.

Tethering Hades to a stand at the curb, he paused on the

sidewalk to peer at the structure, painted in monochrome moonlight, stark and foreboding in the gathering fog. This property had served as Douglas's secret residence. Understanding his brother's choices remained a challenge, but loving Douglas was never in question.

Lantern glow from a post at his shoulder cast his elongated shadow up the three-stepped stoop, arrowing his path. He willed his feet to follow.

Repressing a shudder, he claimed the stairs and dropped the knocker. He repeated the process and waited several moments before a candle lit, the weak light visible through the sheer ivory curtains framing the entry hall. The door opened, hardly a crack.

"I need to speak to Mr. Scotts. It's a matter of great importance." Lunden slid his calling card through the narrow opening and surveyed the butler's countenance. The servant's cool hauteur faltered as he read the inscription, revealed through the slight narrowing of his eyes, but he did not speak and Lunden grew impatient, confused by the man's inept service. "Fetch Mr. Scotts at once. I won't be turned away."

The door opened wider and Lunden stepped through. He removed his coat, offering it into the butler's waiting hands and followed as he was led into a drawing room decorated in shades of crimson and cobblestone gray. An air of masculinity was evidenced in every aspect of decor, from the large writing desk situated near the far wall to the thick velvet curtains draping the mullioned windows. The knowledge that his brother once inhabited the rooms disrupted his self-imposed calm and he scanned the interior in search of liquid fortification. Several crystal decanters sat in wait on a nearby credenza and he wondered again at the butler's reluctant hospitality.

"Please inform Mr. Scotts I need to speak to him immediately. I'll help myself to brandy." He strode toward the sideboard, his hands clenched in fists, but he'd only taken two steps before the butler stalled his progress.

"I'm Scotts. How may I help you?"

Momentarily dumbfounded, Lunden completed his path and poured a generous amount of liquor. He took a long swallow before he turned to confront the situation. "The butler? My brother left this dashing town house to a servant, virtually rent free and for the length of your life?" The idea made no sense and Scotts's awkward, suspicious behavior confirmed there was more to be revealed. Was it simply the case of rewarding excellent service there would be no need to keep the will's contingency cloaked in secrecy. Douglas bequeathed many items upon his death. Why not leave Scotts the town house outright? It would have eliminated the problem currently complicating his life.

"It's not how you state, Your Grace."

For the first time since his entry, Scotts showed due respect and the simmering tension in the room eased the slightest.

"Explain then. I find my patience on a short wick." Lunden finished his brandy and set the glass down. "I saw my brother here the night of his death. I understand the circumstances, if that makes your confession any easier."

"Your brother employed me to keep his discretion. Were I to consult the occupant—"

"An occupant? Of whom do you speak? You leave me at odds to understand."

With visible reluctance, Scotts released a long breath, his earlier austere disposition nonexistent. This time it was the butler that strode to the sideboard and poured two fingers of brandy. He downed it in a quick gulp, then replaced the glass and eyed Lunden across the room. "Your brother left the town house in my name with the agreement I'd keep it invisible for its true purpose. No one has resided here for years and there's rarely correspondence, so I live simply, taking care of a home that knows no life. Yet I owe a responsibility to the late duke and I will not falter in my commitment."

"Very well, Scotts. Tell me what you know and I'll pursue the matter without your involvement. You need not worry about being put out on the street." His words held a lethal edge, the butler too astute to misunderstand Lunden would not be deterred.

"I'm afraid that's impossible. I vowed my loyalty to your brother and I fear violating the terms of our agreement were I to reveal the gentleman's name. I could never live with myself if I sullied my promise to His Grace."

Something akin to jealously ignited in Lunden's veins. His brother had seen fit to confide in a servant, someone of non-blood, before trusting him. The knowledge burned deep, sparking old wounds and rekindling buried emotion. His ever-vigilant conscience reminded him he was hardly the candidate by age or behavior to warrant his brother's trust, but he pushed the rationale aside and welcomed the pain instead.

"Shall I post a footman across the street to await your master's arrival? I'm not a patient man. Regardless of your misplaced loyalty, I need to resolve a legal matter and must speak to the assumed tenant at once." Irritation forced his words out in a strong tone, yet the butler appeared un-nerved.

"Perhaps if you left your card, I can see it received as soon as possible."

Lunden darted forward, his hurried paces finally garnering a reaction. "I'm not fond of riddles, Scotts, so listen carefully. I will return tomorrow, at which time I expect to either speak to the tenant or extract his name." He dropped his voice to a lethal tone. "Have I made myself clear?"

"Yes, Your Grace."

Lunden spared not another moment and rushed to the

hall, snatching his coat from the hook and escaping into the night.

It was later in the evening when Amelia gathered the courage to confront Matthew. Unable to do little besides speculate upon her brother's agreement with Lord Collins and contemplate her options for the future, her heart's unrest propelled her to face the dilemma head-on. It was so unlike her to quit his study earlier. She wondered at her newly developed cowardice and shunned the notion the trait would somehow take root and hold.

With a mere breath's length of hesitation, she paused before the study door and knocked, although she waited for no one to bid her entry. She opened the panel and turned the lock, resolute no one would interrupt their discussion.

At first glance the room appeared empty, but then her eyes, drawn of their own accord, settled on Lunden, his dark silhouette bathed in a golden gleam where he stood at the hearth in contemplation.

"Excuse me. I didn't mean to intrude." He returned her regard, his eyes dark, the planes of his face harsh in the firelight, and she drew closer for a wealth of reasons. All her considerations evaporated. With a mixture of inquisitiveness and affection she yearned to alleviate his sadness.

"You are well?" His voice was gruff, as if unused or perhaps raw and scarred by distraught emotion.

She answered with a barely perceptible nod as he stepped nearer. "I might ask you the same." Her eyes flitted about his person, taking in his jaw shadowed with a day's worth of whiskers, the rolled cuffs and discarded cravat, all indication she'd interrupted a bout of personal turmoil. "I should leave you." The words surprised as she wanted nothing more than to comfort him in the circle of her embrace.

"Do nothing of the kind. Your company is welcome." He

attempted some semblance of a smile and failed. They stood in quiet, facing one another until the fire hissed and popped as if insisting they break the weighty intimacy of their soundless exchange.

She stepped back in restless agitation, otherwise she knew well she'd find her way into his arms. Her mind scrambled for a suitable topic to break the uncomfortable silence. The remembrance of his intimate kiss at the lake brought heat to her cheeks. Emboldened against the impossible sense of spinelessness her brother evoked, she latched on to the subject with zeal before her courage fled.

Could it be her actions of the past hadn't held importance? Her heart hammered in her chest. She'd never experienced such intense emotion of any range, not even when she'd knocked Lord Lennox into the Thames leaving him to drown. The remembrance caused her eyes to flare. Still, while Lunden might pretend their swim lesson was a perfunctory favor, she entertained no illusion.

She swung her attention upward catching his eye. He looked dismantled. His hair stuck out at awkward angles and his eyes were bleary, as if desperately in want of sleep.

"You need rest." No matter his wretched appearance, he looked exceedingly handsome.

"What is it you need?" His question delved inward, his voice gone gravelly.

Unnerved by his whisky-brown regard, she willed her brain to engage her tongue. Was he sick? Had he been drinking? Or perhaps come from some other type of activity? An involvement with another woman? Damn her brother for suggesting Lunden visit a pleasure house. Matthew's blithe comment had eaten away at her innards all afternoon, overriding the information he'd shared concerning Lord Collins.

Now her mind juggled the disconcerting possibilities, suggesting and rejecting them with rash decisiveness. "I need to talk to you concerning my swim lesson."

Something close to desire flashed in his eyes, but then his expression hardened and he arched a dark brow. "I believe I met your demands"—he paused, his stare steadfast—"and overstepped the boundaries of our agreement."

"But I haven't fulfilled my portion of our agreement." She dared to lean closer, too aware of his virility, the heated span of his chest, the spicy scent of his cologne. When he made no reply, she reconsidered and swiftly changed the subject. "Lord Nilworth interrupted my walk with Charlotte this morning." The words were far from those intended when she ventured down the hallway to knock on the door, but the sudden statement erupted from her mouth beyond control. *Or good sense.*

Lunden's jaw worked but no words came out, seemingly content to let her carry the conversation.

"He asked about your return and . . ."

"Nothing uttered by that man is of interest to me. Have a care, Amelia. Your brother won't be pleased if you continue your association." A note of warning colored his words.

"I have no association. He interrupted my walk with Charlotte. There was little I could do beside fend off his odious questions with innocuous answers." Something in his posture relaxed. Did he believe she would pester him in the same mode as Nilworth? Driven by shallow curiosity? "That wasn't my reason for requesting your attention. My swim lesson . . . we never finished."

"We finished." He cleared his throat and readjusted his stance. "You cannot expect the skill to rescue you from an unhappy marriage. Face the facts and understand your brother has already arranged your betrothal to Collins. He won't listen to reason. I doubt proficiency as a skilled swimmer will provide the escape you desire."

His matter-of-fact reply cut deep. Disappointment coursed through her, brutal and unyielding. On an emotional level, void of reason, she'd believed he cared for her, would rescue her . . . and somehow open his heart. But no. He was a private, mysterious man. The news he imparted was callous and calculated, as if he'd given great thought to the delivery and considered his responsibilities fulfilled.

And yet he was wrong. As long as he kept his end of the bargain and taught her to ride, shoot, and swim, she'd have a measure of freedom to escape an unhappy marriage and find a man who'd capture her heart. Love was the guarantee, the one thing that ensured a blissful future. Pity the emotion was elusive as stars at daybreak.

"We had a deal." A knot of emotion clogged her throat and would not clear.

"That point is moot considering your brother's actions. No matter I've produced no candidate worthy of your attention. I'm the wrong one to fix your problems when I've made a mess of my own life." The sober press of his lips emphasized the statements and he stared at her for several breaths, his expression as grave as his words until his eyes altered the slightest.

"I'm doomed to an equally bleak future." Tears threatened and she bit back the quiver in her voice and struggled to maintain her composure.

"Because of an abbreviated swim lesson? I doubt it will make the difference, but I'll make it up to you. I have something specific in mind and well-suited for your list of corruption. You have my word. Tomorrow evening. Is that acceptable?" A reluctant grin pulled at the side of his mouth.

A shiver of anticipation skittered down her spine to chase away uncertainty, never mind she vowed to stop her wishful thinking. Still, the fact remained he wished to please her. "Yes, very much so."

"What is it about marriage that frightens you?"

His voice had gone soft and the question knocked on

her heart with conviction, pleading for confession of her deepest fears.

"Choosing a husband is not something to be taken lightly, entered into as a business agreement or a debt to be repaid. A wife is little more than a possession of a husband, expected to bow and concede to his every whim, while he has access to her mind and body at every advantage. A husband can assert his rights and demand relations whenever or wherever he prefers, and ignore those same relations, or worse take his affections elsewhere without nigh recrimination. If angry, he may beat his wife, treat her poorly, deny her funds, for no other reason than a whim or surly disposition or perhaps, the sun did not shine when he wanted it fair. He needn't practice the same moral code, yet expects the highest degree of loyalty and virtue from his bride, else she suffers the stricture of not just his displeasure, but all society. Should I continue?"

She took a breath and dared a glance to gauge his expression, but the same stony grimace lined his lips as if he heard her words but thought little of her complaint. She forged ahead against his silence. "But a well-chosen mate, one who understands, respects, and cherishes his bride, as I've seen with my parents and other love matches within the *ton,* why that type of marriage is heaven on earth and all I seek for my future. It's not an irrational request, no matter how well my brother asserts it is."

Somehow through the course of her confession, they'd moved closer. She'd wandered about the room as she'd spoken and he'd apparently followed her on stealthy steps because only inches separated them now, her bottom pressed against the puzzle table in negligent retreat.

"The very same conditions may occur with a man of your choosing."

He appeared pleased with the suggestion.

"True enough, although I believe I'm an impeccable

judge of character. It's the reason I remain unattached at this late date. Although how a man presents himself through a courtship is not always indicative of his behavior once the marriage vows are spoken, nor when age robs his bride of beauty."

"And what do you see in my character?" His eyes closed briefly and opened again with a hard blink as if he waged some internal struggle of which she'd never know.

His question surprised her. Did her opinion matter? She stared into the liquid intensity of his gaze, realizing he waited for her answer. Her heart kicked against her ribs. "I know little of the situation that pains you, yet I suspect you suffer regret and loss so greatly felt, you've banished all happiness from your world and withdrawn into obscurity, moving through the days as if a monotonous march leading to your final demise. As self-imposed punishment, you allow yourself no pleasure—"

"I take exception to the latter." His eyes seared into her.

"I don't believe you. Since your arrival, I've never seen you smile. Not during a casual meal or a joke shared between friends. I've no evidence you permit any jovial emotion, nothing to dissipate the shadow that clouds your brow." With fingers that trembled she wiped a fallen lock from his forehead, the intimate gesture causing her breath to catch even though she'd initiated the contact. "What brings you pleasure, Lunden?"

His heated gaze raked over her, rife with potent undercurrents. She ebbed closer, the smallest degree, as if pulled by intangible instinct, powerless to deny its beckon.

"Pleasure? You pose an interesting question."

The sensuous devil inched nearer. Breathing became a conscious effort.

"You won't light me afire, will you? Knock me unconscious? You wish to know what brings me pleasure?" He paused, all amusement gone from his voice. "Should I answer or demonstrate?"

The question scorched her to ashes, yet the words lingered, no completion necessary, his eyes aglitter with improper thoughts. Her lips trembled, unwilling to form a coherent response while her body surged with awareness. Her fingers fluttered at her sides, fumbling behind for the edge of the desk. For long, fraught moments they stood there, silence and tremulous emotion stretched between them.

His chest pressed against her, crowding her into the corner so close they breathed the same air, his exhale hot against her cheek. His mouth was set in a determined line, his eyes alight with an amused gleam. The intoxicating proximity of his nearness flung her off balance. Lord, he was handsome. The devastating combination of rampant virility and tantalizing male scent was enough to scramble her thoughts permanently. But she would think later. There was no room for reason between them.

He towed her forward, lifting her at the waist and sitting her atop the desk, and she allowed it, lost in the physicality of the moment. The inkwell overturned, bleeding onto her skirts and seeping through the layers, likely staining a black tattoo on her outer thigh. Still she did not move away, mesmerized by his sudden actions.

His fingertip traced the outline of her mouth, pausing at one corner before sweeping gently across her lower lip, tugging it the slightest degree. "*You* bring me pleasure, Troublemaker."

His sensual admission caressed her ear. Any objection she might have reserved scattered in haphazard disarray akin to the puzzle pieces flung to the floor when she braced her position. A faraway voice chanted it was time to stop. She shut it out, refusing to listen.

He leaned closer and she reacted in counterpoint, though as she withdrew from his sensual mouth, somehow he gained ground. His lips hovered just above hers where she reclined on the mahogany desk.

Her breath strangled in her throat as she opened her mouth to object or invite. She wasn't sure which. Then his mouth found hers and all conscious thought obliterated. There was no gentleness in his kiss. He took her as if he wished to consume her, hard, as if to sink his teeth into her, devour her, tongue-deep and desperate for the taste of her and her return echoed his potent bid, equally anxious to explore the wonders of his mouth. His fingers laced through her hair, scraped her scalp, and sent pleasure skittering down her spine. In response, she arched against him. He murmured his approval as he tore his mouth from hers, listing kisses along her cheekbone until his lips pressed against her ear, the vibration of his words igniting pleasure through every pore of her being.

"You're exquisite, Amelia. If only I could lose myself in you." He scraped his teeth along the rim of her ear before moving to her neck, the heat of his attention causing a riot of delicious sensation.

"Please." She panted the word in a rough whisper unable to say more in response to his wicked caresses. His kisses liquefied her, shimmering along her nerve endings like electric current, alive and vibrant.

"So beautiful and so stubborn. Every word a contradiction from that deliriously luscious mouth."

He nuzzled her neck beneath her ear and the silky brush of his hair against her earlobe caused another wave of sensation. Her eyes were closed, yet she experienced every caress with acute awareness. She didn't wish him to stop.

He moved with unexpected grace from her neck to her shoulders, licking across her clavicle as if following a path. His fingers trailed behind to tug at fabric, untie ribbons, and bare her breasts to his hot kiss. She bucked with surprise when his hands palmed her breasts, his fingers tight on her nipples, the blissful pleasure-pain almost too intense to bear.

Still, she never felt so free. So wanton, so wonderful, her thoughts a wild tumble—until he took her breast in his mouth and she threatened to shatter at the touch of his hot lips wrapped around her sensitive flesh. Her nipple hardened under the slow stroke of his tongue. She clung to his head, her fingers tight in his hair, as a strange sound erupted from her throat, a whimper no less. He grinned against her skin.

"Beautiful. A beautiful, wild, delicious woman."

She smiled too, heedless of anything besides the wickedness of his kiss. His hands held her firm despite she moved with restlessness atop the narrow desk. Occasionally, something dropped to the floor, shoved over the edge, but she paid no heed lost in the ecstasy of his hands, his mouth, the strong caress of his chin as he trailed kisses lower. Impeded by fabric, he returned to her mouth, nipping at her lips and sucking on her tongue.

He broke away and her eyes fluttered open. He studied her face, his hot breath a whisper against her chin. His arms caged her body on either side, then he slowly moved downward, his palms skimming over her bare flesh, trailing his fingertips down the length of her arms, to where he gathered her skirts, easing them up and pushing them to the side. She stopped thinking, lost in desire, unable to question his actions. If he meant to make her his own, she was ready to surrender. Somehow the fear that gripped her whenever considering her wedding night seemed distant, nonexistent.

His fingertips coasted over her calves, gliding along her silk stockings in the barest of touches until they journeyed above her knees where he laid his palms flat. The hot press of his hands against the intimate flesh of her inner thighs caused her heart to stutter. She quivered with the exalting emotion and wriggled atop the desk, her hips lifting in an unexpected bid for attention. She heard him chuckle softly before his mouth met her skin, the stocking the only barrier between his kiss yet all the more erotic for the sensations he wrought. He trailed sensual caresses down the length of both legs and up again, pausing to nip the skin at the back of each knee before he stopped altogether, his breath hot against her thighs.

Amelia stared at the ceiling, lost in a sea of sensation and excitement, on the verge of some magnificent discovery she could not label, while urgency built with each stroke of Lunden's sensual explorations. He eased his hand between her thighs and she parted her trembling legs, closed her eyes, and shut out the world. Her breath caught in her lungs as he traced one fingertip along her flesh, caressing the most private part of her. She shuddered with sensitivity. Surely she'd shatter if he touched her again, yet she yearned for it. "Yes, please." She shifted on the desk, as if to persuade him to repeat the caress.

"There?"

He stroked the slightest touch against her core and she whimpered her assent.

"Like this?"

He rubbed a little deeper, his finger delving into her heat, and her bones melted, her body weightless, and at the same time dissolved against the hard wood desk. "Yes." Her answer was no more than a weak rasp.

"And here?"

He sunk his finger into her depth and she moaned with pleasure. Surely she would die, perish in this same spot for the wicked, wonderful things he did to her, which she allowed him to do. He rubbed his thumb against her sensitive folds as his finger retreated and advanced with delicious grace, her hips adopting the entrancing rhythm until she couldn't keep still, the pleasure too great.

Deep inside her, something tightened and built with ferocious need. She struggled to contain the sensation, yet it overcame her as she gripped the edge of the desk and rocked helplessly in an effort to release the intensity. Something, whatever it was, lingered on the cusp of her periphery, out of grasp yet taunting with promises of delight and rapture, and she reached for it, yearned for it with every aspect of her viscera. What was this sensation, so new, so powerful? An adventure, an inner rebellion that obliterated every demure etiquette lesson and social scripture learned.

Freedom.

Her body begged for it, throbbing with want, and she couldn't wait a minute longer. "Please, Lunden. Please." She forced her eyes open as her hips arched upward, desperate to stop the clamoring demand inside her soul. "Please!"

He stroked her flesh again and the world shattered. There on the desk amid spilled ink and puzzle pieces, she met her demise. She embraced the pleasure as it shimmered through her with unmitigated force and allowed herself to become lost, without control, utterly free. She drifted on a cloud of sensitivity, over the edge of a waterfall, down, falling into oblivion, somewhere with no end, drawn to an emotion she could not name but necessary, as vital as her heartbeat, never wishing to return. She lay spent until the undulations of sensation subsided and reality intruded.

What had he done? In an act of self-indulgence and wildly driven passion he'd broken every vow, dishonest to the depths of his soul, all resistance frayed by her begging whisper. Only a selfish bastard would behave this way, callously grasping at pleasure when he surely deserved none. How could he be so disloyal to Matthew? So disrespectful of his sister? Here in the study on the desk, no less.

In silence he watched Amelia's eyes flutter open, a mixture of hazy contentment and mild confusion evident. She sat up and attended her clothing. All the while he stood immobile, locked in condemnation of his horrible behavior.

At the deciding moment, his conscience and good intentions never stood a chance. All he wanted was to lose himself in Amelia, her sweet velvety skin, her full sensual kiss. To offer her pleasure. But at what cost?

"Are you all right?" Her voice was hardly a whisper as she laid her hand against his sleeve.

"Yes." How was it she inquired of his welfare? Did he appear distraught?

"Amelia, I—" His voice shook, the reasons too difficult to explain.

"Don't say anything." She moved off the desk and smoothed her skirts into place. "Please. There's nothing you should say."

He watched her speak, her eyes nearly meeting his. Did she despise him? Well, she should. It would be no different than his selfsame reaction. But he hadn't long to consider her expression as she rushed past him and out the door.

Chapter Twenty-One

Lunden kicked Hades into a steady gallop and maneuvered the traffic-clogged streets of Rotten Row. Skill as a horseman proved second nature, his mind far removed from the bulky conveyances and bothersome curricles crowding the thoroughfare.

Last night he could have devoured Amelia, anxious to fill the emptiness of his soul with all the spirited goodness she represented. The peace and pleasure found within her arms lived in him and now he'd only find respite in the memory.

A litany of curses rode on the wind. He'd prepared himself in every way possible to resist the temptation she offered, but to no avail he'd succumbed to desire. The words to refuse her had remained as elusive as the remnants of her jasmine scent this morning.

Guilt swamped him, heavy and overwhelming. Yet, burying emotion, locking it away where it could fester and spread like a disease of the worst kind, didn't cure his misery. The past decade proved that theory.

His heart struggled to ignore Amelia's unspoken plea. Perhaps he should confront his feelings, expose them to light so they held no power over his future. The devil knew she needed someone to rescue her from impulsivity. If only he were a better man.

Lost in recrimination and contradiction, he maneuvered Hades down an alley adjacent to Lamb Street. Damn, she was as reckless as she was beautiful. Her headstrong temper and acute determination breeched every level of resistance he presented last evening. Still the fault lay in his hands.

Tentacles of regret clutched at his heart and he straightened his shoulders as if to shake from their reach. Much to his shame, he'd rejoiced in the act, unwilling to imagine Collins or any man enjoying Amelia's sweet curves and creamy skin, singeing the sheets in the same manner. A pain gripped his chest, so sharp he nearly reined his horse to stop.

Damn fool. When she asked for his assistance, the blood thrummed in his ears with such force, he'd hardly heard her question. Twice he'd jumped to the same insane conclusion, her words resurrecting hope in his long-dead heart.

Jealousy.

Another inconvenient complication. One that would kill a man easier than the most accurate bullet, and the best reason to pack his bag and leave London forever.

He reined Hades in before the town house. A host of conflicted emotions shoved personal matters aside and he glanced to the sky where clouds obscured the afternoon sun. The air held the promise of rain. He hoped it wouldn't prove true. He meant to escort Amelia this evening and end their confused relationship with reparation of sorts. It posed the best solution and a means of survival, if not a dismal, lonely conclusion.

The town house stood cloaked in shade, modest and solemn in this fashionable neighborhood. Inside, Russell Scotts held the key to his brother's distress and could provide the information needed to settle his affairs once and for all.

He tied off his horse, climbed the stairs, and made quick work of the knocker, but Scotts didn't answer. In frustration, he dropped the brass harder and accompanied his entreaty with a demanding pound of his fist. At last the door opened, a stranger on the other side.

Lunden gave no opportunity for dismissal and pushed past the man through the entryway and farther into the foyer. "I expected Mr. Scotts. I'm Scarsdale. We have an appointment this afternoon."

"Scarsdale." The stranger repeated the title with calm determination. "I'm afraid you have wasted your time. Mr. Scotts no longer resides here."

"Rubbish. My brother, the late duke, provided for Scotts's employ and housing until death. We discussed the matter yesterday in this very same place. You're mistaken." He paused and assessed the gentleman before him. "Who are you and why are you here? Are you the tenant?" His questions were laced with barely contained anger, although the authoritative tone rang through.

"I don't see how my identity is of your concern, most especially after you've arrived on my stoop and forced your way into my home."

Lunden eyed the man before him, middle-aged and in fine physical condition. His features provoked some thread of familiarity, vaguely prompting there was more to be discovered here. He growled his retort. "Make no mistake who pays the bills and where you place ownership. I want you out, whoever you are."

"Douglas wouldn't approve of this decision. He guaranteed my security in his will. One would assume you'd honor his final wishes, most especially after causing his death, Your Grace."

The words were an unexpected blow and Lunden did everything in his power not to stagger back. He *had* caused his brother's death. He knew well the fact, but to expose it aloud after all these years while he stood in the place his brother last breathed was almost too much to process. He walked to the sideboard and poured a brandy, throwing it back in one swallow.

"It's obvious you know much of my brother's last evening, but that proves little. Perhaps it's time we clear the air." Anger sharpened his tone. He'd struggled for nearly a decade to keep this secret concealed and yet since returning in a mere handful of days, two people had made their awareness known. The stranger coughed once and Lunden turned in his direction.

"Douglas was a good man and I won't allow anyone to besmirch his memory. The conditions of his will provide for my residency here. Your sudden desire to sell this town house has reopened raw wounds, but I've only arrived yesterday. Last night was the first evening I've slept here since the week following your brother's death ten years ago."

"I don't understand." Lunden left the sideboard and walked to the hearth, his eyes skimming over the articles that littered the mantel. A glass-cased clock stood at the center, a selection of leather-bound books held tight by marble bookends at either side. He stroked a finger over the gold embossed title stamped along the spine of a tome of poetry and felt an internal shiver.

"As you know, your brother led a private life. Scotts was our butler here on Lamb Street and kept our secret as if his own. We trusted him implicitly. Neither one of us wished our personal preferences made public, as we'd be ostracized and forced to separate, no matter we shared a great affinity for each other. Your brother was a peer of pristine reputation, and I, an accomplished viscount. With the help of Scotts, we were able to achieve our goal, and keep a quiet, respectful relationship in this household. But soon after your brother's death, while you dealt with insinuation and accusation, the butler schemed a plot for his own gain. Nefarious strategy, actually. He forced me out and threatened to expose my intimate relationship with your brother to the newspapers if I didn't vacate London. Much akin to your fate, I exiled myself in fear Douglas's memory and my future would be drenched in the deepest scandal. Neither one of us deserved shame and humiliation to replace the genuine affection we shared. Meanwhile Scotts lived here for ten years, virtually rent free, an act of extortion and cruelty, comfortable in the knowledge I'd never expose the unorthodox preference of my personal life or my actions upon your brother's death."

Dumbstruck, Lunden returned to the brandy decanter only to discard the idea with equal alacrity.

"Are you implying Scotts, that mealy little man, black-mailed you with regard to your relationship with Douglas so he could stronghold the fine address bequeathed to you?"

"Yes." The stranger flinched as he spoke, as if the admittance caused him physical pain. "A dishonest opportunist, I'm afraid."

"The very idea is devious and unscrupulous." Lunden's brow rose in consideration. "I wouldn't have thought a servant to initiate such bold disloyalty." He digested the information, aware he'd perpetuated yet another injustice. Had he returned to London to investigate his brother's will, he'd have exposed the butler's distasteful plot years ago. "I discovered my brother's preferences that evening by accident. He saw me at the window as he embraced someone . . . you." His hand rose in an inquiring gesture and the space of two breaths stalled his explanation. "I fled, but as always, Douglas bested me. Familiar with the area, he outmaneuvered me on the dark streets until it was I chasing him, in hope of explanation and reassurance his secret would remain safe. If he'd stopped and allowed me to speak, he would have known I held no judgment. Instead, the blind chase, instigated by my pettiness and intrusive curiosity, led to his death." He took a step closer, his expression a mirror of the sorrow displayed on the stranger's face. "When you met with Scotts's extortion, why didn't you appeal to me?"

"At the time, my emotions were high and unstable. I blamed you for the death of the man I loved. Later, I believed you would not look kindly on the man who attempted to end your life." A long pause stretched across the drawing room as the information settled. "I reacted rashly that evening. Confused and angered, I sought to protect Douglas or at the least prevent what he feared most: exposure. Without intention, I added another layer of dangerous scandal to an already complex situation."

"You followed me that evening? You shot at Matthew in the stable?"

"I was overwrought, my reasoning shaken by emotion, and frightened that the one person I cared about more than life had been taken from me. After you recovered your brother's body and returned to the stables, I observed your actions from afar. Douglas feared exposure, and the threat of disgrace brought to his family's honor lived in him. I couldn't allow him to die in vain as I had no notion of how you'd react. All I knew was two men obstructed my goal and so I fired a shot. I needed to keep our secret. It was all I could offer Douglas at this point.

"When Lord Whittingham fell, I no longer possessed the bile or opportunity to continue. I'd left the town house in a distraught panic, forgotten the powder bag, and therefore the discharged gun was useless. The night, thick with emotion and confusion, led me to retreat, choosing self-preservation, as I could do little to solve the problem once you'd returned home with your brother's body. It proved penance justly served for me to leave after my foolish choices. I loathed being cut off from these rooms where Douglas and I shared happiness." Silence took hold as both men, lost in remembrance, scanned the room.

"There's no returning to the past." Lunden's words were

soft-spoken. If only he could persuade himself of the same advice given.

"True enough, although the decisions of that night have haunted me, and often caused me to deliberate the fiber of my being. I should have gone to you, defended Douglas's honor against the rash of gossip, or at the least, eased your burden as you dealt with not just your brother's death, but society's harsh judgment and your newly acquired title. I owed that to Douglas and I failed him. Had I not reacted by retreating in silence, Scotts would have never hatched his malevolent plan."

Lunden shook his head in acknowledgment, searching for solace in the assorted facts of the stranger's explanation, familiar with his lamentations. Regret, his constant companion for a decade, asserted itself full force until an unexpected thought intruded, nudging it aside.

Amelia.

She'd brought light into the darkness of his life; but soon that light would be extinguished with the same anguished finality as his brother's death. Tonight he must make memories powerful enough to last the rest of his days.

The stranger continued, forcing him from his maudlin considerations.

"Your return here bodes well. I've had this residence watched for years. After your inquiry, Scotts abandoned the property straightaway, likely in fear of the magistrate after the message you delivered."

Lunden nodded, the newly acquired information providing a balm of relief. His brows climbed as his thoughts resolved. There was only one question left unanswered, the inquiry on the tip of his tongue since he entered Douglas's town house. "And you are?"

Stark solemnity consumed the stranger's features before he offered a brittle smile. "Lord Gavin. I believe you're acquainted with my father, Lord Nilworth."

* * *

Deep in thought, Amelia curled farther into the comfort of the drawing room hearth, her mind a mottled mess of emotion and distress, her body equally affected. "I love him." New tears formed in her eyes as she addressed the cat cuddled in her lap. "I've lost my heart and I've lost my way, Pandora."

The cat twitched with the admittance, sensing the deep sorrow of her mistress.

"Whatever will I do?" Amelia wiped the tears from her eyes and released a stilted breath.

"There you are."

Caught unaware, she startled and the anger displayed on her brother's face abolished all other emotion. The sudden movement jostled Pandora who leapt atop the coal scuttle and then to the mantel as Amelia stood and shook out her skirts.

"Best flee or I'll skin you alive."

Belatedly she realized her brother addressed Pandora, and reached for the animal in an act of protection, although with a slink, the cat pounced to the floor, wove through Matthew's legs, and fled the room.

"What are you about?" Her voice shook, but from her brother's furious tone or her heartsickness she could not decipher.

"That infernal beast made a shambles of my study. Haven't I warned you to keep Pandora from my rooms? Yesterday she woke me from a nap when she used my leg as a scratching post. Now today my desk is disheveled, ink spilt, paperwork ruined, hours of diligent progress on my puzzle destroyed."

A bubble of relief volleyed for release against her ribs, but she dared not let it free. "I do my best to keep Pandora contained." *Much the way I struggle now with emotion.*

"Contained? She should be boiled in a pot. Another brilliant reason to see you matched, so I may be rid of that hellish animal." He turned halfway, as if satisfied with his tyrannous exit line, but at the last minute reconsidered. "Let this serve as fair warning, dear sister. If I see Pandora in my study again, I'll thrash her with my cane and use her hide to shine my boots."

"You'll do no such thing. I should think you'd feel the least bit of compassion for my situation. Pandora is my companion, my only ally, once you barter me off to serve your own purpose." Amelia straightened her shoulders, her chin thrust high.

He surprised her then and collapsed into a nearby chair, his left hand propping his cane while the fingers of his right worked his temple. "Why must you be so vexatious?"

She was taken aback at his sudden loss of bluster. Did pain in his leg cause the change in posture? Aware the weather affected his injury, her eyes flittered to the window and confirmed a threat of rain existed, the sky already cloud-covered. A twinge of compassion arose but she refused to linger on the feeling. Instead she took a breath to compose her thoughts, pushing aside the immediate concern and focusing on her goal. "Is it so uncommon for me to choose the course of my life? To want more than a mediocre future? To wish for love and happiness?" She hated the vulnerability in her voice.

"Aah, so now you'll put your claws away and aim for reasonable conversation after you've given me naught but the cold shoulder for the past two days." He glanced in her direction, his expression hard as he groused. "You believe you have choices, and for that reason you'll never be happy. Who has pumped you full of pipe dreams? Created belief you have a say in the matter? It's not the way of things. Father and I need to see you settled."

His reply held a palpable lack of compassion and she

swallowed past the lump in her throat. "Yes, *settled*. A most important word. I want more from life than a mediocre marriage. You speak as if it's a simple transaction. Something you must get accomplished in your daily errands." She gulped down the panic rising in her throat. "I can't marry Lord Collins."

"Of course you can. And you will." His pithy dismissal and conciliatory tone stung, yet unaffected, he straightened his sleeves and settled more fully into the chair. "Do you worry over your appeal? I assure you, there's no need. Shake the dust from your feminine wiles. Too long you've played at independence while Father and I permitted you to do so. It was poorly done of me to allow you freedom here in London, but I'll wait no longer to see you matched. Not when an opportunity as ripe as this one lies within reach. You need to try harder. When next you entertain Collins, offer him a charming smile and bat your eyelashes in coquettish appeal."

"I'd rather stick a needle in my eye."

"Therein lays the problem," he cautioned, his face hard with ruthless determination. "And a foolish notion to boot. You worry over control, but control is an illusion. You can have all the control if you employ your resplendent virtues instead of your sharp tongue."

"This is my future. I should determine whom I marry." She tossed him a peevish glare then ran a hand along the back of a nearby armchair to fortify her stance. In truth, his resolute indifference unnerved her.

"Do you have any idea how ridiculous you sound?" He sniffed as if stifling a sudden bout of laughter. "You should be grateful. *Grateful*. How convenient to have someone arrange and settle your future. How reassuring to know someone else bears responsibility to eliminate the uncomfortable wooing and awkward courting."

His words reflected his situation more than hers and that

earlier feeling, one of compassion and empathy of his life's situation, threatened to replace her determination. Like a bell left neglected, Matthew had grown tarnished and dimmed, where once, much like Lunden, his future seemed shiny and bright. The revelation caught her unaware and she answered with quiet reproach. "I don't mean to be difficult, yet I know you're up to something. You would trade your sister for personal ambition? What have you to gain by encouraging this union? Have a care, Matthew."

He continued as if her words meant little. "Don't contradict me. I believe your anger is subterfuge for your fear. How else would you explain knocking a suitor unconscious or pushing another into the Thames?"

"It wasn't the gentleman as much as his viewpoint."

"Perhaps, but expectation most often leads to disappointment. In many ways, your concerns mirror my own. As a male I have opportunities and choices to distract my displeasure, but the same is not true for you, Amelia. Marriage is your future." He looked at her a long moment as if measuring her reaction. "Do not doubt my attention to this decision." He squared his shoulders to rise, snatching his cane from a nearby perch and her anger reignited.

"You care more for your boot blacking than my happiness."

He gave a harsh laugh although a touch of amusement laced his reply. "Forever the mouthy chit, are you not? Spare me the histrionics. I'll warn Collins of your harridan tendencies although I won't dissolve this betrothal."

She blinked back the sting of tears, unwilling to expose her vulnerability. "How could you be so cruel?" Her spine stiff with staunch disapproval, she slashed him a look of outrage.

"How can you not realize this serves your best interest? Your future is at stake as well as Father's failing health. Don't be fooled by appearances. While he seemed improved since your visit earlier this month, it's common for one's health to show quality before a sudden turn for the worst."

Her indrawn breath served as answer to his last statement, her voice quieter as she continued. "I haven't forgotten Father. I only ask for more time." She eyed him across the room, unwilling to step closer although her words begged him to relent.

"Damnation, Amelia. There is no more time. You've wasted it all on whims and careless preoccupations. The time is now. And don't entertain an appeal to Lunden. He's here for business purposes of a personal matter. Leave him be." He paused, his mouth tight with frustration as if considering his next words with great care. "There's more in the balance than your marriage. Take note, I won't be denied the opportunity to improve my prospects as I settle yours. Nothing will stand in my way, not your stubbornness, nor my shortcomings, when it all overlaps and offers easy resolution."

"I never doubted there existed more to this plan than an attempt to see me wed."

"Collins is a good man. This evening, all members of the society are honoring his departure and celebrating his upcoming relocation because he's served as a fair leader. You should spend the night taking inventory of your upcoming future. Write letters, visit Charlotte, and ready yourself for your pending nuptials. Most importantly, adjust your attitude toward Collins. You could do far worse, no matter you've alienated every other prospect I've put in your path."

"I always believed I'd have a choice."

"Naive chit." He shook his head with the comment. "Life offers us little opportunity for choice. It's better you learn that lesson while you still have time to adjust your disposition. You wouldn't wish to spend the remainder of your days regretful and saddened with disillusion."

Did he refer to Lunden with the blithe comment or was

it that she saw herself aligned to his condition no matter the circumstance? And what of Matthew? She never considered her brother's impairment as detrimental to his future. Until recent discussions, he'd seemed adjusted and otherwise content. Too many unanswered questions badgered.

There seemed no adequate answer and unwilling to allow Matthew to witness her distress, she turned on her heel and left. The tears she fought to contain slid down her cheeks, hot and angry. She wiped at them with the back of her hand and safely tucked in her bedchamber, sagged against the back of the door.

With little effort her mind flittered to Lunden, the comfort and pleasure of their intimacy vibrant within her. How could she survive, married to another, when her heart, soul, and passion lie intertwined in his attention? He meant to leave the city. Tonight was her last chance to change his mind. Then whatever fate delivered she would be forced to accept. When he departed and she was foisted into a marriage devised to serve her brother's selfishness, she'd draw strength from tonight's memories to assuage her heart's wrenched desolation. She still had this chance. One night, to alter the rest of her days.

Chapter Twenty-Two

Lunden paid the hackney driver and turned to grasp Amelia's elbow as he led her down the multitiered slate steps where a small skiff waited to transport them across the Thames. Conversation within the hack proved stilted and sparse. Perhaps it was better that way, although he yearned to decipher the question in her eyes. Was it simply the anticipation of not knowing their destination or did something else puzzle her mind? He detected a note of sadness even though she smiled, her eyes wide as they progressed to the embankment.

The choice of a hack proved convenient, the foremost reason to obscure his identity, in kind to the hat pulled low on his brow; more an act of deception than intrigue, although the two walked hand and hand. It would serve no one for the Whittingham crest to be on display by use of Matthew's coach. Tonight was an evening for secrets, not disclosure. Vauxhall served them well, a destination no refined young lady would dare seek and therefore one sure to delight his companion.

They took their seats and the skiff glossed across the water, cutting through the shroud of low-lying fog. He eyed the clouds with skepticism, an impending storm almost certain, his survey momentarily obscured as they passed beneath Vauxhall Bridge. He hoped the weather would hold long enough for Amelia to view the fireworks. He'd taken a special thrill in the spectacle as a child. On some incomprehensible level, he hoped to give her the same enjoyment. A lasting memory of the evening, a parting gift of sorts.

Wavering lamplight lit the approaching shoreline and with their target in sight, he turned to view Amelia, breathtaking in the twilight, mist kissing her cheeks, as light and delicate as her jasmine perfume. She smiled and something twisted in his chest with disconcerting softness, but he shifted his eyes and busied himself with contemplation of the approaching gate rather than consider the tumultuous emotion.

They disembarked at the riverbank and her gloved hand in his felt *right,* for lack of a better descriptor. He smothered the observation into silence as soon as it formed, resolute he would say farewell this evening, conclude his business, and leave London at last.

He'd been hard-pressed to view his reflection in the mirror while he'd shaved this evening, having sunken to the lowest level of misconstrued gentleman. Although nothing good could come from overthinking the matter. He would not regret Amelia's delicious kisses, the soft velvet of her skin beneath his mouth, her molten heat as he brought her to climax. His choices in the study possessed the shape of colossal misjudgment; utter madness, to exploit an innocent woman, the sister of his closest friend, *his only friend*. He swallowed audibly. Truly, the devil owned his soul.

He shortened his stride to walk beside her as they progressed in amiable silence toward the narrow gravel path leading to the main row of tall trees, expertly manicured and now ornamented by a throng milling through the gardens. Visitors came into view, some decked in masks or dominoes, all eager to escape the strictures of London if only for one short evening. He dared a look at his companion, her eyes glittering with delight and he released a long breath. At least in this, he'd chosen correctly.

"Would you like to discuss things?" There would be no ease in the evening until he determined if she harbored ill feelings concerning their intimacy.

She nodded in the negative. "I wish to live in this moment only." Her smile, slow to start, spread across her face until it lit her emerald eyes with enchantment. "By week's end, I will no longer enjoy the freedom offered here. I will be packed and relocated to the countryside, away from every-thing and everyone familiar to me, my closest friend and childhood home. Tonight, I want to create memories to last a lifetime." She paused and he noticed the sudden rise of her chin, as if to burgeon her courage. "I only have this one night."

He understood, although anger, cruel and sharp, surged through him. She should experience no pain. Harbor no regret. Yet he could give her so little. "Then that's what you will have, Troublemaker. An evening of nefarious adven-ture."

When they reached the wrought-iron gate at the entrance to the gardens, his fingers fumbled with the latch. Society waited on the other side, no matter the gardens were more shadow than light. With a touch to his brow, he lowered the brim of his hat another inch, and led Amelia amidst the evanescent crowd, at times clustered and then nary a small grouping, strangers lost in provocative silhouettes seeking a distraction to relieve their longing, each possessing a private goal.

He ran his eye along the decorated booths lining the walkway. Merchants offered syllabub, sweetmeats, and wine. He purchased two glasses of champagne and much to Amelia's delight, a short velvet mask, mysterious as the night that welcomed them. He gathered the ribbons and tied the mask securely behind her head, although his fingers itched to sink into her lush curls, to push them aside and press kisses to the nape of her neck. With effort, he retreated below a pair of globe lanterns to sip his refreshment. He studied her over the rim of his glass and all tension abated, lost in the fog that shrouded the night.

"Look." She indicated a thick rope suspended between two poles, high above the booths and beyond the water cascade. "A tightrope walker. How very brave and extraordinary."

He followed her indication to the performer perched precariously over the crowd. The man hesitated, his steps delicate and concise, aware the slightest misstep would plummet him to the net below and reveal his worst nightmare. Still, he continued gingerly to the suspended platform at the opposite pole. "Brave fellow. Daring enough to walk a line between success and failure. The past and the future . . ."

Dare he step forward in the same fashion? Or would he remain paralyzed in the past? Perhaps that was his destiny, suspended between two worlds, unable to find happiness because of the sadness in his history.

He swallowed the sudden emotion in his throat.

Amelia flicked her eyes to his and he looked away, concerned she might detect a hint of vulnerability in his expression. Instead he caught the attention of a passerby, the stranger's gaze narrowed as she strove to decipher his interest. He leveled a hard-edged stare and the woman dashed her curiosity elsewhere. What the devil had he been thinking to escort Amelia to a pleasure garden? Her reputation would be in tatters were she discovered among those secreting away for amorous assignations. And what of his welfare? He'd nearly concluded his business in London, yet he risked discovery by his attendance. With any hope, a decade had erased his face from recognition, once a young boy, now returned a man. He would depend on it to ensure his anonymity tonight and not spawn a wave of gossip aimed at exploiting his circumstances.

With a recriminating scoff, he owned his habit of poor judgment. In kind to his past, little had changed. He was selfish, tunnel-visioned, when an idea captured his attention, and not unlike the man the gossipmongers described in their exaggerated tales.

His shook away the realization and returned his gaze to Amelia, her attention riveted to the entertainment at the far end of the gardens. Longing fissured through him. If only life offered alternatives. He'd not purposely hidden under remorse and regret. They were his destiny, his mourning turned lifestyle to protect his brother's secret.

Yet at what point did his suffering become his existence, one of denial not pleasure? He set his glass on a nearby tray and pushed a hand into his pocket. Douglas's watch remained safe. An ever-present reminder of the exact moment he'd taken his brother's life.

Amelia kept her attention glued to the dancers positioned near the end of the cascade although she detected every emotion written in Lunden's expression. What inner demons did he battle tonight?

A grand orchestra, at least fifty musicians, readied their instruments inside a magnificent hall lighted with an incredible number of lamps, the faint notes of their preparations discordant with her inner turmoil. She managed to keep her smile intact, determined to enjoy the evening, yet nothing erased her ill ease. During the carriage ride she'd remained silent, stifling the dismay that gnawed at her nerves, taunting this would be the last evening she'd spend with Lunden. The skiff proved no balm as it rocked across the Thames, as unsteady as her plans for the future.

She forced her attention to the ebb and flow near the Grand Cross Walk and beyond to the Grove. Supper boxes lined the avenue and delectable scents met each inhale. Laughter and conversation overflowed from the dimly lit area dissolving into a background of tinsel and plumes. Tonight was meant for indulgence, not reflection. She'd swallow her dismay as neatly as the arrack punch and lose herself to the night, a path more inviting than analysis of the emotion stabbing her heart. In truth, she had little else to look forward to and with a vow, she reached for Lunden's escort.

Her hand rested at his elbow, aware of the tense set of his muscles as they progressed farther into the garden. Most visitors seemed engrossed in their pleasure seeking, although at times she caught a stranger's intense scrutiny, their restless murmuring rippling through the crowd like a stone thrown into water. No doubt Lunden detected the same. More than once she felt his arm flex beneath her grasp, his jaw set firm.

"I fear I'm more trouble than I'm worth." She strove to keep her expression deferential.

"There's no value to be placed on your worth, Trouble-maker." He angled his head in answer, his eyes filled with teasing, warmed to a rich shade of brown. "You, my lady, are priceless."

His compliment arrowed straight to her heart. He was a man who revealed little, a tight rein wrapped around his emotions at all times, yet he risked his own censure by venturing to Vauxhall, all in an effort to please her.

"Thank you." The words failed, inadequate in expressing her heartfelt emotion. "I'll remember this evening always, no matter how the night unfolds."

* * *

They advanced down the walkway. Mist climbed the lamp poles while darkness filled every corner and alcove, sketching the perfect backdrop for a romantic tryst or stolen affection. They'd nearly reached the end of the Grand Walk when Lunden noticed the occupants of the final dinner box. Matthew was there, as were several other gentlemen, most specifically Lord Collins, accompanied by a female, one free with her favors from his brief survey. The guest of honor appeared to enjoy his send-off with unadulterated zeal. His current activity proved an eyeful, his uncensored celebratory entertainment provided by a woman of questionable morals.

Lunden flicked his eyes to Amelia, blessedly unaware. Devil take him, he had no experience with tender emotion, but he'd be damned if he'd witness her hurt perpetuated. He slowed, angling his arm to steer in an alternate direction. If Matthew spotted them, there would be hell to pay and a guaranteed scene to ignite speculation and misery. Still, that consideration didn't motivate him nearly as much as his desire to remove Amelia from the distasteful display only ten steps away.

She resisted and tugged at his elbow, his feet having decreased to a sluggish pace at the same moment a raucous outburst from the dinner box rose above the noisy throng. A potential nightmare threatened to unfold as she twisted to the right, drawn to the commotion by curiosity. Matthew and Collins, the scantily clad female wrapped tightly around his person, stood in plain view as the small circle of men exited the box and continued their loud cajoling. Another few steps and they'd all merge together in a grouping of outrage and discovery. Amelia persisted as she strained to angle him toward the right.

With the crowd at his back and few viable options, he gathered her close, spun her in his arms, and thrust left in a swift parry that pinned her against the buffeted resistance of a bloom-covered arbor located behind the spectacle. In the shadows of the trellis he pressed his body flush against hers, his mouth descending, seeking, and finding her delicious pout with expert accuracy. She hesitated no longer than a breath, although he suspected she itched to know what scene unfolded beyond their dusky alcove. Then he stopped reasoning altogether and lost himself in loving Amelia.

She tasted sweet, at odds with the tart words she often delivered, and his body reacted with sharp longing, as if an opium eater long denied and then all of a sudden drenched in the euphoric rush of addiction. Reprimands flittered through shreds of his consciousness. Wavering agitation reminded he should not encourage what could never be, but he silenced the thought with effective supplication. *He kissed her to obstruct her vision and avoid a disastrous scene.* The lie took hold and devoured all other considerations.

Soft sweetness molded against him in the same manner the night disguised their embrace. His heart banged against his chest. She offered no resistance, perhaps as certain as he this would be their last kiss and equally as determined to make it last a lifetime. The notion sparked his passion and he reacted instinctively, capturing her delicious mouth in another long openmouthed assault. Reckless, beautiful Amelia, not a timid bone in her warm curvaceous body, returned his kiss, her tongue as eager to explore as his, to taste and tempt. Her hands climbed his shoulders with bold caresses and persistent touches, until they settled at his collar, her fingers wrapped in a firm hold to anchor her close.

The weight of her breasts against his coat and stir of skirts against his thighs caused every nerve ending he possessed to ignite with raw hunger. He couldn't have her—he knew that well—but he could have this: a hot, heated kiss, cloaked by darkness, in the center of a gathering comprised of sin.

He'd allowed himself so little for so long, he could have this.

She brought her palms to his face and the tenderness in her gesture kicked his heartbeat harder. Fire flooded his veins. Did she mean to break free? She made a noise deep in her throat, a whimper of infinite pleasure, and it erased all doubt. He deepened the kiss, his hands sliding down her arms, farther to her slim waist. The memory of her sprawled across the desk, her silky black curls strewn in passionate disarray and skin flushed, all splendidly shaped calves and delicate ankles, her tight, wet heat, caused his grip to tighten. His fingers itched to tear the gown from her shoulders and bare her body to his touch.

The peal of a loud gong signaling the start of evening entertainment broke through his haze of passion.

Damn it all to hell.

The kiss was meant as a diversion, not a seduction. He broke every rule he'd made only hours earlier. He pulled away, his restraint barely contained.

"Lunden?" She remained perfectly still, the word a heated breath against his cheek. Then she slid her palm down the front of his waistcoat to rest atop his heart and his eyes found hers in the discrete shadows. "Are you all right?"

"Of course." He lied. Her touch banished loneliness and regret; he would never be *all right* again. He pushed the persistent thought to the dark recesses of his soul. "Across the walk, I detected trouble." He stepped a pace away.

"So you secreted me into this arbor?" She shook her head in confusion and her curls swayed charmingly.

"It seemed a good plan at the time." Hardly. He'd meant to avoid conflict. Instead he'd allowed her to steal his heart and fracture his resolve. Another poor decision to add to the list.

Worse still, the crowd now filled the Grand Walk to capacity, the visitors aimed at locating the best vantage point for the imminent fireworks display. He'd need to keep his head down and conversation to a minimum until he secured them a private spot. He grasped her hand and locked it into the crook of his elbow before steering toward the slow-moving procession.

She looked at him from beneath dark lashes, her sultry whisper befitting their surroundings. "What were you trying to avoid?"

Emotions, affection, a reason to stay in London when I know I must leave. "A rowdy bunch in one of the dinner boxes. The last thing I desire is to be seen or have you bothered by a few fools unable to hold their liquor." Even he heard the desperate note in his reply.

He pushed farther into the throng and eyed a dimly lit area behind a distant gazebo. It would provide them privacy and yet a fairly adequate view of the skies once the fireworks began. He'd almost reached his goal when he was jostled from the back, his hat nearly toppled from his head due to the unexpected inconvenience. While he reached with his free hand to secure his identity remained hidden, he felt a deliberate press against his person.

Releasing Amelia, he whipped around with a lightning grasp to capture a child's hand as it slipped into his pocket aimed to abscond with the goods. Little did the thief realize he'd chosen a man's history, the only tangible memory of Douglas, with his nonchalant pickpocket attempt, rather than a few shillings.

The urchin struggled to free himself, forcing the throng of visitors milling toward the firework pavilion to react and avoid the commotion. Lunden released the boy into the crowd, unwilling to draw further attention to the scene, but the action proved too late.

"Thief!"

The call of a nearby gentleman echoed over the hum of the crowd, setting everyone on notice. Anxious to rid the area, Lunden locked Amelia to his side and pushed on. She hesitated for some reason he could not name, and with a curse, he pivoted to the right to determine the trouble.

Nilworth stood in her path, seemingly amused as he reached to lower Amelia's mask with a flick of his finger. She blanched. How dare he? Lunden struggled to keep his temper contained as he bolted forward, locking his grasp around Nilworth's extended hand and preventing the man's intrusive touch. Unconcerned by the pressure he exerted, he crushed Nilworth's fingers in his grip and thrust his arm away.

"So I have deduced correctly."

To his credit, Nilworth made no attempt to massage his fist, although Lunden might have cracked a finger or two.

The crowd along the Grand Walk had thinned, most guests having reached their viewing destination, and Lunden darted his eyes left and right, concerned who might witness the conversation, or worse, spread ugly rumors about the altercation come morning. He didn't wish Amelia's reputation left in tatters due to his poor judgment. His welfare mattered little in comparison. No one might recognize his face, but his name remained another matter altogether.

"Don't touch the lady." There was no mistaking his deadly tone. "Ever."

"How very gallant, Scarsdale. Perhaps time has been kind to you after all and taught you to respect one's privacy."

The barb struck its mark and answered a pointed question riddling Lunden's mind. Nilworth knew of his son's preferences and vehemently protected his interest. Perhaps so much as to purchase a piece of property his son desired.

The anonymous man in the coach—Lunden grasped the thought before it evaporated.

"You should sell it, settle your affairs, and be gone. Why risk exposure when the whole matter can be resolved without messy gossip and harmful rumors?"

Was the damned man clairvoyant? Could Nilworth read his contemplations so easily?

"I'll proceed as I see fit without your midnight subterfuge or cryptic advice." Little had changed in a decade. London remained as unforgiving as always. He needed to rid himself of all reminders of the past. Every last one of them. Beckford Hall never seemed more appealing. At last to be gone from this infernal city with its societal pressure and predisposed conclusions. He paused to consider the consequences. He'd lose Amelia in the process, but that proved a suitable penance. He didn't deserve her.

Yet no matter his rationalizations, that one realization created a wound he knew would never heal.

"Very well, then. We'll conclude our business at a later date." Nilworth nodded. "As long as you stir up no further trouble, the past will remain where it belongs."

Lunden took in Amelia's unforgiving glare. She too despised the man. As Nilworth departed, he soothed her temper the best he was able. "It is of no consequence, Troublemaker." He hoped the term of endearment would soften the anger alive in her emerald eyes. "We'll both rid this city before week's end."

She lowered her eyes and he was unsure of her reaction although distress radiated from her, a result of their near altercation with Nilworth or his concluding words, he could not know. A moment later, brilliant yellow sparks lit the sky, a rainstorm of fireworks overhead.

He shifted their position so he embraced her from the back, his chest supporting her shoulders, his arms in a loose circle around her waist while she looked to the sky. He lost himself in the jasmine beauty of her scent, silky comfort of her midnight curls, desperate to press his lips to the delicate pulse at her temple, but he would not allow himself.

Tonight was their good-bye. It was better this way. Any further affection would make the hurt that much sharper. It already cleaved his heart in two with a desperate ache only equaled in depth by the pain experienced as he stood beside his brother's coffin.

Chapter Twenty-Three

It was well past midnight when they parted, and as Lunden paced his bedchamber, brandy in hand, he considered the twisted path of his stay at the Whittingham town house and how he'd managed to make his life more complicated while endeavoring to make it less so.

Amelia enjoyed Vauxhall as he knew she would. The minx. He'd miss her, *terribly,* but she deserved so much more than a regretful husband with a tormented history. She wished for freedom in marriage, strove for independence, and he represented the opposite in every manner imaginable. A caged bird could never fly. He wouldn't clip her wings.

Lost in despair, he startled when a light knock sounded at his door. He'd relieved the valet. His eyes flicked to the clock, the intrusion unexpected.

He opened the panel and breathed a sigh of *relief? Frustration?* His thoughts were too muddled to determine which. His eyes soaked in Amelia on the threshold of his bedchamber.

"May I come in? My brother will be displeased if he sees me at your rooms or worse, gains the information from one of the servants."

He ran his fingers through his hair as he sought to assuage an inner battle.

"Besides, I'll get a pinch in my neck looking up at this angle. It would be most considerate."

Against his better judgment, he stepped to the left and allowed her entry. She scuttled inside without delay, and he imagined her concerned he would change his mind and bar the proposal she'd likely mentally rehearsed. He closed the door and leaned one shoulder against the farthest bedpost, his arms crossed over his chest in what he hoped was a negligent pose. She needed to find her tongue before his brain melted and he no longer harbored the ability to reason.

"Thank you." She sighed with the words.

"What can I do for you?" Damn it all to hell. From where had that question sprung? Not his brain, nor his gut. Apparently, his cock had taken control. One glimpse of Amelia's plump, kissable lips and he turned inside out. What caused this lack of judgment?

Amelia.

She appeared at his door, full of wild hope and untamed goodness, with an earnest appeal for a dishonest man incapable of solving his own problems. The irony was not lost on him. He dared another glance in her direction, the battle to repress anticipation lost by the eager twinkle in her emerald eyes. Why did she torture him so? She wore a silky white wrapper, decorated with lacy pink roses, and the image struck him as ethereal, an angel come to Earth, although he knew her temperament to be anything but heavenly. He needed to dispel these thoughts and quell his desire.

She took a step in his direction and every muscle tensed.

"I need your help. I know you wish to complete your business as soon as possible and this will delay your departure . . . unless something else keeps you here?"

Her quiet question eroded his stoic resolve. Muted candlelight caught the green-gold flecks in her eyes and lent sheen to her magnificent mane of curls. Trapped by her gaze, he forced himself not to react, to deny her pull. He'd decided a decade ago to claim a solitary existence and live outside society. Loneliness inured him to silence and so it should. Due to life's unexplained ironies, he now battled against the unexpected result and the discovery a strong part of him wished to remain in London.

All due to Amelia and her seductive kiss.

An ache of disquiet settled in his chest.

She searched his face, her eyes huge in the reflected light, full of blind belief and some other emotion he couldn't name. Her voice was barely a whisper. "I want you to stay."

Her words of irresistible enticement shone like a crevice of light in his dark soul, as if she'd heard his heart's contemplations and voiced the yearning he struggled to suffocate. He banished the surge of longing, his only defense against the startling power she yielded. Deep down, he would move heaven and earth to have her, if only he wasn't bound for hell, love no longer welcome in his heart.

"You need to go. This can't happen. It won't happen." He shook his head for emphasis, all the while striving in desperation to convince himself the words were for the best, that he didn't need her as a fish needed water, that one glance in her direction did not cause his pulse to lurch. "I owe loyalty to your brother and you deserve better." *Far better than me.*

She pressed her lips together, as if she thought to reply in one manner and then reconsidered. "I deserve better than Collins, but my brother, the man to whom you pledge your loyalty, feels no such allegiance to his sister. I pleaded with him today at luncheon, but the decision has been made. As a boon, I'm granted a one-week courtship to become acquainted with my new husband. Then I am to acquiesce, say my vows, and leave London for a country estate, all without objection." Her voice held a reluctant quiver. "My brother asks too much."

Good God, Matthew hadn't told her about the children. Was her brother mad? How could he condemn her to a drastic change in lifestyle and not confess the outrageous terms? He knew she yearned for a love match, not an uncommon idealistic female vision, but to uproot her from everything familiar and thrust her into marriage and motherhood in one sweep of the pen seemed callous at the least. She fought hard to present a visage of bravery, but the way her voice shook revealed unadulterated fear.

If only he could offer her fortitude. He entertained no illusions of love. Pretending emotions did not exist remained his favored preoccupation, but memories often served as more formidable enemies. Memories brought with them emotion and somehow he knew he would always remember Amelia and the time they'd shared, never mind their kisses and shared intimacies.

He drew a long breath. "You were aware marriage loomed in the near future. There's your father's health to consider and your brother's determination."

"My brother's selfishness," she countered with a bitter note. "He wishes to shirk his responsibility or finagle an enticing gain from this union. How else could he suggest Collins as the most sensible choice? Matthew is so consumed by his involvement with that intellectual society he rarely socializes enough to understand relationships from a woman's point of view." Her voice softened and some of her anger dissipated as she leaned against the opposite bedpost in a reflection of his pose.

"What is it you want?" Foolish question with no good answer, but he asked it anyway.

Their eyes met and held for several breathless minutes. Unable to maintain her crystal gaze, he dropped his eyes to the bed's coverlet, stretched between them as blank as a piece of paper in wait of words left unsaid.

Amelia's heart skipped a beat at his question. What did she want? How could he not know? Had their time together meant so little?

I want a man who makes me feel like you do. Alive. Free. Cherished. I want you. She substituted the words. "I want what every woman desires. A love match, or at the least, a relationship built on friendship and mutual respect."

"Your brother knows this."

"My brother deceives me for his own purpose."

"And you don't believe a congenial relationship with Collins is possible?" The tight set of his mouth revealed how preposterous he considered the proposition.

"No." A wild note curled into her voice and the answer erupted with quick finality. "I want more. I feel nothing when I look at him." She raised her chin and stared into the warm brown depth of his gaze. "Not at all how I feel when I view you." The words fell from her lips as easily as her heart had taken the plunge. She scrutinized his reaction, wandering first from his eyes to the hard set of his jaw, then lower where his shirt parted to a careless vee and exposed the tanned skin of his neck. His pulse lived there and she yearned to place a kiss against his heartbeat.

"Amelia." There was a dark quality in his voice, a husky low timbre, and his stare focused on her mouth as if he wished her words returned. "I should never have taken liberties during your swimming lesson or in the study. I forgot myself. You should be angry with me, at least half as much as I regret the action."

"I have no regrets, nor should you. The loyalty you pledge to Matthew is a virtue he doesn't uphold, epitomized by his selfish decision." She pushed forward from the post and took a single step.

She loved him.

She loved Lunden.

A blissful shiver chased the realization down to the middle of her bones. Faced with the awareness she remained helpless to her brother's machinations, the newly born fact empowered her. "I've no control over my future, but I control now." The soft tread of her feet punctuated each word. "I may have few choices left to me, but I know my mind and own my heart, free to give it to whoever I choose." She stopped before him, her heart drumming against her ribs in a wild tattoo. "And my body . . ." She untied the belt of her wrapper and let it slither to the floorboards. "I offer my body to the man I choose."

"Amelia."

"Yes?" With fingers that trembled only a little, she reached behind her neck and unbuttoned her night rail. Then before she could think otherwise, she angled her shoulders and sent the gown sliding downward in a soft whisper of silk against skin. She stood before him vulnerable and never in more control.

His throat worked as he swallowed whatever objection he meant to voice, his attention a palpable heat.

A cloud passed over the moon, sinking the room in shadow and obstructing the generous glow that flooded the uncurtained windows. The steady rhythm of rain began against the glass panes. If she were of a superstitious nature, she would label the change in weather foreboding, but instead she relaxed, finding comfort in the blue-gray reflection, and exhilaration in her bold decision.

"Amelia."

It was the third time he'd voiced her name, but this time it was no admonishment, the single word a velvet caress. The look in his eyes affected her like warm cognac and she moved forward, no more than the width of one step left between them. Her hands twitched with restless desire. She wanted to run her fingertips across his unshaven jaw, explore the rough sensation before skimming his soft, sensuous mouth, absorbing his strength, his warmth, but she could not. She offered; he must accept. It could be no other way.

The low rumble of thunder underscored the tremulous beat of her heart. The air became too taut to breathe. Why wouldn't he say something? Do something? Time stalled as if she lived the experience in a faraway dream. A sharp strike of lightning rent the sky and exposed the room within a flash of brilliance. She saw his face revealed, amber eyes smoldered with passion, a muscle at work on the side of his jaw.

At last he wet his lips and forced words.

"Put your robe on." His words cut a husky pitch in the stillness.

"No."

Damn her boldness.

He wanted her. He ached for her. But she was not his to take. He'd ended Douglas's life, compromised Matthew's in turn. Ruining Amelia would be unforgivable and deadlier than any of his former sins.

"This isn't a game, Amelia." Heat surged through every nerve as he struggled to recover some sense of equilibrium, his body hard and impatient.

"I'm aware of every choice I make." She sounded unworried, as reckless as her decision. "If you want me clothed, you'll have to do it." Her words were a velvet command, her voice enticement.

A long, drawn silence took hold until he could bear it no longer. Before him, bare as a pagan goddess and perfectly formed, stood his dream come to life. How many evenings had he lain awake envisioning her in the same pose, an elusive deity of lust and pleasure at the edge of his mattress, at the ready to offer him everything he desired but did not deserve?

He knelt near her feet. She made a soft sound in her throat and he felt it on his skin. He kept his eyes forced to the floor and gathered her wrapper, cool against the heat of his palms. He dared not drag his gaze upward. It would take little for his rampant desire to obliterate all control, but while the singular decree burned his brain and his fingers collected the silky cloth puddled near her ankles, his eyes disobeyed, skimming the fluid curve of her calves, the soft skin at the back of her knees, the divine sweetness between her legs. He burned to taste her there, to feel the thrum of her pulse, to press hard kisses to the sensuous velvet of her thighs.

Damn it to hell, he wanted her too much. And wanting was dangerous. Wanting demanded a price, at times so high, he'd become indebted for the rest of his life. Experience taught him this lesson well, but none of it mattered. He ignored logic as his resolve evaporated, and irrepressible emotion took hold.

He rose from where he knelt, smoothing the silk wrapper over each lush curve until in a strong thrust forward he captured her body against his.

Her gasp of pleasure caused an incoherent hurtle of his heart and a wicked grin begged for release. Her lips parted as he leaned in close, his pant of breath warm against her skin. In response he wrapped her tighter, sculpting her luscious feminine form in expensive silk and trapping her arms at her sides.

He lingered on the edge of a treacherous precipice, unable to remember the last time he felt so powerless and so strong, and the more he considered the treasured paradox wrapped within his grasp, the less logic mattered. His world tilted at an incoherent angle, unable to level.

As if on cue, a crack of thunder emphasized the realization, the subsequent flash of lightning illuminating his storm of emotion. Rain beat heavily, thrumming against the windows in an echo of his racing heart. She gave a profound shudder and he allowed his smile freedom.

"My beautiful tempest, is this your wish?" He yearned to capture her delicious mouth in a soul-searing kiss. "Know that life is intractable. There is no second sunrise once the day begins." *He'd learned that lesson well.*

Her nod of agreement sent a rustle of dark ringlets over his fists where they clenched her robe, their satiny softness in competition with the fabric.

"I want this. I want you."

Her oft-maddened reasoning couldn't be trusted, and so he delayed, no matter the blood pounding through his veins and demanded he act.

"You can change your mind. Leave my rooms. Return to your chamber and we'll never speak of this moment." It killed him to voice the words, but he managed, some ill-begotten shred of decency able to pierce his haze of desire. Or perhaps it was his conscience that forced the statements, unwilling to shoulder the blame for further tragedy and careless decision making.

She drew a sharp breath and the tight tip of each breast traced a line on the skin of his forearms, the sensation so intimate, it was as though the silk didn't exist. He fought against the maelstrom of emotions bombarding his better sense.

"Don't you want me?"

Just enough confusion pricked her question.

"Want you? I have all but lost my ability to breathe, my attention honed to your every nuance, my hearing impaired from the blood pounding through my veins." Damn it all to hell, he hated emotion, his body taut as a strung bow.

She appeared dissatisfied with his answer and the corners of her mouth quivered. "Then why do you send me away?"

"Because this is about what's best for you, not me." How long would he be able to hold her close, wrapped in silk and invitation, without giving in to the ferocious urge to take her, devour her, consume the pleasure and freedom her body promised? His hands shook with exigency.

"So, you've decided what's best for me in the same manner my brother plans my future?" She straightened her shoulders, a long breath held.

"Damn it, you know that for a lie." He readjusted his grasp on the wrapper, his fingers threatening mutiny. "You appeared at my door with an innocent plea to my conscience, only to invade this bedchamber, a mythical goddess straight from my midnight dreams, determined to tempt my resistance at a time when I'm fraught with regret and indecision. Don't you dare play victim when you stand here with nothing more than a thin piece of silk to conceal your hidden agenda." The force of his diatribe brought his lips to hover directly above hers, their eyes matched in passionate vehemence, while his fingernails bit into his palms, so hard did he clench the collar of her robe.

The tip of her tongue poked out as she readied a rebuttal, but the careless motion brought the wet heat of her mouth in contact with his, and the stroke of her tongue across his lips reverberated lower as if she'd licked him *there*. A soft whimper escaped her throat and his cock pulsed with arousal. Suppressed desire slipped out of his control and plummeted him over the edge. In a movement of fluid grace and rampant need, he released the silk and swept her into his arms.

Chapter Twenty-Four

He couldn't get enough of her, her jasmine-scented skin an aphrodisiac, the sound of her shallow breath as hypnotic as laudanum. He pressed hot kisses along the lithe column of her neck to her collarbone, licking over the shallow indent where her wild pulse beat hot against his tongue. He relished the gentle vibration of her voice as she uttered her pleasure and progressed across the sensitive shell of her ear to whisper wicked intentions in return before he caught the lobe between his teeth and suckled slowly. He threaded his fingers through her thick mane and drank her gasp, angled her mouth for another ravenous assault.

He hungered for her touch, greedy for more, and when she sighed the sweetest sound, it devastated his soul. She tasted like rebellion and fantasy, everything he ever needed and feared to wish for, no matter how dark the night or desperate the yearning. She destroyed his resolve with enamored images of survival and he drank from her soul, thirsting for every drop of hope she offered.

She set her hand flat to his chest, her fingers at work to free his shirt from his shoulders, the fabric caught by two buttons, soon nothing more than a soft patter upon the floorboards. Her palms spanned his frame, each muscle taut as it jumped in response to her caress, the weight of her breasts against him causing his insides to tighten. Wild heat flooded every nerve ending and settled in his groin. Her skin, smooth as satin, enticed him and enflamed his rampant ardor.

Need overtook logic.

He meant to pull away, to allow them a chance to catch their breath, rethink their actions, but when her right hand stilled over his pounding heart and a smile curled her delicious lips, all reservation broke and he could only answer with a long, deep kiss.

Everywhere he pulsed with need, a desire to which he had no understanding. Her body against his was pure agony and the sweetest torture. Her fingers fumbled with the closures of his trousers. With alacrity she met with success, his sole duty to kick them away as her palms slid over his buttocks, his smalls discarded with similar haste.

He retracted his gaze to measure her expression, and she grinned, her twist of the lips a combination of mischief and delight before she leaned in to offer another kiss, wild and impatient, yet slow and sensual, a contradiction as always, innocence and eroticism combined with every stroke of her tongue. He sought support against the bedpost, all at once intoxicated, his mind a torrent of spinning emotion, the blood rushing lower, where her fingers stroked his erection in a tentative grasp.

He rolled his back against the post and pressed her to the mattress without breaking their kiss, his body a buffer to the fall. With his hands framing her waist, he turned her on the bed, but she fought the motion, overthrowing his attempt and resettling so she straddled him, lady conqueror in rule above. A flash of lightning announced her victory, the consequent thunder akin to the laughter rumbling within his chest. He looked up, reaching in reverence to trail his fingertips along the length of her arms, feel the weight of each breast in his hands.

She lowered her lips to his and placed a slow sensual kiss. Like a fairy atop a mortal, she offered him eternal ecstasy, full knowing no matter how fleeting, once the sun rose, day would reveal the truth of it all.

He'd buried emotion for so long, denied pleasure of any kind, the joy of Amelia astride him, wet, hot, and wanting, threatened to ruin him in far worse a way than the danger he posed to her reputation. His mind struggled to ignore the perilous consequences while his body applauded his actions.

In a subtle movement, she slid lower, leaned in for another kiss, and allowed her soft breasts to trace against his chest. His heart dared to explode from thrice its rhythm. She nibbled at his mouth, licked the corners of his lips, tasted him as if he were a sweet to be savored, and all the while his cock caressed the silky curve of her bottom, nestled against him in a velvet tight fit. It was unbearable delight. Death by wicked fantasy.

He begged to succumb.

He stopped thinking.

He barely breathed.

She moved her hands over him, learning his body, exploring his heat, her innocence abandoned under the demanding force of curiosity. She kissed his neck, licked the indent near his clavicle, inhaled his scent with a murmur of satisfaction as if to memorize every detail of his person. Then she rose again, her palms pressed flat against his chest.

Time ceased, the only reminder of reality the drumming beat of rain against the roof, the refraction of light and echo of thunder in the persisting storm.

She raised her hips and adjusted her body above his. The head of his arousal throbbed against her wet heat. She

lowered herself, guiding him inside in a slow, mind-melting
sensation that left him devastated and aching. Tight. So very
tight, and hot. His vision blurred. His body beseeched her
mercy and he groaned, unable to form coherent words as
she watched him, her expression one of beauty and fervent
need. She rose again, this time sure in her measure, settling
atop him and encasing his thick length in one determined
sweep. He felt resistance and pushed past it as she melted
into him. He growled his pleasure, grasped her bottom, and
held her hips in place. He matched her eyes and allowed his
long-lost joy to break free.

Her hair tumbled about her shoulders in enticing disarray, her kiss-swollen lips formed the slightest curve, and her
full breasts swayed as she leaned forward with another searing kiss. His fingers faltered, tracing the curve of one dark,
silky curl against the alabaster silk of her skin. Then he
skimmed his palms along the length of her legs wrapped
tight against his hips to lock their bodies together as perfectly fit as two puzzle pieces.

"Tonight you are mine, Lunden."

He dared not voice his immediate retort. *Forever I will
remember this moment. Forever you will live in my heart.*
"It appears you've successfully subdued me."

She half smiled in answer before she began a sensual
rhythm, her body revealing every emotion kept concealed.
He could not keep his gaze from her.

Above him, a goddess of pure power, a forbidden dream,
naive yet so enticing, worked his body, *their bodies,* as if
they'd been created for each other. Her eyes were half closed,
yet the passion in their emerald depths tore at his heart. Dark
ringlets spread about her ivory shoulders like a wild storm,
her cheeks kissed pink whether from ardor or exertion he
could not know, and she appeared breathtakingly beautiful, silhouetted in a golden glow by the burning coals in
the fireplace.

He reached for her face, cradling her cheek in a tender caress before skimming his palm down the delicate curve of her neck, across her velvet smooth shoulder and farther to settle both hands on either side of her hips. With a firm hold he anchored her to him and lifted off the bed to bury himself deeper into her lovely warmth. Her delighted moan of approval encouraged him to repeat the motion. Again and again, they moved in faultless unison, stroke for stroke, as if the sweet madness they created was not new, but a practiced symphony, long rehearsed and perfected.

He wanted it to last and last, but she decimated any semblance of his control each time she arced her back in tune to his thrusts. His body throbbed with want. His hands trembled at her hips as he fought back release. She laughed then, a delighted sound, and leaned down for a tender kiss that threatened to destroy the last vestiges of restraint with its beauty. He kissed her back with hunger and yearning, with every emotion he'd locked away for years, the turmoil of loneliness and despair of regret, hoping, wishing, the intimacy of the moment would vanquish his dark secrets forever. And she understood his need, answering his kiss in kind.

He turned her then, bringing her to the bed with care as he positioned above, their frenetic love play turned incredibly cherished in the span of a few heartbeats. He searched her face for any sign of hesitation, but when he saw only desire, he entered her again with gentle fervor, anxious to lose himself in their intimacy. Like the escalating storm outside, the cadence of their pace increased to a level of exquisite torture and he could do little to temper his thrusts, driven by more than need, too captivated by sensation to examine any other emotion.

"Take me. Make me yours." Her husky purr urged him to continue. Her fingers dug into his biceps. Her skin glistened with a fine sheen of sweat. And her eyes fell closed as her muscles tightened and shuddered, a shaky breath coming fast as sensation consumed her.

"Oh God, Amelia." His voice was no more than a strained rasp and he could hold back no longer, his release upon him fast and furious, consumed in heat and passion as if he'd fallen into the sun.

With desperate effort, he pulled from her at the last moment, his climax as powerful as a secret revealed. He spilled himself on the bedsheets before collapsing, exhausted and spent.

Amelia awoke, wrapped in Lunden's possessive embrace. She blinked twice, clearing the contented haze from her mind and sweeping away the last vestiges of sleep. She relished the moment, the delightful soreness of her body a testament she hadn't dreamed the entire episode. How foolish she'd been to fear the intimacies of a wedding night. The sudden twinge of penetration had been fleeting, a sharp pang and then gone, but the aftermath, the incredible loving that followed, was worth any price she'd have to pay.

She stole a glance in Lunden's direction. The first rays of dawn shone through the window limning his profile in newborn sunlight, bringing with it a fresh rush of memories, her body atop his, matched, high and tight. She sighed, the result of her actions the night before settling in her bones with satisfied pleasure. Where she once sought Charlotte's advice, she now trusted her instinct. Lovemaking was not painful, as she'd been told. The deep-rooted fear that consumed her thoughts and perpetuated fear no longer existed. Thank heavens she'd eavesdropped on the scullery maids often enough to learn the proper manner to seduce a man. By the serene expression gracing Lunden's face in sleep, she'd succeeded.

Content, her eyes memorized his features. How differently he appeared in sleep. The worried crease that marred his brow with frequency was gone, and his mouth, his wondrously skillful mouth, was smooth and relaxed instead of pressed into a line of intense constraint. He'd smiled last night—a true, rare, wonderful smile that spoke straight to her heart. What she wouldn't give to cause the reaction more often. Here was a man who made the decision to live apart from society, exiled and neglected by his own choosing, absent from the comfortable companionship of friendship and camaraderie. Was his struggle so different than her own? Life was too short to live without affection, trust, and most importantly, love. Yet he'd shut himself off from those very same emotions, accepting his exclusion as penance for some painful, secretive tragedy years ago. If only he'd confide in her, reveal the torment of his heart, perhaps she could bring him as much happiness as he granted her last evening.

He murmured and turned. His eyes eased open as if he knew she stared at him in admiration and uncomfortable with her assessment, sought to break the contact.

"Good morning."

His voice, a husky thrum, caused a wave of pleasure to wash over her and she smiled, aware warmth crept up her cheeks.

"Good morning," she answered, just as quietly.

"You're still here."

Did she detect a note of surprise combined with a thread of seriousness? Did he think she would skulk away during the night?

"That's not wise." His voice intruded on her musings with a sudden dose of common sense. "If someone enters to tend the fire, you'll be discovered. We can't risk your brother learning your whereabouts."

"I plan to speak to Matthew this morning." She rose from the security of Lunden's embrace, wrapping the sheet around her torso and leaning on her arm, bent at the elbow, to better view his reaction. His eyes searched her face as she continued. "I never intended to marry Lord Collins."

He snapped forward from the bed, his face a mask of stern determination. Something fierce and raw flashed in his eyes and the immediate reaction took her by surprise.

"This changes nothing, our being together. I thought you understood. No matter what pleasure we pursued, I have every intention to resolve my business and leave London permanently." His resolute voice came from deep in his chest.

She hesitated and he continued.

"This"—he motioned between them with a wave of his hand—"doesn't mean I'm going to marry you. Don't misconstrue the situation." He allowed the words to sink in. "I'm not husband material." He ended in a bleak voice that broke her heart more, his unexpected reply stalling her immediate retort.

"I never intended to marry Lord Collins. I've already secured an alternative future." The latter statement gained his direct attention, the intensity in his brown eyes urging her to explain. "My brother cannot barter me if I'm already married to another."

"Don't ask this of me, Amelia. You'll not receive the answer you seek."

For a long moment she said nothing. The sorrowful emotion in his whisky-warm eyes blunted her curiosity and she discarded every question that rose to mind, unwilling to be the source of further sadness. Here was a man that carried the silent contrition of his scars inside, secured behind walls of his own making. Pain speared her heart. What would it take for him to confess the secrets haunting his soul? Perhaps by his nature, it proved an impossibility. Dukes are closemouthed concerning family secrets. Dukes notoriously kept everything important locked away tight, and *her duke* had more to hide than most.

"Hear me out, please. I won't settle, lonely and unloved. I won't by choice, condemn my future, relinquish all control, and sacrifice my freedom."

Gone was the serenity he'd found in slumber. His lips pressed in a flat line of tolerance but he didn't interrupt, though she wondered at how closely her words cut to the bone. "Matthew can't arrange my betrothal if I'm already married. That's where I'll need your help." He made to object and she continued in a flurry of explanation. "Keep my brother at bay while I institute my plan. I've a candidate in mind. I'll need only a few days to secure his agreement. Matthew has given me a weeklong courtship with Lord Collins. With your help, I'll meet with success." She rose from the bed and began to dress. His eyes followed each of her movements, although his expression remained stoic and detached.

"And how will this secure you a happy future, married to some codswallop to please your father and thwart your brother?"

"I have little choice but to act, otherwise I'll find myself given to Lord Collins by the end of the week in satisfaction of some unknown bargain he's struck with my brother." Her voice dropped off in a show of resignation. "At least I will have made my own choice." She pinned him with a heartfelt stare. "Just as I did last night."

The mention of their lovemaking stole his anger. His features softened, his eyes once again warm and clear. "Speak to your brother before you act rashly. Give him the opportunity to hear you out and listen to reason."

She moved to his side of the bed. He'd pushed up during

their discussion, now propped against the headboard. Her wrapper was knotted tightly around her waist, and she shifted with impatience, her bare feet cold against the wooden floorboards. "I will, but I doubt I'll find compromise where there's been nothing but autocracy." She raised her eyes to his. "Why must it be like this?"

"Because I wish the best for you." He reached forward and stroked her cheek in a tentative caress. "I want for you to dance at balls, make friendships unmarred by secrets, move through society with the respect you deserve."

His words did little to soothe the blunt truth he wouldn't reveal the burden of his past and share a future in her arms.

"I understand." Her answer was mostly deception.

"What you've given me is most precious."

She closed her eyes for a long blink, absorbing his words. "Repay my gift with your help in this matter."

A hard knock at the door dashed any hopes of further discussion. In a series of curt movements, he managed his smalls and trousers before motioning for her to hide behind the drawn bed curtains, out of sight.

"Open up, Lunden. It's an emergency and I need to speak to you." Her brother's voice intruded, a note of urgency punctuating his commands.

With caution, she watched through a slit in the fabric as Lunden raked his fingers through his hair, perhaps assembling his thoughts, before he cracked the door hardly an inch. Still, her brother burst into the room.

"This is no time for hesitation." Matthew's harried distress resounded within the quiet. "Amelia's gone. Run away, I suppose. She's impulsive, selfish, and irrational, yet I suspect I pushed her too hard and she's taken matters into her own hands."

"How do you know this?"

Amelia dared not peer around the edge of the curtains, although she breathed easier at the calm Lunden managed.

"She hasn't slept in her bed and she dismissed her maid before yesterday evening. Mary hasn't seen her since. A footman reported he saw her enter a hackney last evening. The pieces fit, and it adds up to her worst feat yet. She has no idea what's at stake. Collins will wring my neck."

"What power does he hold over you?" A splash of water indicated Lunden's use of the wash basin. His nonchalance would either mollify or exacerbate the situation, Amelia knew not which.

"We've already made arrangements and signed petitions. Collins is impatient to see this done. Never mind the contracts are soaked with black ink from Pandora's interference. That infernal cat's purpose aims at causing me misery. I'll be relieved when Amelia marries for no other reason than to take that evil feline with her."

Amelia recognized the clip of boot heels as her brother paced the room, his body casting a narrow shadow as he passed the slim break dividing the velvet curtains. She tried to summon concern for his discontent, but found she hadn't any. Instead a faint smile curled her lips at his misconstrued conclusions.

"Find Collins another bride." Lunden's tone grew stronger, and her smile bloomed. He was her hero, no matter he refused the role.

"That's impossible. Everything impinges on Amelia's hand in marriage." Matthew paused, his voice so near, he likely stood beside the bed with only a panel of fabric separating them. A shiver of dread whispered through her.

"Amelia has no desire to marry that odious man. Have you considered your part in this problem? Perhaps you'd do well to speak to her with compassion instead of command."

"Suddenly you're the master of delicate emotions?" Matthew's question sliced the air and his pacing resumed. She drew the curtain aside the scarcest breadth and peered out with one eye. "My sister rarely makes the right decision.

She's ruled by emotion and is shortsighted. Had she not done such a splendid job of alienating society's finer gentlemen, she would have more choice in her future. Instead she acted without a care while Father's health steadily declines. It's selfishness, pure and simple."

Unable to voice her retort, she fisted the sheets to satisfy her anger. How dare Matthew speak of her with blatant disrespect and accusation as if she'd disregarded Father's health? He would label *her* selfish, when he machinated her marriage for personal gain?

"I disagree. She deserves to make her own choice. No one's future should be dictated. I'm acquainted with the outcome of that course of action." Melancholy laced Lunden's angry tone and her heart squeezed at the price he'd endured for his decisions.

"Perhaps, but your situation is far from convention. Our actions that night foretold our futures. What happened afterward . . ." Matthew tapped his cane against the side of his boot.

"You've fared well enough." Lunden's words snapped sharp and Amelia's eyes flared with the sudden vehemence.

"Truth. And the path you chose—"

"I had little choice. How much better had a bullet pierced my heart instead of your leg? Your wounds healed. Mine remain infected."

She bit her lower lip to prevent a gasp as Lunden's admittance spiked through her.

"It didn't have to be that way. No one expected you to sacrifice your youth." Matthew's rebuttal escalated the disagreement and his voice rose with anger.

"No? I kept the funeral a private affair, yet it still fueled the fire of suspicion and condemnation. I withdrew to the country, but guilt and regret followed me, anxious to haunt my nights and darken my days. Don't speak to me of choice."

The room fell strangely quiet and Amelia barely breathed.

Heartache clogged her throat. At last, Matthew's voice rent the silence.

"We digress. Dragging up the past serves little purpose now. My sister's missing and needs to be found. The time for compromise is over. Left to her own device, I have no doubt she'd choose some impudent pup for a husband, one barely out of leading strings, with a plan to run roughshod over him. Meanwhile the oaf, beguiled by her beauty, would thank her afterward for the humiliation. That's a recipe for boredom, which quickly evolves into trouble. Dismissing the mollycoddled husband, her well-being would fall to my shoulders and the responsibility of unraveling her future tomfoolery threatens me with a megrim."

"You paint your sister in a very poor light and oversimplify the matter in an effort to ease your conscience and dismiss your personal gain."

Her brother laughed in response, but the sound was bitter, not amused. "Clever girl. So she's dragged you under her spell and somehow solidified your support, an admirable effort, but all for naught. There's nothing she can do to deter me." His voice brooked no compromise. "Running away will accomplish little. I have men seeking her whereabouts right now. Collins expects his bride and he will have her."

"Not if I've given myself to another." Temper unfurled, Amelia stepped from behind the bed curtains. She angled her chin with a confident thrust and locked eyes with Matthew. "I refuse to be owned nor bartered."

Comprehension flared in her brother's eyes as he took in her disheveled assembly. With a grunt of outrage, he flung his cane to the floor and launched at Lunden with fists raised.

"Traitor!" His jaw hard with fury, he spat the word. "I

asked you to find her a husband, not seduce her, you lying bastard."

Lunden made no motion to move, nor raise his fists.

"Matthew!" Amelia rushed across the room, but her brother thrust his arm out to ward her away.

"Stay back, Amelia. This doesn't concern you."

Something in his tone stopped her cold. There'd be no reasoning with him.

"Of course not." Her stomach clenched in a tight hot knot and her voice shook with sarcastic emotion. "Just as my marriage is none of my business."

She darted her eyes to Lunden. He made no retreat as Matthew advanced, and when her brother landed the first punch to his midsection, the dull thud of his fist against Lunden's bare body brought tears to her eyes. She released a strangled cry as the impact sent Lunden backward, only a step, yet he remained stoic, with no attempt to deflect Matthew's attack.

"So I'm good enough to call friend, but unfit to court your sister."

Lunden's voice sounded calm, although Amelia's heart beat a mad rhythm. Matthew charged with effort, his limp a hindrance; still, Lunden didn't take advantage. Her brother landed a sharp jab, a red weal forming near Lunden's clavicle and lower, across the skin of his ribs.

"Court her? Do you believe me a fool? I understand what happened here, under my roof, at the extension of my hospitality." Matthew lunged, catching Lunden in the sternum. Still Lunden stood unprotected, making no effort to defend the onslaught. "Fight, for I won't hold back no matter your refusal to engage." Another punch landed and an agonizing moan escaped her.

"I have no reason to fight you." The words were said through clenched teeth.

"Matthew, you must stop." Tears flowed down her cheeks and she wiped them away, her plea broken by emotion. "Please." Her brother paid no heed.

"I asked you to help see her wed, not take her to bed, you lying arse." His limp more pronounced, Matthew repositioned on one leg before resettling with another advance.

"I've never lied to you." Lunden grunted and staggered, impacted by the power of Matthew's left hook as it caught his right shoulder.

Again Amelia approached, but this time Lunden warned her away, his eyes gleaming with resolve. "Leave us."

She would do no such thing.

"Raise your fists and let's finish this." Matthew connected with Lunden's jaw and the punch snapped his head back, the sound accompanied by Amelia's demand they cease at once.

"Have I ever bemoaned my leg? Blamed you for the results of that night? I have not." Matthew swung and missed, Lunden having swayed to the side. "I accepted my fate for our foolhardy plan because I urged you to follow Douglas. I hold partial blame for the tragic events. Don't think I live without bitter regrets."

"Aah, but your life wasn't ruined, was it? Your reputation not maligned. Instead society viewed you as the victim and carved another scar into my soul. Dare I forget the *London Times* and their callous headlines or the scandalous inquiries of my motives while I attempted to accept my brother's passing. I alone dealt with the insult and ostracism." As if shoring himself for the next blow, Lunden straightened his shoulders and faced Matthew undaunted.

"My parents carted me to the country to heal while speculation circulated. By the time I returned to the city, you had left, your home locked tight. Your butler refused to accept messages on your behalf." Matthew rolled his shoulders and leveled a solid punch to Lunden's stomach.

"I'd begun mourning." Lunden's words were low, his back pressed against the bedpost, his eyes dimmed by resignation.

"You've never finished." Matthew drew his arm back, set to pummel Lunden despite his refusal to shield himself against the strike.

"Fight him, Lunden. Hit him. Make him stop. Please." Amelia's high-pitched demand countered her brother's action, stalling his arm midair.

"So I see where your loyalty lies. Perhaps my remorse shouldn't be so great that I bargained you to Collins." Matthew shot her a glare, a fast flick of warning, then threw his arm back again.

"I love him!" She nearly shouted the words and the room fell eerily quiet, so much so, the sound of the hallway clock chiming the hour cut through the heavy tension as if to break a terrible spell. She struggled to breathe, her breast rising and falling with the extent of her fury.

Both men turned in her direction and she brought herself to words, emotion fighting for attention regardless an enormous vulnerability consumed her. "Leave him be, Matthew. I love him. Nothing you do or say can change the way I feel."

Lunden's expression softened. A peaceful calm replaced the usual shuddered darkness and as time stretched, she couldn't sever the intensity of the moment. Her heartbeat filled her breast with a steady thrum. She ignored her brother in her peripheral vision, his profile blurred by fresh tears. Instead she stared into Lunden's whisky-warm gaze in hope her eyes conveyed the depth of emotion growing stronger with every breath.

"I want you out." With a silent vengeance Matthew threw a final punch, and Lunden crumbled to the floor.

Chapter Twenty-Five

Beaten. He deserved to be punished. Lunden clenched his teeth as a cloth pressed against his sore jaw forcing reality to sweep clear the foggy shadows of his mind. He peeled his eyes open and raised a hand to fend off the unnecessary ministrations, only to meet with smooth, soft skin. He retracted his fingers at once. Amelia hovered over him, her brows knit with worry, her lips set in a determined line.

"Don't move until I stop the bleeding."

Her voice, as rigid as her shoulders, conveyed her concern and he grimaced in knowing he'd caused her distress. Mistaking his expression for one of pain, she tutted a small sound and moved the cool cloth to his right cheekbone. He might have smiled were his lower lip not swollen and clumsy.

Pockets of light from the fire cast a warm glow outlining her profile, as if an avenging angel intent on mending his soul, her halo a billow of dark curls. Surrendering to the care, he closed his eyes and absorbed the luxury of her touch. All too soon he would be left bereft, but he locked away those feelings, crowding them down in the dark, lonely corners where they belonged.

Still a bit disoriented, he allowed a dormant memory to take hold, too defeated to squelch it in his usual practice. He was a child, chasing his brother about the countryside, left behind no matter how hard his short legs pumped in a struggle to keep pace, reaching Douglas only when he'd reclined beneath a tall oak to enjoy an apple as if taunting he had time for leisure, his younger brother never fast enough. As he approached, Douglas discarded the half-eaten fruit and swung to the lowest branches of the tree, climbing with an efficiency afforded by his strong build and long legs. Lunden stood at the base, eyes cast upward. He leapt for the lowest branch, but failed, the limb scant inches from his reach. His brother's laughter rained down around him in kind to the leaves shaken loose from his ascent; Lunden, far below on the ground, peered after him, longing and admiration intertwined in his gaze, devastated to be left behind.

He flicked his eyes open and a vague restlessness blanketed his heart as he blinked hard. It was nothing more than warped hero-worship that goaded him to shadow Douglas all those years ago, although perhaps his brother cultivated that competitiveness in envy of a spare's carefree purposelessness in life, rather than the strict demands endured as the future duke.

The memory left him damnably raw and in search of distraction. He focused on Amelia as she crossed the room with a snifter of brandy and set it on the floor near his elbow. She leaned across his form to examine his injuries in the window's light, pressing two fingers along a particularly tender bruise.

Lunden felt no pain.

Instead, with eyes heavy-lidded, he assessed her bodice, mere inches from his bare chest and confined in the same silky wrapper that ignited his defeat. The delicious scent of jasmine lulled his senses and soothed the hurts, only to fuel his yearning. Despite the inappropriateness of the situation and the action of the last hour, he swelled with heat for her. His was a hopeless soul.

"That's the best I can do." Seemingly pleased with her efforts, she released a faint sigh and drew back from where she'd kneeled beside him on the floor. "Would you like to stand?"

He wouldn't voice what he truly desired.

"Thank you." He brought himself to his feet too quickly and set a hand on the bedpost to regain equilibrium. "I deserved the thrashing, but I appreciate your attention all the same." He did well in keeping the bite of regret from his words. Matthew had called him a traitor, and the insult cut deep, no matter it proved an appropriate label.

She bent and retrieved the snifter from the floorboards, pressing it to his chest. Her fingers, cool and delicate in their featherlight touch, reached beneath his skin to caress his heart and remind of her power to disrupt his balance. He'd allowed her to distract him from his purpose, and in turn instigated more problems than alleviate them. Yet on some indistinct level, he remained aware her kiss was the cause he'd returned to London, her love the reason he hadn't perished under a mountain of self-loathing years ago. Still, he couldn't allow himself the extravagance of her affection regardless the aching desperation of his soul.

"I meant what I said earlier." She smiled, her eyes twinkling as warm as the afternoon sun. "Mine were not careless words."

He knew that well. Her declaration had slammed into him with more force than Matthew's punches, yet he dared not return the sentiment. Love equaled pain. History taught that lesson twice through the unexpected deaths of his parents and brother. He wouldn't develop the affection, wouldn't fall in love. The despicable emotion was complicated and inconvenient, more weakness than strength. And were he to love Amelia and then lose her, death would not be enough to end his suffering.

He raised his eyes to hers. A fringe of black curls framed her cheek and his fingers itched to brush them away as he pulled her into kisses, fierce and ravenous. With a resolute effort, he shook off the absurd preoccupation and readied an answer.

"I don't take your words lightly." He paused for a contemplative swallow of brandy, shoring himself for the hurt he would inflict. "Although I can't speak in kind. I've overstayed my welcome and will be packed and gone by dinner this evening. Whatever unsettled business remains can be resolved from a room at an inn." He spoke more to himself, yet the words fell, hollow and meaningless, into the void between them.

"I'm sorry. I'm so sorry, Lunden. I . . ." She swallowed, emotion causing her lips to tremble. "I only thought of myself when I stepped from the bed curtains. I acted in fear of losing you—" A stilted exhale shuddered through her. "I will never forget you."

She looked entirely too young, afraid, and most of all, vulnerable. His heart, that traitorous organ that betrayed him repeatedly, nearly stopped beating with her honest admittance.

An indefinable stillness blanketed the room.

"I assure you, I'm unremarkable." He turned away, unwilling to watch as he destroyed the bond they'd created only hours before. "Someday you'll give your heart to another, a man worthy of your loyalty and devotion, and I'll become a distant memory, perhaps forgotten altogether. That's my hope, at least." He cleared his throat as if to dismiss the subject.

"I'll have nothing to give. I love you with everything I am."

The words sliced through his heart, shredding it to ribbons.

"No, you will forget." He whispered the reply, a world of resignation in his words. Still she persisted, her soft padded steps at his back.

"In the same fashion you've forgotten your brother?"

Had she not already destroyed his heart, her inquiry would have accomplished the task, yet he couldn't summon his usual cloak of anger and self-recrimination. Perhaps it was time to stop lamenting the past and look forward. She deserved to understand the extent of his despair. He could offer her that, if not what she truly asked of him.

With a resounding exhale, he settled against the bedpost and conjured the events of that evening a decade past.

"Matthew and I were comrades in tomfoolery, often in trouble and no doubt an irritant to my brother. The vast difference in age and my persistent desire to gain Douglas's approval added fuel to a fire that often threatened to consume our tenuous relationship. Douglas assumed the responsibilities of the duchy in much the same fashion as I came to the title years later. Having a dukedom thrust upon you as you mourn the loss of a loved one is no simple undertaking, no matter he'd been groomed for the role since birth. Our parents' death came unexpectedly and he quickly discovered his life greatly altered. I took the news hard and turned to him for comfort, yet he turned away. I will never know why. We did not discuss such things. Douglas was forbiddingly private, often lecturing my behavior and warning of scandal that could disparage the Scarsdale reputation.

"On the night of his death, my birthday, Matthew and I took to celebrating. I had no idea Douglas would arrive at the tavern or a public scene would ensue. Nilworth was there, as were several other gentlemen of our social circle. Douglas and I argued, and I spoke hastily. Yet despite my ill ease, I continued to make poor decisions. I sought him out when I returned home, hoping to repair my most recent digression, but he wanted no part of a conversation, disgusted with my behavior and in a hurry to continue his evening elsewhere. It was his usual habit. He existed as a vault with his personal affairs, as it should be, despite I questioned him often. I felt rejected and confused that he, my only living relative, would not spare time.

"When Matthew suggested I shadow Douglas and discover where he went, where he chose to spend his time rather than with me on the day of my birth, I foolishly believed I could still make amends. So I saddled my mount and followed him to Lamb Street. I watched from afar as he climbed the steps to a neat town house and let himself in by key. Intrigued by the secret location, I dismounted and went to the window, glued to the scene I witnessed inside. My brother embraced another gentleman in passion. I was unprepared for the shock of my discovery and couldn't move from that spot. Another foolish decision. Though the light burned low, my brother noticed me. I will never forget his look of betrayal, and for a heartbeat, the flash of utter fear in his eyes.

"The rest exists as a blurry memory, although I lived it, time has preserved it in distant flashes of chaos and pain. Afraid I'd destroyed any shred of relationship existing between us, I fled, but Douglas knew the area well, while I did not. He circumvented my escape, intent on arriving home first. I chased after him, to explain and to offer acceptance. At last, I possessed understanding of his reserved nature."

Lunden darted his eyes to Amelia, poised near the foot of the bed. Her expression gave little away, although her brows dipped in a show of compassion and encouragement.

"I'd nearly caught up when his horse stumbled on a loose cobblestone and threw him. His body fell so still I knew the unthinkable truth before I ever knelt beside him. Then I panicked, youth and emotion in control of my actions.

Douglas feared scandal, exposure, and yet I wept in a London street beside his dead body. I needed to act. I needed to bear responsibility, a foreign concept in my youth.

"Struggling, I managed to return home with Douglas's lifeless body. Your brother waited in the stables and in a rush of broken explanation and confusion I urged him to assist me in carrying Douglas into the house. We exited the stable when the shot was fired. The agony that eroded every cell of my being was duly replaced with fear for Matthew's life, for I couldn't have his death on my conscience as well. Stable hands emerged at the sound and together, we returned Douglas and Matthew to my home. A few servants sought the gunman, but no one was ever discovered." He grimaced, a forlorn emptiness dragging at his soul. "Now you know what I would never confess to another living soul. Even Matthew knows little of the truth from that night."

Lost in the bitter retelling, he didn't notice Amelia beside him until the tentative touch of her fingers on his shoulder gained his attention. He backed away, a pang of regret lancing his chest, unwilling to accept comfort for the circumstances punishing him.

"Mistakes are forgivable. The very definition of the word declares it an action without intent."

Her soft-spoken reassurance was well intended, but forgiveness was unheard of. "For a year after Douglas's death I hardly spoke a civil word to anyone who dared cross my path. It's a wonder a single servant remained in my employ when I consider my obstinate surly demeanor. I'm still that man, although I've buried my anger rather than wear it as a flag for all to see. I'm a blight, unequal to your measure."

She snapped her eyes upward with a furious flash of green, but something in his expression must have stopped her words.

How could he face a lifetime without her? If only . . .

Wretched hope dared high in his chest, but he dispelled the misplaced emotion and strove to recover his composure. He would endure, learn to live without Amelia much the same way he survived without Douglas. She deserved better. She deserved a full, rich life. And he would remember her always. Her breathless sigh caught on his lips, her incredible beauty, much the same way he treasured his brother's pocket watch.

"You will marry Collins and obey your brother's bidding." He ran a finger along the rim of his glass and forced the words past his lips in an unbreakable voice. She looked instantly appalled, although her chin rose a full inch. Then she stared at him with a mixture of determination and impunity that exposed her heart.

"I vowed long ago not to be forced into a loveless match and I remain resolute to that promise. If you will not have me, I'll marry another. A gentleman of my choosing. I've already decided."

The minx had someone in mind. How convenient. *How irritating.* Though it mattered little. It was better this way.

"Then so be it." He lowered his eyes to veil true emotion, though a hint of annoyance crept into his voice. "We both knew this day would come and to pretend it wouldn't was pure folly. I came to London to complete unfinished business with every intent to return to Beckford Hall immediately after." He paused to allow the words to settle. "I wish you much happiness in your future, Amelia."

But she may not have heard his latter statement as the door closed with an emphatic click.

Chapter Twenty-Six

"So what will you do?" Charlotte posed the question with an equal amount of concern and curiosity.

Amelia searched for an easy answer. She despised her neediness, imposing on her friend at an hour likely to ignite Lord Dearing's censure, but at a loss to remain home where the walls weren't thick enough, resolve not strong enough, to keep her from Lunden while he prepared to leave. It had taken every ounce of survival she possessed to turn her back and walk out of his rooms.

"I can't marry Lord Collins. If ever I feared becoming nothing, he would prove it to be true. I'd be less than nothing actually, letters on a line, a nonentity." Her breath left her lungs in a despairing exhale and Charlotte squeezed her hand before setting to work on the tea tray.

"And Scarsdale?"

"I don't wish to speak of it." She tempered her declaration with an apology. "I'm sorry. Forgive me." She closed her eyes, recalling the haunted expression on Lunden's face as he shared the dark secrets locked so tightly to his soul. Her vision blurred from fresh tears, not for her heartache, but for his. He believed himself blackened, when she knew him to be loyal to a fault, passionate, courageous, and above all else, loving. How ironic, *she* epitomized hypocrisy. She sat beside Charlotte, resolute no man would hold her at a disadvantage, yet Lunden owned her heart. What greater disadvantage existed than unrequited love? She'd forever remain stranded in turmoil if she didn't discover a path through her misery.

"Is Lord Collins so very distasteful?"

"He's decidedly older and bold in his opinion." She wrinkled her nose in blatant disgust, recalling his lecherous leer and innuendo as she'd accompanied him through the garden after dinner. "Of course, his advanced years could be held as an advantage. Widows have ample freedom, above societal censure."

"Amelia!" Charlotte's teacup rattled on the saucer as she replaced it with haste. "You're not thinking clearly." She adjusted the sugar bowl and creamer as if to reorder her thoughts. "Besides, how much freedom would you enjoy caring for six children were Lord Collins to expire quickly?"

"Little. Although I doubt he's interested in the children beyond their monetary value or else he wouldn't be in such a rush to secure a wife to relegate the task."

"Let's hope his inheritance is sufficient enough to guarantee you a comfortable life."

"Money is my least concern. Father's health has steadily declined, despite his relocation." Her voice dropped to a melancholic tone, her conscience pricked whenever she thought of her father. "I doubt my relationship with Matthew will ever mend and Lunden—I fear I will never see him again, no matter he consumes my every thought." Whenever she recalled his words, her future shattered in so many pieces she worried she'd never feel whole again. Fear of the unknown held great power, but as she'd often advised Charlotte, the militant motivator should not dictate life's path. How trite her advice sounded when applied to her personal condition.

"Lady Amelia, this is an unanticipated visit, I presume." Lord Dearing stood within the threshold of the doorway, his posture as crisp as the pristine folds creasing his Gladstone collar. He bowed politely before treading farther into the room, his attention focused solely on Charlotte. "Is this not your scheduled hour for pianoforte practice? I wasn't notified you chose to forgo your routine and take tea with Lady Amelia." He scowled to emphasize his disappointment although his chiding tone and choice of phrasing served as sufficient.

"Lord Dearing, how wonderful to see you again." Amelia offered her greeting in an attempt to defuse the awkward hostility in the room.

Charlotte managed a contrite, yet amiable smile, although Amelia could feel the tension radiating from her dearest friend. Pushing aside her inner turmoil, she grasped onto the unexpected opportunity to improve Charlotte's situation, despite her own future dangling by a thread.

"You must pardon my intrusion. I encroached on Charlotte's routine. I wouldn't have done so if her caring nature and kindhearted friendship weren't such a balm to my soul at this troubling time." She met his gaze squarely although she stood a tad taller than he. Despite his sour attitude, he cut a fine figure, his hair the color of fresh cut hay, his eyes a deep brown that could offer affection and warmth if he allowed the sentiments. Still, he represented a tone of domestic comfort, as much as Lunden's appearance suggested forbidden secrecy and dark adventure.

"Indeed." He measured her admission with the scope of his glance and Amelia straightened her shoulders. "I only mention it because I'm accustomed to Charlotte's musical accompaniment as I review correspondence in my study. The absence of her melodies went noticed."

Would he not smile? Would he not expose the veiled

compliment and brighten his wife's view of their relationship by expressing how much he enjoyed her skill on the pianoforte? No wonder Charlotte balanced on eggshells, living each day in precarious confusion of her husband's expectations. What was it Lord Dearing withheld with his forbidding reserve? And did his restricted attitude permeate all shades of his personality? In a revelation, Amelia understood why Charlotte shared little concerning marital intimacy. Viewing the man in front of her, Amelia doubted he would recognize passion were it to climb the steps to the door and drop the brass knocker. And yet there was a flicker of something, a vague, curious sentiment that lit Dearing's eyes whenever he turned his attention toward Charlotte.

"I'll practice before dinner is served. Twice as long if that brings you pleasure, Lord Dearing."

Charlotte's capitulation had Amelia's brow raised high and she eyed her friend with a mixture of outrage and compassion. Here was a marriage in dire need of rescue. Charlotte would wither and die under such constrictive scrutiny and good heavens, *Lord Dearing*. The formality was nigh unbearable. He appeared staid and pensive, although some niggling suspicion told Amelia more was at play than a need to control.

Regret took up residence in her heart. She'd neglected her friend's distress when she'd become embroiled in her own turmoil, but clearly the Dearing relationship existed in an equally precarious status. What to do now? She wrestled her conflicted emotions into submission and stood to leave.

"I won't impose on you a minute longer." She moved toward the door, waving away Charlotte's immediate objection. "My attention is needed at home, no doubt. My best to you both." And with the cordial farewell, Amelia scuttled out the door.

She took the longest route home, in no hurry to face

Matthew, while the thought of seeing Lunden reduced her gait to languid steps. The weather proved pleasant, a swath of blue sky overhead with a moderate, refreshing breeze, yet the state of her heartache overshadowed any happiness to be found in the temperate weather. Lunden was leaving, her declaration of love abandoned as if meaningless, her heart as broken as an hourglass with its sands spilled, never to be whole again. She loved him enough for the two of them, but that wasn't sufficient, nor the lopsided emotion on which to build a marriage.

Meanwhile Matthew waited to bind her future to a man who took little interest in a wife except to tend children and warm his bed. Matthew would not listen to reason on these counts.

What would cause her brother to deflect logic at the sake of her happiness? Hardly cut from spontaneous cloth, his decision making had never proven rash in the past, his actions usually deliberate and well considered. What could be at stake? He pursued few interests aside from his puzzle obsession and weekly attendance to the meetings of the Society for the Intellectually Advanced. The society. Lord Collins had boasted of his position as chief officer when he wasn't attempting to ogle her décolletage in the garden behind the town house. Perhaps whatever drove Matthew was fundamentally connected to his participation at the society. With a grin that bespoke of satisfaction and determination, Amelia made haste at the next corner, her boots tapping the cobblestones in a lively rhythm.

Lunden signed the paperwork strewn across the canvas blotter on Bolster Hamm's desk. The solicitor made no mention of the unusual conditions or the steadfast expedience with which he'd expected his requirements met, no matter Lunden had entered the office unannounced, and without appointment.

With a resolute exhale, he vowed to complete his obligations and rid the city before dusk. In cyclical repetition, London had shown no kindness, and his body hummed with an urgency to leave at last.

His eyes strayed to the window and his heart begged to conjure an image of Amelia, her confession of love an intoxicating potion swirling in his blood. No. He snapped his attention to the desktop and lifted his glass of brandy, finishing the liquor in one fiery swallow. The burning sensation did little to restore his calm; still he forced his eyes to the work spread before him. He refused to consider Amelia, or Matthew for that matter, shirking obligation and ignoring the determined emotions that tangled around his heart like a barbed thicket. Emotions proved distasteful poison. His attention should be on resolving the bothersome legalities he'd inherited with the duchy.

He picked up his pen and blew a cleansing breath to dispatch his distraction as his eyes scanned his brother's documents. Of late his memories of Douglas had lost their potency to knife his reserve. Responsibility replaced self-loathing. How easy it had become to blame his loneliness on his brother's passing. But Lunden existed as his own man. He'd created a loathsome world and withdrawn into it. Time waited for no one, least of all those immersed in pity. Holding further self-recrimination at bay, he sanded another contract and set it aside, despite his stubborn conscience refusing to release the last of its vigilant hold.

He'd wasted so much time—weeks, months, years—squandered in nothingness, a shell of meaningless existence. Now he wished every day returned for no other reason than to mourn his brother properly. He scoffed at his duplicity, the former conclusion a partial lie. He wished the years returned so he might celebrate every minute with Amelia. To relive his life, start again. But the words reverberated within him, a reminder of those softly spoken as they'd embraced the night before. There were no new beginnings.

He stared at his brother's signature, scrawled across the bottom of the paper before him. Each stroke of black ink, smooth in its balanced flourish, provoked his past. He let the remembrance come, the bittersweet memory no longer accompanied by a rush of anguish and despair, yet he braced himself nonetheless.

His parents had been placed in the ground nearly a year, and in a rare occurrence, he'd stumbled upon Douglas in the study. Lunden did not bother with books, nor did he frequent the room where his father led aristocratic discussions and political debates. He was a second son, his pursuit of pleasure superseded most everything else, and this evening he'd been on the hunt for a bit of brandy. Douglas, on the other hand, hardly spared a moment for leisure time, their vocations aimed in perpendicular directions since birth, so it gave Lunden pause to find his brother seated at their father's desk, poring over ledgers with a disheartened expression on his face.

When Douglas realized he was no longer alone, he shook off his peevish expression, and drew Lunden forward. Expecting a stern reprimand, he'd been shocked when Douglas proceeded to explain the columns of numbers and yearly incomes, listed with meticulous care by the estate solicitor and presented for review. The camaraderie so rare and cherished, Lunden had watched with wide eyes and piqued interest, until his brother's glib comment ended their fleeting amity. *Listen well, little brother, and practice your maths, though I doubt you'll have need of these skills unless I die an early death.* The fulfilled prophecy haunted him to this day and contributed to his fatalistic perspective.

He released a long exhale and touched his hand to his brother's watch pocketed safely away. Sorrow laced the motion. If only they'd had more time together.

"I believe you'll find everything in order, Your Grace."

Hamm's baritone pulled Lunden back to the present and after sparing the paperwork a final glance, he stood and retrieved his greatcoat from the coatrack near the door. "Yes, I'm on my way to smooth the finer details now." If the solicitor noticed his bruised face, he possessed enough good sense not to mention it.

"Then things will proceed as planned."

Lunden repressed a bitter laugh. Rarely was the instance.

He bid the solicitor farewell and directed the hackney driver to Lamb Street, yet instead of considering the dossier of litigious paperwork clenched in his grasp, Amelia's heartfelt admission replayed in his brain like a litany. She'd stated, *no, actually* she'd proclaimed, her heart's affection. Amelia, who was all light and energy in his dark, dark soul. Somehow she'd managed to erode the mortar and topple his walls, leaving him in a pile of ruin.

And now she would be bartered to Collins, her brother the victor in his game of personal gain. Meanwhile Lunden had contributed to her misery. Had he not come to London, not appealed to Matthew for help, he'd never have intruded on Amelia's life, nor instigated her misguided feelings.

Possessiveness, bold and virulent, swelled in his chest. How he wished for what he couldn't have. Love, and the swath of complicated emotions intertwined with relationships, remained beyond his capabilities. Never mind Amelia would never experience the lifestyle she deserved.

Before Douglas's death, he might have had a chance to win her hand, regardless of his birth order as a second son. His parents were favored by the *ton*, his father's work in Parliament considered innovative and his mother revered as a benevolent volunteer to many charitable causes. When his parents died, London grieved for the loss of two respected peers, all perspicuity turned in the eldest son's direction, intent he would honor their untimely passing by fulfilling the responsibilities expected by a man of his lineage. How would Lunden have evolved were his parents not taken so early? He'd like to believe his world would have included more than tomfoolery and brainless fabrication. But fate had the last laugh.

A spiral of grief twisted his soul. He once possessed the capacity to love. Perhaps he loved too deeply. Still, love meant loss. Deep wounds that never healed lest one stir up the past and destroy his family's fine reputation. He wouldn't expose Amelia to the threat of shame and embarrassment. Were Douglas's preferences made known to the public, the extent of scandal would damage her beyond repair; and he cherished her far too much to take that risk, most especially when Nilworth threatened to exhume his past, his brother's death, and the potential indignity, were he not to leave the city with haste. Resolve filled the hollow ache in his chest.

And what of Nilworth? What impetus, aside from his rampant appetite for gossip and desire to be favored by the *ton,* served him to threaten exposure? Did Nilworth know of his son's arrangement with Douglas? Was his goal to rid Lunden of the city in order to conceal his son's preference or coerce cooperation in obtaining the Lamb Street town house? Surely Nilworth couldn't have known of Russell Scotts's extortion. The man would never stand for such a thing. Yet why wouldn't the son have confided to his father when the situation arose? Too many questions remained unanswered and Lunden could spare no further patience in seeking resolutions.

The hackney arrived, and he unfolded from the seat, paid the driver, and climbed the town house steps with solemn determination. The sooner he delivered the paperwork to

Lord Gavin, the better. Then Lunden needed to make one final stop before ridding the city forever.

A butler opened the door with prompt attention and this time, Lunden was shown into the drawing room without delay. Gavin waiting inside and Lunden shrugged off his offer of spirits, intent on completing his business without lingering a minute longer.

"Good day, Gavin. I assume you're well." He rested the packet of documents on a nearby table.

"Yes, thank you." Gavin indicated two wing chairs near the fire, but again Lunden dismissed the hospitality. He couldn't sit, not with his nerves vibrating with impatience.

"I've signed all the documents necessary to secure this property in your name. It's yours to enjoy for the length of your life, and then to bequeath thereafter." *And Lunden wouldn't have to consider it ever again. Neatly done.*

"How did you manage? I believed Douglas had the property tied in knots."

"Not difficult to untie once the circumstances were understood and that scoundrel Scotts fled the premises. I regret we can't pursue the thief and prosecute, although I'm not fool enough to trust he wouldn't ingratiate someone to assist in slandering our reputations."

"I agree." Gavin nodded, his expression relieved.

"And your father? He knows of your residence here?" Lunden skimmed his eyes along the room's perimeter while waiting for a response, uncomfortable with the queries no matter the questions needed to be asked.

Gavin examined the tips of his boots a long moment. "My father and I haven't spoken in many years. There was a time when I sought his help, but the result was less than favorable. We had a falling-out that has yet to be repaired."

"I see. Your answer explains much, although it does present me with yet another matter to resolve. On that note, I'll take my leave." He turned away, making quick strides to the hall before he realized Gavin meant to continue their conversation. The sincerity in the man's farewell gave him pause and he reentered the room.

"I can't express my gratitude well enough. This home, the one Douglas and I created here, was our sanctuary. By returning it to me, you've brought peace to my soul and restored Douglas's final wishes. I hope you realize your act of good faith has honored your brother's memory."

Words seemed unnecessary and Lunden nodded his acceptance, clasped Gavin's extended palm in a firm handshake, and hurried to the waiting hack. He barked Nilworth's address to the driver and the horses took office, their hooves beating an impatient rhythm in kind to Lunden's continued unrest.

"I'm sorry, milady, but you're not allowed entrance." The stoic doorman managed to peer down his nose regardless she stood as tall as he. "Perhaps you'd enjoy a visit to the tearoom on the corner while you await the gentleman in question. You may also leave a message for Lord Collins if—"

"I've no time to stand on formality. This is a matter of great importance." Raising her chin, Amelia employed her haughtiest tone, one that usually achieved the desired outcome, but this servant remained steadfast, barring her entry with his body and inflated self-importance.

"Again, my apologies. Females are not welcome at the society. It's a long-standing policy that I enforce. Let me provide paper and pen for you to write your missive."

He turned to a small writing desk near the wall and Amelia pushed past, bounding up the staircase and into the meeting hall foyer. Aware the doorman shadowed her, she followed the cacophony of baritone conversation and bolted into the second room on her right. She penetrated the double paneled doors, the force of her sudden entry enough to cause each to bank against the wall with a resounding thud. Silence blanketed the room as every male head swiveled in her direction.

Her eyes darted left and right, taking quick inventory of the gentlemen inside, thankful her brother was not in attendance.

"See here, miss, you're not allowed in this portion of the building. Didn't our doorman inform you of the rules? You must wait in the hall if there's some sort of emergency."

A tall, overbearing sort was the first to break loose from the pack, lurching forward on long strides as if her very presence would contaminate their intellectual discussion. Amelia stood undaunted, her eyes glued to Lord Collins where he waited at the podium. She noticed his Adam's apple bobbed with a sudden case of angst.

"Back away." Surprised by her bold command the forthcoming gentleman stopped in his tracks. "I'm here to speak to Lord Collins and believe me, it's quite the emergency." His voice echoed with seething determination and a deep murmur rode out over the crowd. All eyes riveted to the front of the room where Collins inched backward as if to disappear without notice.

"Good luck, old boy. You'll have little peace until you get this one in hand, although in hand might be her most useful place."

The crude comment was a slap in the face and, momentarily distracted, Amelia speared the outspoken heckler with a glare meant to convey she considered him a nodcock. She quickly regained her purpose, no longer affected by the swell of disrespectful tripe rippling throughout the chairs. She gathered her skirts and strode farther into the room, but when she flicked her eyes to the podium, Collins had disappeared. Her shock must have shown on her face, evident by the harsh swell of laughter that filled the room.

"Intellectually advanced, indeed." She spun on her heel, straightened her shoulders, and leveled each occupant with a condescending stare that soon held the room quiet as a church.

"Add this to your inventory of facts, gentlemen. Women are not possessions. Nor do we wish be toyed with or treated as decorations. Our opinions, thoughts, and most of all, feelings, matter. Trifle with the wrong woman, show her disrespect, and you'll find you've unleashed a force undefeatable." She paused to take a deep breath before moving closer to the doorway, though she didn't leave yet. "When Lord Collins skulks back to this place, *this sanctum of high intelligence,* inform him I understand his motive and he needn't pursue his offer of marriage. The answer is a resounding no."

Chapter Twenty-Seven

Lunden reined Hades to a stop and dismounted, handing the straps to the conscientious footman outside Nilworth's estate. Situated on the outskirts of London, the bucolic property was miles from the city center, but offered access to the social Season while still withstanding a conservative level of privacy. The redbrick residence wasn't what he expected, and while the reason for his visit was unpleasant, the rustic landscape reassured he would soon return to Beckford Hall where his life could regain predictability.

Somehow he'd managed to complicate his problems. A talent fast becoming second nature. Amelia's intention to marry any available feather-wit in order to thwart her brother's efforts, burned like an acid in his gut. No matter the candidate she chose, the fool didn't deserve her. Nor did Collins. No one did. Least of all, he. His behavior could only be labeled *reprehensible*. At the end of the day, he was a gentleman, no matter his code of honor evaporated whenever he caught sight of those midnight curls. Better to distance himself from the reality as soon as possible, considering he could offer no solution, regardless their time together was the most peaceful he'd experienced since choosing isolation a decade ago.

Foolhardy hope dared him to envision a pleasant future. A noisy household filled with mischievous children possessing brilliant green eyes. For a reason he could never explain, a smile curled his lips, despite he'd made the difficult decision to squelch the unattainable daydream. It would prove, undoubtedly, another poor choice sure to haunt until he knocked on death's door. Best he mastered his misplaced lust and reordered his life.

Shaking away the bitter considerations, he approached the wrought-iron gate and followed the inlaid slates to the grand entry. He dropped the brass knocker and gained admittance upon offering his card. The foyer was dimly lit and Lunden noted the furniture appeared a bit worse for the wear. He was shown into a drawing room done in celadon green and ivory, the curtains drawn to brighten the room where a pair of French doors led to manicured gardens at the rear. He walked to the glass and looked out, uncomfortable with the confrontation he would instigate, although necessary as a means to an end. He didn't relish the unpleasantness of his business though he yearned to shed the last vestiges of guilt. Perhaps then he would possess the strength needed to live out the rest of his days with a modicum of peace.

"Lord Nilworth will receive you shortly."

The butler's reserved tone, a mixture of stricture and displeasure, roused his attention and Lunden nodded acknowledgment before opening the French doors, anxious for fresh air to alleviate the stifling weight of the anticipated conflict. The insufferable sun lazed high in the sky, birds sang, a ladybug landed on a delicate white rose growing on a trellis covered with ivy. Still, the air hung heavy and suffocating. Restless, he advanced from the stone-laid terrace into the modest walled garden, his feet moving along the path without reason, as if pulled from the distasteful subject he must broach inside the house toward the respite of nature. But the cobbles ended abruptly and a feeling of unfulfilled expectation blanketed his already overburdened spirit.

To the right, under an aged yew tree and nearly swallowed by overgrown weeds, a marble bench sat sentry, for what purpose he could not know. Without heed for his expensive boots, he pushed through the brush to investigate. A marker appeared within the small clearing. Something sharp twisted in his chest as he recognized the plaque as a headstone, similar to the three placed at Beckford Hall in loving memory of his parents and brother. Unbidden, the sound of his mother's sweet voice and his father's baritone bubbled to the surface, but he shoved them away. Now was not the time for sentimentality, the opportunity to beg for forgiveness out of reach. He'd never said good-bye. Not to his parents or his brother, and worse, he'd failed by instigating the circumstances causing Douglas's death. A sigh of wistful sadness escaped and he fisted his hands near his thighs, steeling against the lapse of self-loathing. He'd matured without a father's firm hand or a mother's gentle touch, nurtured by survival and self-reliance. Pity that, but he would forestall his review of failures until he recovered his country existence.

Still one razor-sharp emotion persisted, forcing him to submission. Amelia's laughter, the saucy thrust of her chin, and taste of her kiss, now inured the comfortable loneliness that fit him better than his tailored coat.

Bowing his head, his eyes dropped to the marker at his feet. Sarah Nilworth. He did not know the name, but the year indicated she could only be a child, too young for a wife or sibling. With an abrupt snap to attention, he regained the path and strode to the house, leaving his memories behind on the smooth marble bench.

The drawing room remained empty long enough for him

to close the French doors, but Nilworth entered shortly thereafter. His frosty demeanor implied his adversity to the visit, his belligerent gaze served as confirmation.

"It didn't take long for you to find trouble, did it, Scarsdale?" Nilworth eyed his bruised face, his lofty countenance adding to the tension in the room. "What is your business here? I'm unaccustomed to entertaining purported criminals in my home." Darkness hovered in the set of his brow and his mouth turned in an acerbic grin.

"Be wary of your tone and implication. Hiring an agent to meet me in the dead of night to issue threats and extort my cooperation falls into the same category. Or was that you inside the carriage, disguising your voice and attempting theatrics? To what end?" Lunden replied in a chisel-sharp tone no less uncompromising.

Nilworth stood silent a moment too long, his change of expression indicating an inner war waged. Then he strode to the brandy decanter, perhaps angling for time to assemble his reply. Lunden came back to the question.

"What is it you want from me? I've returned to London to conduct personal business with no intent to provoke your interest, most especially after the slanderous lies you've perpetuated in the past."

"Your reputation has never been of my concern. My son . . ." He paused as if deliberating each word carefully. "Gavin is my heir, my only son. I buried one child and will not allow it to happen again. Protecting his interest is my priority. Your welfare became an unfortunate casualty of the situation, but that evening so long ago, Gavin acted without thinking. He came to me emotionally distraught and terribly confused, with an urgent appeal for help. Mentally disheveled, he blurted out his distress before I rid the hall of servants. I couldn't allow a story that implicated my son to violence and sordid behavior to circulate throughout London, so help him I did, the only way I knew how, by instigating societal gossip and invidious suspicion of my own fabrication. It only took a few words of innuendo and unsatisfied curiosity led to rampant speculation. True, it cast you in a poor light, but the backlash didn't befall my son, nor was his secret exposed."

"You destroyed my future to preserve your son's reputation." He stared at Nilworth, a decade's worth of resentment poured into his glare.

"It's not so different from what you did for your brother." Nilworth took a long swallow of brandy. "You shunned society, seeking the same result."

"I had little choice." Years of resentment and anger coiled in his chest and Lunden spat the words as if he needed to release them or he'd never breathe again. "I protected my brother with cost to no one but myself."

"In reflection it would seem society served you a grievous indignity, but no one could predict you'd become a recluse. At worst, I assumed you'd weather the storm of inquiry and scandal. I planned to turn the tide of gossip once things settled, but you left the city and I saw no need to insight more discussion of the subject." Nilworth released a bitter laugh. "Despite my efforts, Gavin and I had a falling-out concerning my handling of the problem. He suspected quite accurately that it was I who fueled the vicious gossip and thus, hasn't spoken to me in years. Still, I've kept a close eye on his existence. When you returned I feared a revival of old trouble. The stories I could control, but what of your purpose? So I had you watched as well. Your everlasting friendship with Whittingham remains a curiosity as he's the only other person who witnessed the tragedy of that night. I wonder still if he realizes who's responsible for his disability."

"You have the facts confused with your fiction." Lunden's voice dropped to a lethal tone and a prolonged pause ensued.

"Perhaps. Over the years, memories have muddled. Yet

your current position here needed attention. I received reports you'd visited your solicitor and Lamb Street several times. I needed to act and secure the property meaningful to my son. Gavin won't answer my letters and the butler at the property is tenacious; still, I meant to acquire the town house to make reparation, perhaps mend fences. It's why I need you to sell me the property."

"You're too late, but it's of little matter. I would show you no kindness after the hatred you circulated in regard to my family. Society's scorn means little at this juncture. I've no desire to participate in the active *ton*."

"Aah, so you haven't changed. Still stubborn and hell-bent in your decision making. True, ten years brings with it perspective, and while your family scandal may not be the current *on dit*, my actions sought to ensure my son remained free from ridicule. All instinct led me to believe you meant to reside in the city. I assumed Lady Whittingham—"

"Don't speak of the lady. Stay away from her. You're a poison more powerful than any suspected rumor you fed into the *ton*'s addiction." Words could never sufficiently express his remorse. Nilworth gained what he wanted, regardless it was not Lunden's intent. "The Lamb Street address now belongs to your son. I personally delivered the paperwork not an hour ago."

Nilworth appeared dubious before his expression melted into smug approval. "Then there is nothing for it. Our business is concluded."

A swarm of bitter emotions held Lunden quiet. He departed the house and regained Hades, setting down the lane at a breakneck speed, anxious to be rid of everything Nilworth represented—the censure and frivolity of the upper ten thousand, manipulation of good to support evil, and the perpetuation of dishonesty. He steered Hades with a nudge of his knees, his fists wrapped tightly around the leather straps while his mind spun in myriad directions.

His business in London may be concluded, the haunted memories of his past finally laid to rest, but where did that leave him? He remained stagnant on his self-made tightrope, paralyzed between the past and the future, unwilling to move forward and afraid to fall into the oblivion Amelia's love offered. He was a bloody fool, hardly different from himself ten years ago, yet it was no less than he deserved for returning to a city that never showed him kindness. He'd destroyed a valued friendship, broken an innocent heart, and now faced a hollow future rife with more regret than ever before.

"Make each word count, as I'm short on time and patience." Matthew strove to keep his tone civil though a note of warning laced the curt command. He'd shown Lunden loyalty for over a decade. He didn't deserve his friend's blatant disregard. And Amelia. This wasn't the first time she'd betrayed his wishes. Soon, she too would be none of his concern.

Her shadow fell across the desk where he worked to reassemble his puzzle. He'd rebuilt much of the Galapagos Islands and now concentrated on the Adriatic Coast, yet his heart wasn't in the effort, distracted by the ill feelings created when he'd discovered his sister in Lunden's bedchamber, and the confrontations that ensued.

"I know I've made things difficult." She took a long breath as if fortifying for certain battle.

"Correct, although your rebellion has done little except destroy a long-standing friendship. I'm confident Collins will still have you. Your indiscretion shouldn't disturb him, your purity never in question. I dare say he never wanted a missish wife, although you should bid farewell to your recalcitrance."

"Matthew, I'm mortified."

"As well you should be. Your reckless behavior speaks of

your consistent selfishness." He wouldn't succumb to his sister's pleas. Didn't he deserve a satisfactory future as much as she? At last the opportunity to assume the position of chief officer hung before him, a golden ring he merely needed to reach for and grasp.

"What drives you to be so unfeeling? You speak as if I'm some appalling hoyden." Hurt permeated her complaint.

"If the slipper fits . . ." He rounded on her, shifting his weight to his good leg, his voice low with tension, and her surprise was evident, her brows bowed and lips pressed tight. "You begrudge I dare to achieve something for myself, when you've done nothing but perpetuate trouble for your own gain. Happiness is fleeting. Intelligence is lasting. Be smart and make the right decision. You need to be married and Collins needs a wife. You're capable of the math." He speared her with a stare meant to embolden his sarcasm.

She ignored his baited reply and he fixed his attention on the assorted shapes in his palm.

"My feelings for Lunden are true."

He would not weaken with her mislaid emotion. "He's an unsuitable match in every aspect."

Her expression grew chary, yet with a flick of her chin, all defiant confidence returned. "He's done nothing dishonorable. The complete opposite, actually. He's protected his brother and family's reputation while sacrificing his life in return."

"Would that society heard your outrage and indignation, dear sister, but the rumor-mongering *ton* cares little for truth, ever anxious to distort reality in pursuit of a tasty bit of gossip to feed their avaricious appetite. It takes but one whisper into an attentive ear. Your life would be desolate, ostracized by the uppers for the fleeting attention of a broken man devoutly unwilling to marry." He allowed the words to settle. "If he did choose a bride, I'd assume he'd guarantee a measure of peace, rather than a female with a talent for trouble." He could see his words stung, but they needed to be said in an effort to dissuade her misplaced feelings.

"Nevertheless, I won't marry Lord Collins. He doesn't seek a wife in truth, not one in accordance to the wedding vows."

"You're far too intelligent to believe that's the way of the world. Truth is a fanciful notion, and a virtue not often considered when fulfilling obligations or satisfying a need." He dropped the pieces onto the table and grasped his cane, pitching his weight forward, the ache in his leg as sharp as the stab to his pride. "I'm needed at the society. Elections are tomorrow and I have business to settle. I know you view this arrangement as less than satisfactory, but I assure you it's the fear of the unknown that motivates your rebellion. Once you are ensconced in married life you will find a degree of tolerance. Most people do." He moved to the door, ready to take his leave. "And before you bludgeon me with Charlotte's condition, I implore you to consider the whimsical illusions the two of you entertained since childhood. Life is not a fairy tale. Compromise is necessary for some degree of contentment. People grow old, bear sickness, suffer loss. It is the way of things, and as soon as you accept this stark reality you will find peace."

"You're right."

Her immediate complacence had him twisting to view her face, but Amelia's expression appeared passive, all usual fight and bluster appeased. Would that he believed her response to be true, but a flicker of suspicion narrowed his eyes and he had no time to consider it.

Calling for his carriage, he arrived at the society as a misty drizzle began to fall. Damnation, must it rain every time he needed to climb the marble steps leading to the hall? His leg ached like the devil. He clenched his teeth and ambled out of the carriage, batting away his driver's extended hand and grasping tightly to the opened umbrella foisted in his direction. With caution he approached the steps, juggling his cane and umbrella to one hand in order to press his palm against the knotted spasm in his left thigh. Eventually, he managed the stairs, shucked the umbrella, and stood brushing raindrops from his sleeves when Winthrop burst into the foyer, his eyes alight with anxious bidding.

"I've been on watch for your arrival. Have you heard the news?"

"What now?" A ripple of acute pain throbbed down his leg. The last thing he desired was another wrinkle in his rumpled plan. "You've become a veritable magpie when it comes to fresh information."

Winthrop waved away the snipe with no consequence and grasped Matthew's elbow in a frantic tug, intent on steering him from the main entrance to a corner in a blatant attempt at privacy. Matthew scoffed, convinced the low rumble throughout the meeting hall bandied whatever news Winthrop sought to keep confidential.

"Out with it." He regarded his friend thoughtfully. "I've paperwork to see to and people to greet in order to ensure I gain the majority vote. I've no time for idle gossip if I'm to convince the board I present the wisest choice."

"That's just it."

This time it was Winthrop's noticeable pause that drew his attention. As Matthew eyed his friend, a shadow of unease slid down his spine, bringing with it the surety this news would not be welcomed. He pierced his friend with an intense glare and steeled his courage in preparation, desperate for a shred of inner peace.

"Have you secured Collins's recommendation?" Winthrop's voice reduced to a hushed whisper.

The question was not what he expected and annoyance

replaced anxiety. "In a manner of speaking, although the documents will need to be rewritten. There was an accident with my inkwell . . ." His voice trailed off, the last words forced through clenched teeth as an image of Pandora scampered through his mind.

"That's unfortunate." Winthrop's crestfallen expression did little to assuage his unease.

"God's teeth, what is it?" Heads swiveled in their direction at his sudden outburst, but he could no longer stand idle, the curiosity to understand the news Winthrop intended to impart pulsing in his veins with more aggression than the throbbing ache in his leg. Failure to secure the nomination and win the election was not an option. He gave a quick, fierce swallow. "Out with it, so I may get on with the business at hand."

The once-eager expression dropped from Winthrop's face and he leaned a bit closer, dismay causing his brows to furrow his forehead in a deep vee. "That's just it, my friend. There may not be any business for you to get to."

When Winthrop again hesitated, Matthew struck him in the leg with his cane, anger superseding good sense were anyone viewing their interaction. He needed every vote to gain election. Several popular gentlemen vied for the same position.

"Collins has eloped. Run off to Gretna Green with Lord Humber's niece. I heard she was in the family way and Humber planned to send her to Scotland for a convenient stay with the grandparents, but it all proved for naught. As soon as Collins heard of the situation he took prompt advantage." Winthrop paused, his voice taking on a sympathetic note. "Although Humber's good fortune equals your despair."

Matthew swayed, dropped his cane, and leaned against a nearby wall. Gone were his plans of a fulfilling future, his dreams of holding the exalted position of chief officer, his hope of measuring out a portion of happiness. Damn happiness, and damn his pride, as wounded as his damaged leg. It was all Amelia's fault. But his despair was short-lived.

With a mutter of farewell, he ventured into the rain again and returned home, his leg a persistent reminder of unsettled emotion and fickle expectation. This time it was he who barged in unannounced, though when he viewed Amelia standing near her bedchamber window with tear tracks on her cheeks, his anger mollified a degree.

He owed her an apology and explanation. How had things become so complicated?

"I want to speak to you. Are you all right?" He moved closer, await of her reception before he began what he needed to say.

Amelia turned from the window and wiped away her tears. It wasn't like Matthew to storm into a room, but regardless, she wouldn't have him see her upset. So much remained unsaid. If they could manage a civil conversation, free of conflict and struggle for control, she might be able to convince him of her heart. She needed him to know how deeply she loved Lunden.

"I need to speak to you as well." She motioned toward the large upholstered bench at the foot of her bed and waited while he came to sit beside her. "It seems somehow we've both lost our way."

"It didn't begin that way, I assure you." Matthew's expression seemed more relaxed than she'd noticed in weeks. "You should speak first."

"Thank you." She hooked a few stray hairs behind her ear and folded her hands atop her skirts. "All I've ever wanted from marriage is a chance at happiness, a sense of security, and contented future. Mother and Father's love match and the genuine affection they share instilled a desire for the same rare union and I vowed to have no less.

Excepting the circumstances of Charlotte's marriage, I believed the natural course of life would lead my heart to love. I had Seasons, attended parties, and accepted the attention of gentlemen callers, but no one convinced me our futures were fated. As time passed, Father grew anxious and assigned you the impossible task." She paused and brought her eyes to his with a slight smile.

"Indeed." He returned her grin.

"A series of unwelcomed emotions preyed on my confidence. Father's illness complicated matters and fear I would fail to find a suitable husband, a man I could love and respect, transformed every well-intended situation into a battle for control." She paused and hoped her brother would understand the depth of her words.

"Your explanation mirrors my own. I possess the same reluctance." Matthew shifted on the bench and extended his leg. He briefly kneaded the muscles of his thigh. "Time has revealed my disability is not singular." He scoffed a wry sound. "While my leg pains me at times and prevents assorted activities, I've allowed my brain to harbor enough self-doubt to cripple me twofold."

"Matthew." She reached for his hand knowing how difficult his confession.

"No, let me finish." He gently placed her hand within his. "I'm not foolish enough to attend ballrooms, left to admire the waltz and quadrille from the periphery. Nor will I pretend to ignore the pity-filled glances or benevolent conversation cast in my direction while I mentally list my physical limitations. As substitution, I've chosen a path of academic pursuit with a specific goal in mind. Yet blinded by purpose and an intense desire to prove a modicum of self-worth, I've wronged you. I've treated you unkindly in the process. I'm sorry, Amelia." He cleared his throat and exhaled a long breath.

"I am, too." She squeezed his hand with sincerity. "You're

too hard on yourself. I know the ideal woman exists for you and not only in your imagination." She couldn't help but add a tease. "A patient and unique woman, no doubt."

"The same way you believe in your ideal man." Matthew smiled and released her hand.

"Oh, I've discovered him already. He lives in every beat of my heart."

They fell into companionable silence after that. They'd bared their souls and found forgiveness in the process and truly, there was nothing left to say.

Chapter Twenty-Eight

Life no longer made sense. Not so long ago quiet was solace and solitude, a close companion, but now the world turned inside out. Days lingered longer than twenty-four hours, minutes crawled by, marked so slowly, he'd ordered every clock removed from the premises. Beckford Hall, once his salvation, now served as a prison. A stark reminder of his poor judgment much more than the secret he protected from crawling out of the grave. But there was nothing for it. He'd once again made the wrong choice, this time an exile within his heart.

Long, reckless rides on Hades, the usual height of release, were now constant remembrances of Amelia atop her mare, a vivacious bundle of green-eyed temptation. She'd changed him. Lost in the deadly undertow of the past, the vixen had awakened whatever scrap of survival was left in his disquieted soul. She was adventure and rebellion, reckless exploration and contagious excitement, everything his empty existence sacrificed years ago, given back to him in the form of a beautiful woman. And he'd failed her. Turned his back and walked away.

Lunden set down the brass letter opener and moved to the windows, his attention drawn by a passing shadow in the front drive. A carriage approached. Devil deuce it, did it bear the Whittingham crest? Could it be? Would she? After two months' time? What could he possibly say after leaving her without the barest explanation? A familiar ache intensified in his chest and he averted his gaze from the scene unfolding outside, unwilling to invite disappointment.

Yet a breath later his eyes slid back, craving the sight of Amelia. One fleeting glance. The pugnacious tilt of her chin. The liquid silk of her ebony curls.

His heart beat a heavy thud. Matthew exited the coach and bid the driver continue to the stables. He stood alone.

Exhaling his frustration, Lunden clenched his eyes against the sharp pang of regret permanently lodged in his chest and returned to his desk in wait of his visitor. Congenial greetings could be heard from the front hall, followed by the uneven tread of the man he once considered a dear friend.

"Ah, so you've resumed your brooding right where you left off. You do it quite well."

Matthew moved forward, his voice louder than his presence, although Lunden merely narrowed his eyes at the jibe. He couldn't trust himself to speak. Not yet.

"I'm here on a mission. To invite you to a wedding." Matthew raised his palm as if anticipating an immediate refusal. "Before you argue, you should know Amelia is happy with this decision. Overjoyed, actually. She has an appointment at the modiste on Regent Street this afternoon for her final fitting. Her gown and accompanying fripperies are costing me a small fortune, but it will be worth every penny if I never see Pandora again."

Jealousy, searing hot, blinded Lunden as Matthew's words hit home, but he fisted his hands and offered only a long, considering stare, allowing the moment to pass before he dared answer. "While your motive may be abstruse, I appreciate your journey here to deliver this news in person.

Please extend my best wishes to Amelia." He hadn't said her name aloud since he'd left her. He swallowed hard with the effort.

"Nonsense. You must attend. I've found the perfect man for her and as you know, that posed no simple task. Of course, I benefited from her input. It took her a bit of doing, but I realized Amelia knew her own mind and heart from the very beginning. Any matter, Father is much improved by the prospect of a new addition to the family. I'm sure you'll approve. He meets every criterion on my mother's ridiculous list."

A jarring warning shook him from the inside out and he nailed his temper down hard. He would not react; despite Matthew stood there, oblivious to his agony, anxious and cheerful with his blithe news. Perhaps this visit served as a measure of revenge in exception of the amiable greeting. Lunden would escort him to the door and resume his ambition to become as lost and forgotten as an unmarked grave.

The silence stretched into the loudest noise imaginable until Bittles arrived with a refreshment tray. Matthew made to leave before the butler poured tea.

"Oh, I can't stay. Too many details beg attention, but after all that transpired I could never allow this moment to pass. Considering our history . . ." Matthew paused as if unsure of his words. "I didn't like the way we parted and a wedding seemed the smartest idea to bring us all together again. You'll always have my friendship, Lunden. No matter the past, the present, or the future before us."

He extended his hand in a bid for truce and Lunden accepted with a hearty shake. "She's happy?"

"More than I can express, but then who would disagree? The gentleman is a stellar choice."

Honest delight tinged the words, and for the umpteenth time Lunden bit back the question burning his tongue. *Who is the lucky gentleman?* But no, the less information, the more sanity to be found. "Very well then, extend my felicitations to your family." Their hands dropped and time stood still. Then Matthew tapped his cane against his boot and pivoted, leaving Lunden to stare after him as he exited the room.

Lunden forestalled a reaction for nearly an hour until his heart will out and he demanded his horse made ready for a long ride. Faster than the path of his thoughts, he kicked Hades harder, gathering speed like a secret let loose as he rode toward the city with the singular intent to see Amelia one last time before she became another man's wife. Accomplished at keeping his feelings hidden, she'd managed to lay his heart bare. If he could have this one final glimpse at her face, he would relinquish his ill-begotten emotions once and for all and fade into the countryside.

As he neared Regent Street he contemplated his foolish reaction. In spite of everything, he wanted her. It was as honest a confession as he'd allow himself, no matter she would never be his. *Or could she be?* He scoffed at the question. Bloody fool, she's promised to another.

True to the word, a Whittingham coach sat parked on Regent Street. He tethered his horse with haste, unwilling to let better sense impede his progress. He sought only a glimpse of her smile, nothing more, but as his boots brought him to the shop window, he wondered at the depth of his lie.

Frilly bonnets, ornate slippers, and a gown of russet silk obstructed any random passersby from eyeing the ladies inside. He swore with impatience and removed his leather gloves. Entering the shop committed him to consequences. He would see the joy reflected in her eyes as she spoke of her betrothed.

But didn't he wish her happiness? His heart encouraged

him to turn the brass knob while his brain labeled him
a fool.

"May I help you?"

The tinkle of a brass bell above the shop doorway alerted
the shopkeeper to a new arrival. Heads swiveled in his direction, one full of black satin curls, barely contained by a
lovely green ribbon.

"Lunden. You've come."

She glanced up.

He had no words.

She looked delighted to see him.

He could never understand.

Still, happiness hit him like a runaway carriage.

Amelia, breathtakingly beautiful, swathed in diaphanous
white lace from head to toe, her eyes like emeralds, her
smile more radiant than the sun.

"Your brother told me where to find you." His words,
spoken gently, contradicted the thunderous pound of his
heart.

"Of course he did, although the groom is never to see
the bride before the wedding day. Some believe it to be bad
luck."

He swung his head from left to right with reluctant urgency,
anxious to finally identify the groom and equally loathed to
create the memory.

Mary chuckled, the maid seemingly amused by his indecision.

"Forgive me, Amelia. I don't understand." He sounded
more himself with the admission.

This time it was Amelia who laughed, her lovely hands
waving with impatience at the seamstress and assistants
occupying the room. There was little she could do concerning the audience of women watching from the dress-
maker's pattern table, and Lunden eyed the small crowd

with skepticism as a knot of dread formed in his chest. He took a deep breath before returning his eyes to hers.

Amelia struggled to keep her joy contained. Lord, he cut a sharp profile, dark and intriguing, as entrancing as that very first evening. Much like Matthew had promised, Lunden's heart had won the battle. A few carefully positioned comments and he appeared as planned. Joy broke loose and flooded her heart. Now to convince him he was the bridegroom. That might take a bit more doing.

She stepped from the raised platform where her dress had been measured and closed the distance between them to less than one stride. Then in front of Mary and the shoppers, and to the blatant surprise of the most handsome Duke of Scarsdale, she placed both hands atop his and smiled. "I'm yours for the asking, Lunden. I've never been more ready to become your wife."

The humor of the situation was not lost and she watched as a twinkle sparked in his warm whisky-brown eyes. "What mischief are you creating now, Troublemaker?"

Then he laughed and the sound was pure delight to her ears, until he smiled, a true smile, and her heart threatened to burst.

"No mischief, whatsoever. Can you see my smile?"

"Even when you're not with me."

"Then say yes, Lunden. Say yes to the rest of your life. This is our happily ever after." The very idea stole her breath.

"I love you, Amelia, every troublesome, reckless inch." He traced a black curl against her cheek before he cupped her face in a reverent caress. "I've lived life without you and much prefer when you're in it."

He smiled again and the intensity of his love settled deep in her heart.

It didn't matter who watched as their future unfurled. A murmur rode out over the crowd but Amelia was accustomed to causing great scenes. And it didn't matter what they had experienced to reach this moment. Lunden had been through hell and back. She wished to offer him only heaven.

In the end, what mattered most was that they'd found each other, that she'd found Lunden, a man who believed life held only darkness until the magic of their love emblazed a wondrous future. Perhaps it was the city's fault all along, banishing her soon-to-be groom and caging his soon-to-be bride within its social dictates. In truth, it was London's biggest mistake, but Amelia let the thought dissolve as her betrothed kissed her with all the love in his heart.

Can't get enough of those
Midnight Secrets?
Keep reading for a sneak peek
at the next book in the series,

LONDON'S BEST KEPT SECRET.

Coming soon from
Anabelle Bryant
and
Zebra Books!

"A kitten?" Charlotte Lockhart, Lady Dearing, withdrew until her shoulders brushed the embroidered tableau detailed across the upholstered settee in her formal sitting room. "Whatsoever are you thinking, Amelia?" Her voice raised an octave and she forced a calm breath as her friend reached into the basket on the rug and revealed a lively ball of black fur despite the livid objection.

"There we are." Amelia Beckford, Duchess of Scarsdale, grinned with delight as she foisted the impatient feline forward. "Pandora produced a brilliant litter and I'm determined to find each kitten a loving home. It's only natural I choose the sweetest of the lot for my dearest friend."

With reluctance, Charlotte accepted the tiny animal and settled the soft bundle in her skirt. Her posture immediately relaxed. "Lord Dearing will never allow—"

"I don't understand why not. Every woman wants for a little companionship when her husband is inaccessible." Amelia's eyes flared to punctuate her reply. "In your case, that matter can't be understated."

"But a kitten . . ." Charlotte found a secret smile though she dashed it away just as quickly. "Lord Dearing and I have discussed this subject before and I—"

"I won't accept no for an answer. Besides, I've chosen the most docile kit of the five." As if aware of their critical inspection, the kitten emitted a perfectly timed mew and blinked its pale blue eyes. "If the discussion with your husband progressed in the same fashion you've previously described, I suspect it was confined to one syllable. *No.*"

Impatient and adventurous, the kitten attempted a daring leap and became tangled in the folds of Charlotte's skirt, its claws snagging the fine woven muslin.

"She's climbing already."

"Well, of course she is. She's a cat, not a bootjack." Amelia tapped the toe of her slipper against the imported Aubusson carpet in dismissal of Charlotte's concern. "Now let's consider a proper name for her."

"Please." Charlotte gathered the kitten in her palms although she stalled midway through the task when the feline licked her fingertips. The rough caress of the kitten's tongue tickled in the nicest way. "Just because Dearing and I have yet to find our way to marital bliss, doesn't mean we won't. I wouldn't want to cause a disagreement. You don't understand."

"I understand more than you realize and that's why I've decided upon this gift."

"I can't keep her." Charlotte gave a woeful shake of her head.

"I didn't travel all the way to London with the darling to have you refuse. Secret her away to your bedchambers. Dearing will never be wiser." A brief excruciating silence ensued. "You're still practicing that ridiculous sleeping arrangement and retiring to separate rooms, aren't you? Good heavens, I can't imagine waking up anywhere than beside Lunden." A grin of delight danced around her mouth before she continued. "But never mind about that. My recent marriage and wedding trip temporarily derailed my efforts to see you happily settled, but I've returned now with renewed effort."

Accustomed to Amelia's enthusiastic conversational skills, Charlotte sighed and her exhale whispered over the kitten's fur to elicit a soft purr of pleasure. The kitten was a pretty little thing. And how divine it would be to have a confidant who listened rather than strove to contribute or worse, correct all the ills of her relationship.

True to Amelia's assessment, Charlotte had entered into marriage as a stranger to her husband and thereby encountered a unique set of circumstances. She'd returned home from a tea party one afternoon to be informed by her father she would be married within a fortnight. Indeed, Lord Dearing had rescued her family from financial ruin and exemplified several times over he was the epitome of a respected gentleman. Still, ten months proved too long to wait for a first kiss, fond embrace, or dare she imagine, passion-filled evening. Their expedient two-week courtship had overflowed with the planning and preparation most brides accomplished over months and therefore hadn't spared adequate time to promote a sense of comfortability.

"Every time I see that look of longing on your face it pains me." Amelia reached across the oval occasional table and stroked the kitten between the ears. "Even if Dearing discovers your new companion, at least it will begin a discussion."

"Discussion?" Charlotte scoffed. "This rascal will cause an argument."

"All the better." Amelia bit her bottom lip as if fighting to hold another grin at bay.

"In what manner?" Charlotte knew her friend well.

"An argument is exactly what the two of you need. All your polite etiquette has gotten you nowhere. But a confrontation, composed of heated words and reckless sentiment, will lead to unrivaled passion. I daresay all that emotion needs to be funneled out somehow. Dearing is a hot-blooded male. He doesn't fool me for a moment. I see the way he looks at you when he believes no one is watching."

Charlotte narrowed her eyes as skepticism overrode hope. "It's not as if we've never kissed." The weak assertion garnered a snort of disbelief from her friend.

"Those chaste pecks on the cheek? That's no more a kiss than a caper is a banquet. I wonder if there's something we haven't noticed. Do you think he has an injury or other ailment preventing him from—"

"Amelia." It was Charlotte's turn to interrupt.

"I'm only considering the possibility."

"Yes, I know. I can hear you."

"It would explain quite a bit, wouldn't it? Perhaps I should speak to the gardener at Beckford Hall. He's a gypsy from Romania or somewhere far away. He could prepare a healing powder if Dearing—"

"Amelia!" Charlotte all but shouted, and the kitten reacted, sinking her claws into Charlotte's thigh. Thank heavens the multitude of layers beneath her day gown protected from the pain.

"You really shouldn't doubt me." Amelia stood with a firm shake of her skirts and prepared to leave.

"Perhaps he won't notice." Charlotte gathered the kitten closer to her heart. "Except for meals and the rare cordial exchange, Dearing is usually locked away in his study."

"Locked away? Find the key. Open the door." Each well-meant directive brought Amelia closer to the hall, her heels tapping out the words to underscore their intent. "And one last instruction."

"Yes?" Charlotte carefully removed the wriggling bundle from her gown and hurried to follow.

"You must adore your new kitten as I do you." Amelia

flashed a wide smile before she hurried across the threshold and into the foyer.

"Oh, no worry of that." Charlotte found a similar expression and placed a gentle kiss to the kitten's nose. "I already do."

"Faxman."

"Yes, milord."

On alert, the wiry secretary rose from his chair and Jeremy Lockhart, Viscount Dearing, silently commended the servant's attentiveness, assured he'd hired an intelligent, intuitive man to execute his business dealings. Where would he be without Faxman? Now there was a question deserving of examination. The secretary's business acumen paralleled his own.

Faxman had served in the position for five years and proved a cheerful fellow who knew when to speak and when not. He also possessed a sharp mind and refrained from complaint of Dearing's rigorous schedule, which often kept them both into late hours. Thus, Faxman was trusted with all financial transactions, shrewd fiscal contracts, investment maneuvers, and monetary exchanges.

All except one.

Dearing settled his eyes on the corner of his mahogany bureau plat desk where a black leather box rested beside the inkwell, an ivory letter opener, and precise stack of portfolios. The locked box remained a constant reminder of unfinished business. And too, some secrets were best hidden in full view. He returned his attention to his secretary. "Have you completed the documents for the Harrison stock and consols purchase?"

"I've just sanded the page, milord." Faxman angled his head to indicate the foolscap atop his workstation. "Shall we continue our discourse from yesterday concerning the Tasinger and Oliver merger? Or would you prefer to examine the Benson proposal?"

The first notes of the pianoforte, faint and ephemeral, chased Faxman's inquiries and Dearing shifted his eyes to the elegant regulator clock above the hearth.

He'd worked straight through luncheon and beyond, the hour later than he'd realized. At the very least, Faxman deserved time to eat and rest. Otherwise Dearing courted the risk of running the secretary into the ground and he couldn't have that.

"Never mind. Look at the time. You may go for now. Thank you." Dearing didn't say more and waited for Faxman to leave, but instead of gathering his belongings with haste as the servant was apt to do daily, the younger man stalled, his brows drawn low over inquisitive eyes.

"Mozart, isn't it?"

"Haydn's Sonata No. 59 in E-flat major." Dearing drummed his fingertips against his thigh, all at once impatient for Faxman to be gone. This particular piece was his favorite and he didn't wish to spoil it with dialogue.

"Lady Dearing's accomplished skill draws attention in the best method. My father preferred the instrument and oft said music has a way of expressing what otherwise cannot be stated with words. At the risk of speaking beyond my position, when I hear Lady Dearing's poignant offerings, I recall my father's memory with fondness."

Dearing remained quiet another beat. "That will be all then, Faxman." Somehow the secretary's uncanny ability to voice provoking observations unnerved him. It was almost as if the man meant to advise, but that isolated observation posed a ridiculous notion.

"I will return at half eight, tomorrow morning." Faxman collected his satchel and coat from the hook near the door. "Good day, milord."

Dearing watched as Faxman exited though his ears remained attuned to the ariose melody in surrender to Charlotte's clever skill. How would she react were he to enter the music room and become her audience? Was she aware how deeply he favored her masterful ability?

With a deep exhale, he lamented his wife remained a mystery. Ten months past, ten months wasted. They spoke little more than niceties and cordial conversation, and he accepted the blame for the stagnant, awkward tension that grew more pervasive each day. Meanwhile, his body yearned to breach the chasm between them.

He stepped backward, a feeble attempt to detach from the incongruity as much as distance himself from the enchanting summons of her music, each note and chord a beckon. Instead, his legs met the edge of the desk. He thrust his hand out and caught the corner of the leather box. With care, he laid his palm flat atop the surface and closed his eyes to the truth within.

How much easier it would be if he could pack up his emotions and keep them in a secured container. He shook his head at the inanity while truth intruded to remind his heart waited. As each day passed, his soul prodded, the hour grew late.

He'd adored Charlotte from the moment his eyes found her, yet despite he'd executed the most ingenious business maneuver of a lifetime and acquired an ideal wife, the marriage contract left him desolate of satisfaction. He was unfamiliar with the result.

A cascade of precisely timed notes resonated through the hall to permeate his thoughtful reflection. As if they communicated on a level unmarred by indecision, the music syncopated the sentiment and reason at war within him.

All too soon the tempo changed and he fell in stride with each striking chord as it dominated the new rhythm and forced him forward. He arrived at the door of the music room and watched in silence, the pianoforte positioned near the large mullioned windows overlooking the gardens behind the house. Seated with her back to the door, Charlotte would never know the convenience allowed by the judicious placement of furniture. Her fingers caressed the keys, gentle yet purposed to produce the loveliest songs. Many a night he spent wondering how those slender fingers would feel lingered across his skin with the same scrupulous finesse.

The song came to a poignant flourish and he angled his body forward, his heartbeat quickened and interest enthralled. How absolutely fetching she appeared in the throes of concentration, cheeks flushed pink and delicate brows furrowed in attentiveness, though his view of her profile proved fleeting. The candlelit epergne atop the pianoforte lent a burnished glow to her silky brown hair, neatly arranged in a braided coronet. Would she object were he to remove the pins and thread his fingers through the lengths? Would she welcome a kiss placed to the graceful slope of her neck?

A sustained final note pierced through the haze of his admiration and he turned into the hall and made his way abovestairs. Still the questions resonated in kind to the vibrant remembrance of Charlotte's musical composition. What if he'd charged into the room instead of forcing denial? What if he'd dared show without words how well and thoroughly he loved his wife?

Connect with

Visit us online at
KensingtonBooks.com
to read more from your favorite authors, see books
by series, view reading group guides, and more.

for sneak peeks, chances to win books and prize packs,
and to share your thoughts with other readers.

facebook.com/kensingtonpublishing
twitter.com/kensingtonbooks

Tell us what you think!

To share your thoughts, submit a review,
or sign up for our eNewsletters, please visit:
KensingtonBooks.com/TellUs.

Books by Bestselling Author
Fern Michaels

___The Jury	0-8217-7878-1	$6.99US/$9.99CAN
___Sweet Revenge	0-8217-7879-X	$6.99US/$9.99CAN
___Lethal Justice	0-8217-7880-3	$6.99US/$9.99CAN
___Free Fall	0-8217-7881-1	$6.99US/$9.99CAN
___Fool Me Once	0-8217-8071-9	$7.99US/$10.99CAN
___Vegas Rich	0-8217-8112-X	$7.99US/$10.99CAN
___Hide and Seek	1-4201-0184-6	$6.99US/$9.99CAN
___Hokus Pokus	1-4201-0185-4	$6.99US/$9.99CAN
___Fast Track	1-4201-0186-2	$6.99US/$9.99CAN
___Collateral Damage	1-4201-0187-0	$6.99US/$9.99CAN
___Final Justice	1-4201-0188-9	$6.99US/$9.99CAN
___Up Close and Personal	0-8217-7956-7	$7.99US/$9.99CAN
___Under the Radar	1-4201-0683-X	$6.99US/$9.99CAN
___Razor Sharp	1-4201-0684-8	$7.99US/$10.99CAN
___Yesterday	1-4201-1494-8	$5.99US/$6.99CAN
___Vanishing Act	1-4201-0685-6	$7.99US/$10.99CAN
___Sara's Song	1-4201-1493-X	$5.99US/$6.99CAN
___Deadly Deals	1-4201-0686-4	$7.99US/$10.99CAN
___Game Over	1-4201-0687-2	$7.99US/$10.99CAN
___Sins of Omission	1-4201-1153-1	$7.99US/$10.99CAN
___Sins of the Flesh	1-4201-1154-X	$7.99US/$10.99CAN
___Cross Roads	1-4201-1192-2	$7.99US/$10.99CAN

Available Wherever Books Are Sold!
Check out our website at **www.kensingtonbooks.com**